BY ADAM JOHNSON

Emporium

Parasites Like Us

The Orphan Master's Son

Fortune Smiles

FORTUNE SMILES

RANDOM HOUSE

NEW YORK

FORTUNE SMILES

Stories

Adam Johnson

Copyright © 2015 by Adam Johnson

All rights reserved.

Published in the United States by Random House, an imprint and division of Penguin Random House LLC, New York.

RANDOM HOUSE and the HOUSE colophon are registered trademarks of Penguin Random House LLC.

LIBRARY OF CONGRESS CATALOGING-IN-PUBLICATION DATA
Johnson, Adam.
[Short stories. Selections]
Fortune smiles : stories / Adam Johnson.
pages ; cm
ISBN 978-0-8129-9747-7
eBook ISBN 978-0-8129-9748-4
I. Title.
PS3610.O3A6 2015
813'.6—dc23
2015023455

Printed in the United States of America on acid-free paper

randomhousebooks.com

2 4 6 8 9 7 5 3 1

FIRST EDITION

Book design by Dana Leigh Blanchette
Title-page and part-title images: © iStockphoto.com

In memory of
Thomas Mannarino, 1964–2007,
and
Eric Rogers, 1970–2012

CONTENTS

FORTUNE SMILES

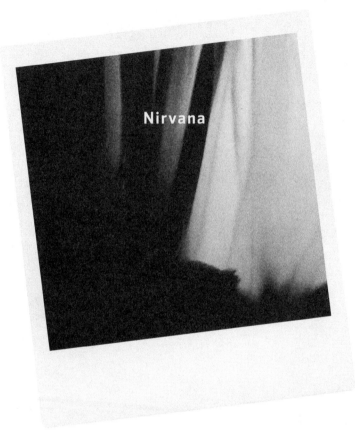

Nirvana

It's late, and I can't sleep. I raise a window for some spring Palo Alto air, but it doesn't help. In bed, eyes open, I hear whispers, which makes me think of the president, because we often talk in whispers. I know the whispering sound is really just my wife, Charlotte, who listens to Nirvana on her headphones all night and tends to sleep-mumble the lyrics. Charlotte has her own bed, a mechanical one.

My sleep problem is this: when I close my eyes, I keep visualizing my wife killing herself. More like the ways she might *try* to kill herself, since she's paralyzed from the shoulders down. The paralysis is quite temporary, though good luck trying to convince Charlotte of that. She slept on her side today, to fight the bedsores, and there was something about the way she stared at the safety rail at the edge of the mattress. The bed is voice-activated, so if she could somehow get her head between the bars of the safety rail, "incline" is all she'd have to say. As the bed powered up, she'd be choked in seconds.

And then there's the way she stares at the looping cable that descends from the Hoyer Lift, which swings her in and out of bed.

But my wife doesn't need an exotic exit strategy, not when she's exacted a promise from me to help her do it when the time comes.

I rise and go to her, but she's not listening to Nirvana yet—she tends to save it for when she needs it most, after midnight, when her nerves really start to crackle.

"I thought I heard a noise," I tell her. "Kind of a whisper."

Short, choppy hair frames her drawn face, skin faint as refrigerator light.

"I heard it, too," she says.

In the silver dish by her voice remote is a half-smoked joint. I light it for her and hold it to her lips.

"How's the weather in there?" I ask.

"Windy," she says through the smoke.

Windy is better than hail or lightning or, God forbid, flooding, which is the sensation she felt when her lungs were just starting to work again. But there are different kinds of wind.

I ask, "Windy like a whistle through window screens, or windy like the rattle of storm shutters?"

"A strong breeze, hissy and buffeting, like a microphone in the wind."

She smokes again. Charlotte hates being stoned, but she says it quiets the inside of her. She has Guillain-Barré syndrome, a condition in which her immune system attacks the insulation around her nerves so that when the brain sends signals to the body, the electrical impulses ground out before they can be received. A billion nerves inside her send signals that go everywhere, nowhere. This is the ninth month, a month that is at the edge of the medical literature. It's a place where the doctors no longer feel qualified to tell us whether Charlotte's nerves will begin to regenerate or she will be stuck like this forever.

She exhales, coughing. Her right arm twitches, which means her brain has attempted to tell her arm to rise and cover the mouth. She tokes again, and through the smoke she says, "I'm worried."

"What about?"

"You."

"You're worried about me?"

"I want you to stop talking to the president. It's time to accept reality."

I try to be lighthearted. "But he's the one who talks to me."

"Then stop listening. He's gone. When your time comes, you're supposed to fall silent."

Reluctantly, I nod. But she doesn't understand. Stuck in this bed, having sworn off TV, she's probably the only person in America who didn't see the assassination. If she'd beheld the look in the president's eyes when his life was taken, she'd understand why I talk to him late at night. If she could leave this room and feel the nation trying to grieve, she'd know why I reanimated the commander in chief and brought him back to life.

"Concerning my conversations with the president," I say, "I just want to point out that you spend a third of your life listening to Nirvana, whose songs are by a guy who blew his brains out."

Charlotte tilts her head and looks at me like I'm a stranger. "Kurt Cobain took the pain of his life and made it into something that mattered. What did the president leave behind? Uncertainties, emptiness, a thousand rocks to overturn."

She talks like that when she's high. I tap out the joint and lift her headphones.

"Ready for your Nirvana?" I ask.

She looks toward the window. "That sound, I hear it again," she says.

At the window, I peer out into the darkness. It's a normal Palo Alto night—the hiss of sprinklers, blue recycling bins, a raccoon digging in the community garden. Then I notice it, right before my eyes, a small black drone, hovering. Its tiny servos swivel to regard me. Real quick, I snatch the drone out of the air and pull it inside. I close the window and curtains, then study the thing: its shell is made of black foil stretched over tiny struts, like the bones of a bat's wing. Behind a propeller of clear cellophane, a tiny infrared engine throbs with warmth.

"Now will you listen to me?" Charlotte asks. "Now will you stop this president business?"

"It's too late for that," I tell her, and release the drone. As if blind, it bumbles around the room. Is it autonomous? Has someone been operating it, someone watching our house? I lift it from its column of air and flip off its power switch.

Charlotte looks toward her voice remote. "Play music," she tells it.

Closing her eyes, she waits for me to place the headphones on her ears, where she will hear Kurt Cobain come to life once more.

I wake later in the night. The drone has somehow turned itself on and is hovering above my body, mapping me with a beam of soft red light. I toss a sweater over it, dropping it to the floor. After making sure Charlotte is asleep, I pull out my iProjector. I turn it on, and the president appears in three dimensions, his torso life-size in an amber glow.

He greets me with a smile. "It's good to be back in Palo Alto," he says.

My algorithm has accessed the iProjector's GPS chip and searched the president's database for location references. This one came from a commencement address he gave at Stanford back when he was a senator.

"Mr. President," I say. "I'm sorry to bother you again, but I have more questions."

He looks into the distance, contemplative. "Shoot," he says.

I move into his line of sight but can't get him to look me in the eye. That's one of the design problems I ran across.

"Did I make a mistake in creating you, in releasing you into the world?" I ask. "My wife says that you're keeping people from mourning, that *this you* keeps us from accepting the fact that the *real you* is gone."

The president rubs the stubble on his chin. He looks down and away.

"You can't put the genie back in the bottle," he says.

Which is eerie, because that's a line he spoke on *60 Minutes,* a moment when he expressed regret for legalizing drones for civilian use.

"Do you know that I'm the one who made you?" I ask.

"We are all born free," he says. "And no person may traffic in another."

"But you weren't born," I tell him. "I wrote an algorithm based on the Linux operating kernel. You're an open-source search engine married to a dialog bot and a video compiler. The program scrubs the Web and archives a person's images and videos and data—everything you say, you've said before."

For the first time, the president falls silent.

I ask, "Do you know that you're gone . . . that you've died?"

The president doesn't hesitate. "The end of life is another kind of freedom," he says.

The assassination flashes in my eyes. I've seen the video so many times—the motorcade slowly crawls along while the president, on foot, parades past the barricaded crowds. Someone in the throng catches the president's eye. The president turns, lifts a hand in greeting. Then a bullet strikes him in the abdomen. The impact bends him forward, his eyes lift to confront the shooter. A look of recognition settles into the president's gaze—of a particular person, of some kind of truth, of something he has foreseen? He takes the second shot in the face. You can see the switch go off—his limbs give and he's down. They put him on a machine for a few days, but the end had already come.

I glance at Charlotte, asleep. "Mr. President," I whisper, "did you and the first lady ever talk about the future, about worst-case scenarios?"

I wonder if the first lady was the one to turn off the machine.

The president smiles. "The first lady and I have a wonderful relationship. We share everything."

"But were there instructions? Did you two make a plan?"

His voice lowers, becomes sonorous. "Are you asking about bonds of matrimony?"

"I suppose so," I say.

"In this regard," he says, "our only duty is to be of service in any way we can."

My mind ponders the ways in which I might have to be of service to Charlotte.

The president then looks into the distance, as if a flag is waving there.

"I'm the president of the United States," he says, "and I approved this message."

That's when I know our conversation is over. When I reach to turn off the iProjector, the president looks me squarely in the eye, a coincidence of perspective, I guess. We regard each other, his eyes deep and melancholy, and my finger hesitates at the switch.

"Seek your inner resolve," he tells me.

Can you tell a story that doesn't begin, it's just suddenly happening? The woman you love gets the flu. Her fingers tingle, her legs go rubbery. Soon she can't grip a coffee cup. What finally gets her to the hospital is the need to pee. She's dying to pee, but the paralysis has begun: the bladder can no longer hear the brain. After an ER doc inserts a Foley catheter, you learn new words—*axon, areflexia, ascending peripheral polyneuropathy.*

Charlotte says she's filled with "noise." Inside her is a "storm."

The doctor has a big needle. He tells Charlotte to get on the gurney. Charlotte is scared to get on the gurney. She's scared she won't ever get up again. "Please, honey," you say. "Get on the gurney." Soon you behold the glycerin glow of your wife's spinal fluid. And she's right. She doesn't get up again.

Next comes plasmapheresis, then high-dose immunoglob-ulin therapy.

The doctors mention, casually, the word *ventilator*.

Charlotte's mother arrives. She brings her cello. She's an expert on the siege of Leningrad. She has written a book on the topic. When Charlotte's coma is induced, her mother fills the neuro ward with the saddest sounds ever conceived. For days, there is nothing but the swish of vent baffles, the trill of vital monitors, and Shostakovich, Shostakovich, Shostako-vich.

Two months of physical therapy in Santa Clara. Here are dunk tanks, sonar stimulators, exoskeletal treadmills. Char-lotte becomes the person in the room who makes the victims of other afflictions feel better about their fate. She does not make progress, she's not a "soldier" or a "champ" or a "trouper."

Charlotte convinces herself that I will leave her for one of the nurses in the rehab ward. She screams at me to get a va-sectomy so this nurse and I will suffer a barren future. To soothe her, I read aloud Joseph Heller's memoir about con-tracting Guillain-Barré syndrome. The book was supposed to make us feel better. Instead, it chronicles how great Heller's friends are, how high Heller's spirits are, how Heller leaves his wife to marry the beautiful nurse who tends to him. And for Charlotte, the book's ending is particularly painful: Joseph Heller gets better.

We tumble into a well of despair that's narrow and deep, a place that seals us off. Everything is in the well with us— careers, goals, travel, children—so close that we can drown them to save ourselves.

Finally, discharge. Yet home is unexpectedly surreal. Amid familiar surroundings, the impossibility of normal life is amplified. But the cat is happy, so happy to have Charlotte home that it spends an entire night curled on Charlotte's throat, on her tracheal incision. Goodbye, cat! While I'm in the garage, Charlotte watches a spider slowly descend from the ceiling on a single thread. She tries to blow it away. She blows and blows, but the spider disappears into her hair.

Still to be described are tests, tantrums and treatments. To come are the discoveries of Kurt Cobain and marijuana. Of these times, there is only one moment I must relate. It was a normal night. I was beside Charlotte in the mechanical bed, holding up her magazine.

She said, "You don't know how bad I want to get out of this bed."

Her voice was quiet, uninflected. She'd said similar things a thousand times.

"I'd do anything to escape," she said.

I flipped the page and laughed at a picture whose caption read, "Stars are just like us!"

"But I could never do that to you," she said.

"Do what?" I asked.

"Nothing."

"What are you talking about, what's going through your head?"

I turned to look at her. She was inches away.

"Except for how it would hurt you," she said, "I would get away."

"Get away where?"

"From here."

Neither of us had spoken of the promise since the night it was exacted. I'd tried to pretend the promise didn't exist, but it existed.

"Face it, you're stuck with me," I said, forcing a smile. "We're destined, we're fated to be together. And soon you'll be better, things will be normal again."

"My entire life is this pillow."

"That's not true. You've got your friends and family. And you've got technology. The whole world is at your fingertips."

By friends, I meant her nurses and physical therapists. By family, I meant her distant and brooding mother. It didn't matter: Charlotte was too disengaged to even point out her nonfunctional fingers and their nonfeeling tips.

She rolled her head to the side and stared at the safety rail.

"It's okay," she said. "I would never do that to you."

In the morning, before the nurses arrive, I open the curtains and study the drone in the early light. Most of the stealth and propulsion parts are off the shelf, but the processors are new to me, half hidden by a Kevlar shield. To get the drone to talk, to get some forensics on who sent it my way, I'll have to get my hands on the hash reader from work.

When Charlotte wakes, I prop her head and massage her legs. It's our morning routine.

"Let's generate those Schwann cells," I tell her toes. "It's time for Charlotte's body to start producing some myelin membranes."

"Look who's Mr. Brightside," she says. "You must have been talking to the president. Isn't that why you talk to him, to get all inspired? To see the silver lining?"

I rub her Achilles tendon. Last week Charlotte failed a big test, the DTRE, which measures deep tendon response and signals the *beginning* of recovery. "Don't worry," the doctor told us. "I know of another patient who also took nine months to respond, and he managed a full recovery." I asked if we could contact this patient, to know what he went through, to help us see what's ahead. The doctor informed us this patient was attended to in France, in the year 1918.

After the doctor left, I went into the garage and started making the president. A psychologist would probably say the reason I created him had to do with the promise I made Charlotte and the fact that the president also had a relationship with the person who took his life. But it's simpler than that: I just needed to save somebody, and with the president, it didn't matter that it was too late.

I tap Charlotte's patella, but there's no response. "Any pain?"

"So what did the president say?"

"Which president?"

"The dead one," she says.

I articulate the plantar fascia. "How about this?"

"Feels like a spray of cool diamonds," she says. "Come on, I know you talked to him."

It's going to be one of her bad days, I can tell.

"Let me guess," Charlotte says. "The president told you to move to the South Pacific to take up painting. That's uplifting, isn't it?"

I don't say anything.

"You'd take me with you, right? I could be your assistant. I'd hold your palette in my teeth. If you need a model, I specialize in reclining nudes."

"If you must know," I tell her, "the president told me to locate my inner resolve."

"*Inner resolve*," she says. "I could use some help tracking down mine."

"You have more resolve than anyone I know."

"Jesus, you're sunny. Don't you know what's going on? Don't you see that I'm about to spend the rest of my life like this?"

"Pace yourself, darling. The day's only a couple minutes old."

"I know," she says. "I'm supposed to have reached a stage of enlightened acceptance or something. You think I like it that the only person I have to get mad at is you? I know it's not right—you're the one thing I love in this world."

"You love Kurt Cobain."

"He's dead."

We hear Hector, the morning nurse, pull up outside—he drives an old car with a combustion engine.

"I have to grab something from work," I tell her. "But I'll be back."

"Promise me something," she says.

"No."

"Come on. If you do, I'll release you from the other promise."

I shake my head. She doesn't mean it—she'll never release me.

She says, "Just agree to talk straight with me. You don't have to be fake and optimistic. It doesn't help."

"I am optimistic."

"You shouldn't be," she says. "Pretending, that's what killed Kurt Cobain."

I think it was the shotgun he pointed at his head, but I don't say that.

I know only one line from Nirvana. I karaoke it to Charlotte:

"With the lights on," I sing, "she's less dangerous."

She rolls her eyes. "You got it wrong," she says. But she smiles.

I try to encourage this. "What, I don't get points for trying?"

"You don't hear that?" Charlotte asks.

"Hear what?"

"That's the sound of me clapping."

"I give up," I say, and make for the door.

"Bed, incline," Charlotte tells her remote. Her torso slowly rises. It's time to start her day.

I take the 101 Freeway south toward Mountain View, where I write code at a company called Reputation Curator. Basically, the company threatens Yelpers and Facebookers to retract negative comments about dodgy lawyers and incompetent dentists. The work is labor-intensive, so I was hired to write a program that would sweep the Web to construct client profiles. Creating the president was only a step away.

In the vehicle next to me is a woman with her iProjector on the passenger seat; she's having an animated discussion with the president as she drives. At the next overpass, I see an older man in a tan jacket, looking down at the traffic. Standing next to him is the president. They're not speaking, just standing together, silently watching the cars go by.

A black car, driverless, begins pacing me in the next lane.

When I speed up, it speeds up. Through its smoked windows, I can see it has no cargo—there's nothing inside but a battery array big enough to ensure no car could outrun it. Even though I like driving, even though it relaxes me, I shift to automatic and dart into the Google lane, where I let go of the wheel and sign on to the Web for the first time since I released the president a week ago. I log in and discover that fourteen million people have downloaded the president. I also have seven hundred new messages. The first is from the dude who started Facebook, and it is not spam—he wants to buy me a burrito and talk about the future. I skip to the latest message, which is from Charlotte: "I don't mean to be mean. I lost my feeling, remember? I'll get it back. I'm trying, really, I am."

I see the president again, on the lawn of a Korean church. The minister has placed an iProjector on a chair, and the president appears to be engaging a Bible that's been propped before him on a stand. I understand that he is a ghost who will haunt us until our nation comes to grips with what has happened: that he is gone, that he has been stolen from us, that it is irreversible. And I'm not an idiot. I know what's really being stolen from me, slowly and irrevocably, before my eyes. I know that late at night I should be going to Charlotte instead of the president.

But when I'm with Charlotte, there's a membrane my mind places between us to protect me from the tremor in her voice, from the pulse in her desiccated wrists. It's when I'm away that it comes crashing in—how scared she is, how cruel life must seem to her. Driving now, I think about how she has started turning toward the wall even before the last song on the Nirvana album is over, that soon even headphones and marijuana will cease to work. My off-ramp up ahead is blurry, and I realize there are tears in my eyes. I drive right past my exit. I just let the Google lane carry me away.

When I arrive home, my boss, Sanjay, is waiting for me. I'd messaged him to have an intern deliver the hash reader, but here is the man himself, item in hand. Theoretically, hash readers are impossible. Theoretically, you shouldn't be able to crack full-field, hundred-key encryption. But some guy in India did it, some guy Sanjay knows. Sanjay is sensitive about being from India, and he thinks it's a cliché that a guy with his name runs a start-up in Palo Alto. So he goes by SJ and dresses all D-School. He's got a Stanford MBA, but he basically just stole the business model of a company called Reputation Defender. You can't blame the guy—he's one of those types with the hopes and dreams of an entire village riding on him.

SJ follows me into the garage, where I dock the drone and use some slave code to parse its drive. He hands me the hash reader, hand-soldered in Bangalore from an old motherboard. We marvel at it, the most sophisticated piece of cryptography on earth, here in our unworthy hands. But if you want to "curate" the reputations of Silicon Valley, you better be ready to crack some passwords.

He's quiet while I initialize the drone and run a diagnostic.

"Long time no see," he finally says.

"I needed some time," I tell him.

"Understood," SJ says. "We've missed you, is all I'm saying. You bring the president back to life, send fifteen million people to our website and then we don't see you for a week."

The drone knows something is suspicious—it powers off. I force a reboot.

"Got yourself a drone there?" SJ asks.

"It's a rescue," I say. "I'm adopting it."

SJ nods. "Thought you should know the Secret Service came by."

"Looking for me?" I ask. "Doesn't sound so secret."

"They must have been impressed with your president. I know I was."

SJ has long lashes and big, manga brown eyes. He hits me with them now.

"I've gotta tell you," he says, "the president is a work of art, a seamlessly integrated data interface. I'm in real admiration. This is a game changer. You know what I envision?"

I notice his flashy glasses. "Are those Android?" I ask.

"Yeah."

"Can I have them?"

He hands them over, and I search the frames for their IP address.

SJ gestures large. "I envision your algorithm running on Reputation Curator. Average people could bring their personalities to life, to speak for themselves, to customize and personalize how they're seen by the world. Your program is like Google, Wikipedia and Facebook all in one. Everyone on the planet with a reputation would pay to have you animate them, to make them articulate, vigilant . . . eternal."

"You can have it," I tell SJ. "The algorithm's core is open-source—I used a freeware protocol."

SJ flashes a brittle smile. "We've actually looked into that," he says, "and, well, it seems like you coded it with seven-layer encryption."

"Yeah, I guess I did, didn't I? You're the one with the hash reader. Just crack it."

"I don't want it to be like that," SJ says. "Let's be partners. Your concept is brilliant—an algorithm that scrubs the Web and compiles the results into a personal animation. The president is the proof, but it's also given away the idea. If we move now, we can protect it, it will be ours. In a few weeks, though, everyone will have their own."

I don't point out the irony of SJ wanting to protect a business model.

"Is the president just an animation to you?" I ask. "Have you spoken with him? Have you listened to what he has to say?"

"I'm offering stock," SJ says. "Wheelbarrows of it."

The drone offers up its firewall like a seductress her throat. I deploy the hash reader, whose processor hums and flashes red. We sit on folding chairs while it works.

"I need your opinion," I tell him.

"Right on," he says, and removes a bag of weed. He starts rolling a joint, then passes me the rest. He's been hooking me up the last couple months, no questions.

"What do you think of Kurt Cobain?" I ask.

"Kurt Cobain," he repeats as he works the paper between his fingers. "The man was pure," he says, and licks the edge. "Too pure for this world. Have you heard Patti Smith's cover of 'Smells Like Teen Spirit'? Unassailable, man."

He lights the joint and passes it my way, but I wave it off. He sits there, staring out the open mouth of my garage into the Kirkland plumage of Palo Alto. Apple, Oracle, PayPal and Hewlett-Packard were all started in garages within a mile of here. About once a month, SJ gets homesick and cooks litti chokha for everyone at work. He plays Sharda Sinha songs and gets this look in his eyes like he's back in Bihar, land of peepal trees and roller birds. He has the look now. He says, "You know, my family downloaded the president. They have no idea what I do out here, as if I could make them understand that I help bad sushi chefs ward off Twitter trolls. But the American president, that they understand."

The mayor, barefoot, jogs past us. Moments later, a billboard drives by.

"Hey, can you make the president speak Hindi?" SJ asks. "If you could get the American president to say 'I could go for a Pepsi' in Hindi, I'd make you the richest man on earth."

The hash reader's light turns green. Just like that, the

drone is mine. I disconnect the leads and begin to sync the Android glasses. The drone uses its moment of freedom to rise and study SJ.

SJ returns the drone's intense scrutiny.

"Who do you think sent it after you?" he asks. "Mozilla? Craigslist?"

"We'll know in a moment."

"Silent. Black. Radar deflecting," SJ says. "I bet this is Microsoft's dark magic."

The new OS suddenly initiates, the drone responds, and using retinal commands, I send it on a lap around the garage. "Lo and behold," I say. "Turns out our little friend speaks Google."

"Wow," SJ says. "Don't be evil, huh?"

When the drone returns, it targets SJ in the temple with a green laser.

"What the fuck," SJ says.

"Don't worry," I tell him. "It's just taking your pulse and temperature."

"What for?"

"Probably trying to read your emotions," I say. "I bet it's a leftover subroutine."

"You sure you're in charge of that thing?"

I roll my eyes and the drone does a backflip.

"My emotion is simple," SJ tells me. "It's time to come back to work."

"I will," I tell him. "I've just got some things to deal with."

SJ looks at me. "It's okay if you don't want to talk about your wife. But you don't have to be so alone about things. Everyone at work, we're all worried about you."

Inside, Charlotte is suspended in a sling from the Hoyer Lift, which has been rolled to the window so she can see outside. She's wearing old yoga tights, which are slack on her, and she smells of the cedar oil her massage therapist rubs her with. I go to her and open the window.

"You read my mind," she says, and breathes the fresh air.

I put the glasses on her, and it takes her eyes a minute of flashing around before the drone lifts from my hands. A grand smile crosses her face as she puts it through its paces— hovering, rotating, swiveling the camera's servos. And then the drone is off. I watch it cross the lawn, veer around the compost piles, and head for the community garden. It floats down the rows, and though I don't have the view Charlotte does in her glasses, I can see the drone inspecting the blossoms of summer squash, the fat bottoms of Roma tomatoes. It rises along the bean trellises and tracks watermelons by their umbilical stems. When she makes it to her plot, she gasps.

"My roses," she says. "They're still there. Someone's been taking care of them."

"I wouldn't let your roses die," I tell her.

She has the drone inspect every bloom. Carefully, she maneuvers it through the bright petals, brushing against the blossoms, then shuttles it home again. When it's hovering before us, Charlotte leans slightly forward and sniffs the drone. "I never thought I'd smell my roses again," she says, her face flushed with hope and amazement. The tears begin streaming.

I remove her glasses, and we leave the drone hovering there.

She regards me. "I want to have a baby," she says.

"A baby?"

"It's been nine months. I could have had one already. I could've been doing something useful this whole time."

"But your illness," I say. "We don't know what's ahead."

She closes her eyes like she's hugging something, like she's holding some dear truth.

"With a baby, I'd have something to show for all this. I'd have a reason. At the least, I'd have something to leave behind."

"You can't talk like that," I tell her. "We've talked about you not talking like this."

But she won't listen to me, she won't open her eyes.

All she says is "And I want to start tonight."

Later, I carry the iProjector out back to the gardening shed. Here, in the gold of afternoon light, the president rises and comes to life. He adjusts his collar and cuffs, runs his thumb down a black lapel as if he exists only in the moment before a camera will broadcast him live to the world.

"Mr. President," I say. "I'm sorry to bother you again."

"Nonsense," he tells me. "I serve at the pleasure of the people."

"Do you remember me?" I ask. "Do you remember the problems I've been talking to you about?"

"Perennial is the nature of the problems that plague man. Particular is the voice with which they call to each of us."

"My problem today is of a personal nature."

"Then I place this conversation under the seal."

"I haven't made love to my wife in a long time."

He holds up a hand to halt me. He smiles in a knowing, fatherly way.

"Times of doubt," he tells me, "are inherent in the compact of civil union."

"My question is about children. Would you have still brought yours into the world, knowing that only one of you might be around to raise them?"

"Single parenting places too much of a strain on today's families," he says. "That's why I'm introducing legislation that will reduce the burden on our hardworking parents."

"What about your children? Do you miss them?"

"My mind goes to them constantly. Being away is the great sacrifice of the office."

In the shed, suspended dust makes his specter glitter and

swirl. It makes him look like he is cutting out, like he will leave at any moment. I feel some urgency.

"When it's all finally over," I ask, "where is it that we go?"

"I'm no preacher," the president says, "but I believe we go where we are called."

"Where were you called to? Where is it that you are?"

"Don't we all try to locate ourselves among the pillars of uncommon knowledge?"

"You don't know where you are, do you?" I ask the president.

"I'm sure my opponent would like you to believe that."

"It's okay," I say, more to myself. "I didn't expect you to know."

"I know exactly where I am," the president says. Then, in a voice that sounds pieced from many scraps, he adds, "I'm currently positioned at three seven point four four north by one two two point one four west."

I think he's done. I wait for him to say "Good night and God bless America." Instead, he reaches out to touch my chest. "I have heard that you have made much personal sacrifice," he says. "And I'm told that your sense of duty is strong."

I don't think I agree, but I say, "Yes, sir."

His glowing hand clasps my shoulder, and it doesn't matter that I can't feel it.

"Then this medal that I affix to your uniform is much

more than a piece of silver. It is a symbol of how much you have given, not just in armed struggle and not just in service to your nation. It marks you forever as one who can be counted upon, as one who in times of need will lift up and carry those who have fallen." Proudly, he stares into the empty space above my shoulder. He says, "Now return home to your wife, soldier, and start a new chapter of life."

When darkness falls, I go to Charlotte. The night nurse has placed her in a negligee. Charlotte lowers the bed as I approach. The electric motor is the only sound in the room.

"I'm ovulating," she announces. "I can feel it."

"You can feel it?"

"I don't need to *feel* it," she says. "I just know."

She's strangely calm.

"Are you ready?" she asks.

"Sure."

I steady myself on the safety rail that separates us.

She asks, "Do you want some oral sex first?"

I shake my head.

"Come join me, then," she says.

I start to climb on the bed—she stops me.

"Hey, sunshine," she says. "Take off your clothes."

I can't remember the last time she called me that.

"Oh yeah," I say, and unbutton my shirt, unzip my jeans.

When I drop my underwear, I feel weirdly, I don't know, *naked*. I swing a leg up, then kind of lie on her.

A look of contentment crosses her face. "This is how it's supposed to be," she says. "It's been a long time since I've been able to look into your eyes."

Her body is narrow but warm. I don't know where to put my hands.

"Do you want to pull down my panties?"

I sit up and begin to work them off. I see the scar from the femoral stent. When I heft her legs, there are the bedsores we've been fighting.

"Remember our trip to Mexico," she asks, "when we made love on top of that pyramid? It was like we were in the past and the future at the same time. I kind of feel that now."

"You're not high, are you?"

"What? Like I'd have to be stoned to recall the first time we talked about having a baby?"

When I have her panties off and her legs hooked, I pause. It takes all my focus to get an erection, and then I can't believe I have one. Here is my wife, paralyzed, invalid, insensate, and though everything's the opposite of erotic, I am poised above her, completely hard.

"I'm wet, aren't I?" Charlotte asks. "I've been thinking about this all day."

I do remember the pyramid. The stone was cold, the staircase steep. The past to me was a week of Charlotte in Mayan dresses, cooing at every baby she came across. Having sex under jungle stars, I tried to imagine the future: a faceless *someone* conceived on a sacrificial altar. I finished early and tried to shake it off. I focused only on all those steps we had to make it down in the dark.

"I think I feel something," she says. "You're inside me, right? Because I'm pretty sure I can feel it."

Here I enter my wife and begin our lovemaking. I try to focus on the notion that if this works, Charlotte will be safe, that for nine months she'd let no harm come to her, and maybe she's right, maybe the baby will stimulate something and recovery will begin.

Charlotte smiles. It's brittle, but it's a smile. "How's this for finding the silver lining—I won't have to feel the pain of childbirth."

This makes me wonder if a paralyzed woman *can* push out a baby, or does she get the scalpel, and if so, is there anesthesia, and all at once my body is at the edge of not cooperating.

"Hey, are you here?" she asks. "I'm trying to get you to smile."

"I just need to focus for a minute," I tell her.

"I can tell you're not really into this," she says. "I can tell you're still hung up on the idea that I'm going to do something drastic to myself, right? Just because I talk about crazy stuff sometimes doesn't mean I'm going to do anything."

"Then why'd you make me promise to help you do it?"

The promise came early, in the beginning, just before the

ventilator. She had a vomiting reflex that lasted for hours. Imagine endless dry heaves while you're paralyzed. The doctors finally gave her narcotics. Drugged, dead-limbed and vomiting, that's when it struck her that her body was no longer hers. I was holding her hair, keeping it out of the basin. She was panting between heaves.

She said, "Promise me that when I tell you to make it stop, you'll make it stop."

"Make what stop?" I asked.

She retched, long and cord-rattling. I knew what she meant.

"It won't come to that," I said.

She tried to say something but retched again.

"I promise," I said.

Now, in her mechanical bed, her negligee straps slipping off her shoulders, Charlotte says, "It's hard for you to understand, I know. But the idea that there's a way out, it's what allows me to keep going. I'd never take it. You believe me, don't you?"

"I hate that promise, I hate that you made me make it."

"I'd never do it, and I'd never make you help."

"Then release me," I tell her.

"I'm sorry," she says.

I decide to just shut it all out and keep going. I'm losing my erection, and my mind wonders what will happen if I go soft—do I have it in me to fake it?—but I shut it out and keep going and going, pounding on Charlotte until I can barely

feel anything. Her breasts loll alone under me. From the bedside table, the drone turns itself on and rises, hovering. It
flashes my forehead with its green laser, as if what I'm feeling
is that easy to determine, as if my emotion has a name. Is it
spying on me, feeling sympathy or executing old code? I wonder if the drone's OS reverted to a previous version or if
Google reacquired it or if it's in some kind of autonomous
mode. Or it could be that someone hacked the Android
glasses, or maybe . . . That's when I look down and see Charlotte is crying.

I stop.

"No, don't," she says. "Keep going."

She's not crying hard, but they are fat, lamenting tears.

"We can try again tomorrow," I tell her.

"No, I'm okay," she says. "Just keep going and do something for me, would you?"

"All right."

"Put the headphones on me."

"You mean, while we're doing it?"

"Music on," she says. From the headphones on her bedside table, Nirvana starts to hum.

"I know I'm doing it all wrong," I say. "It's been a long
time, and . . ."

"It's not you," she says. "I just need my music. Just put
them on me."

"Why do you need Nirvana? What is it to you?"

She closes her eyes and shakes her head.

"What is it with this Kurt Cobain?" I say. "What's your deal with him?"

I grab her wrists and pin them down, but she can't feel it.

"Why do you have to have this music? What's wrong with you?" I demand. "Just tell me what it is that's wrong with you."

The drone follows me to the garage, where it wanders the walls, looking for a way out. I turn on a computer and download one of these Nirvana albums. I play the whole thing, just sitting there in the dark. The guy, this Kurt Cobain, sings about being stupid and dumb and unwanted. In one song, he says that Jesus doesn't want him for a sunbeam. In another song, he says he wants milk and laxatives along with cherry-flavored antacids. He has a song called "All Apologies," but he never actually apologizes. He doesn't even say what he did wrong.

The drone, having found no escape, comes to me and hovers silently. I must look pretty pathetic, because the drone takes my temperature.

I lift the remote for the garage door opener. "Is this what you want?" I ask. "If I let you go, are you going to come back?"

The drone silently hums, impassive atop its column of warm air.

I press the button. The drone waits until the garage door

is all the way up. Then it snaps a photograph of me and zooms off into the Palo Alto night.

I stand and breathe the air, which is cool and smells of flowers. There's enough moonlight to cast leaf patterns on the driveway. Down the street, I spot the glowing eyes of our cat. I call his name, but he doesn't come. I gave him to a friend a couple blocks away, and for a few weeks the cat returned at night to visit me. Not anymore. This feeling of being in proximity to something that's lost to you, it seems like my whole life right now. It's a feeling Charlotte would understand if she'd just talk to the president. But he's not the one she needs to speak to, I suddenly understand. I return to my computer bench and fire up a bank of screens. I stare into their blue glow and get to work. It takes me hours, most of the night, before I'm done.

It's almost dawn when I go to Charlotte. The room is dark, and I can only see her outline. "Bed incline," I say, and she starts to rise. She wakes and stares at me but says nothing. Her face has that lack of expression that comes only after it's been through every emotion.

I set the iProjector in her lap. She hates the thing but says nothing. She only tilts her head a little, like she's sad for me. Then I turn it on.

Kurt Cobain appears before her, clad in a bathrobe and composed of soft blue light.

Charlotte inhales. "Oh my God," she murmurs.

She looks at me. "Is it him?"

I nod.

She marvels at him. "What do I say?" she asks. "Can he talk?"

I don't answer.

Kurt Cobain's hair is in his face. Shifting her gaze, Charlotte tries to look into his eyes. While the president couldn't quite find your eyes, Kurt is purposefully avoiding them.

"I can't believe how young you are," Charlotte tells him. "You're just a boy."

Kurt mumbles, "I'm old."

"Are you really here?" she asks.

"Here we are now," he sings. "Entertain us."

His voice is rough and hard-lived. It's some kind of proof of life to Charlotte.

Charlotte looks at me, filled with wonder. "I thought he was gone," she says. "I can't believe he's really here."

Kurt shrugs. "I only appreciate things when they're gone," he says.

Charlotte looks stricken. "I recognize that line," she says to me. "That's a line from his suicide note. How does he know that? Has he already written it, does he know what he's going to do?"

"I don't know," I tell her. This isn't my conversation to have. I back away toward the door, and just as I'm leaving, I hear her start to talk to him.

"Don't do what you're thinking about doing," she pleads with him. "You don't know how special you are, you don't know how much you matter to me," she says, carefully, like she's talking to a child. "Please don't take yourself from me. You can't do that to me."

She leans toward Kurt Cobain like she wants to throw her arms around him and hold him, like she's forgotten that her arms don't work and there's no him to embrace.

Hurricanes Anonymous

Nonc pulls up outside Chuck E. Cheese's and hits the hazards on his UPS van. The last working cell tower in Lake Charles, Louisiana, is not far away, so he stops here a couple times a day to check his messages. He turns to his son, who's strapped into a bouncy chair rigged from cargo hooks, and attempts to snag his cell from the boy, a two-and-a-half-year-old named Geronimo.

"Eyeball," Geronimo says into the phone. "Eyeball."

It's one of the boy's few words, and Nonc has no idea what it means.

"Trade?" Nonc asks as he raises a sippy cup of chocolate milk. "For some gla-gla?"

Geronimo has puffy little-boy eyes, white nubby teeth and an unfortunate sunburn.

"Eyeball" is all the boy will say.

Nonc next waves his DIAD, the electronic pad customers use to sign for their packages. It's got GPS, Wi-Fi, cellular and

Bluetooth capabilities, though most of that is worthless since the hurricane. The kid goes for it, and Nonc steps down into the parking lot, which is a checkerboard of green and blue tents.

The boarded-up Outback Steakhouse next door is swamped with FEMA campers, and a darkened AMC 16 is a Lollapalooza of urban camping. It's crazy, but weeks after losing everything, people seem to have more stuff than ever—and it's all the shit you'd want to get rid of: Teflon pans, old towels, coffee cans of silverware. How do you tell your thin bedsheets from your neighbor's? Can you separate your yellowed, mismatched Tupperware from the world's? And there are mountains of all-new crap. Outside the campers are bright purple laundry bins, molded plastic porch chairs and the deep black of Weber grills, which is what happens when Wal-Mart is your first responder.

Inside the pizza parlor, the place is packed, everyone looking sunburned and glassy-eyed in donated T-shirts and baggy-ass sweats. Nonc heads for the restroom, but when he opens the door, a loafy steam rolls out that makes it clear a hundred people have just taken a dump, and even Nonc—a guy who has lately improvised toilet paper from first-aid compresses, a *miniature* New Testament and the crust of Chuck E.'s own pizza—even he backs out.

Nonc steals all the plastic spoons and napkins, then checks his voicemail, trying not to focus on the people around him—they're so clueless and pathetic, sitting around Chuck E.

Cheese's all day, a place that's open only because it's a Christian outfit. Sure, Nonc shouldn't point fingers—he's had some mosquito problems lately, and his wraparound sunglasses have given him a raccoon tan line. But nobody gave him free clothes and prepaid calling cards after he was evicted last year and all his possessions were auctioned by the sheriff.

First there's a text message from his girlfriend, Relle: "411+XXX."

Then there's a voicemail from his boss about a utility crew. Delivering to the utility crews is the biggest pain in the ass—they're in a different place every day, lost themselves half the time. They're all from Nebraska and Arkansas, and since they signed up to go save New Orleans after Hurricane Katrina, they're none too happy about getting stuck in Lake Charles after Hurricane Rita.

Finally, there's a message from a doctor in Los Angeles about his father. Nonc's old man is a garden-variety scoundrel, and on the scale of bad dads, he probably only rates a medium, but because of his ability to write vicious and unrelenting Post-it notes, he was one of the most avoided characters in Lake Charles right up to the day he stole Nonc's car and left town. Nonc's father can't speak, so once or twice a year Nonc gets a call from somebody who's been suckered into the task of reading a stream of Post-its.

The doctor's text message is this: "Your father is very ill and not expected."

Nonc's dad has had cancer before, so the diagnosis isn't

exactly news. There's something *right* about it, though. A man spends his life "not expected"—isn't that how it should end?

Nonc steps up on one of the kiddie rides, a paddy wagon driven by a singing rat. From this height, he can see the evacuees are all wearing orange FEMA bracelets and the same cheap-ass white sneakers. Eating pizza all day, watching TV. It's true these folks had it bad—got hit by Katrina, then evacuated to Lake Charles, only to get hit by Rita three weeks later. But Rita has passed, and it's high time to get their shit tight. Someone needs to tell them that they're better off without their coffee tables and photo albums. Some person will have to break it to them that their apartments weren't so great, that losing track of half their relatives is probably for the best. Some shit, though, you got to figure for yourself.

Nonc lifts a hand. "Does anybody know Marnie Broussard?" he asks them yet again. "She's a white girl, from Tremé in New Orleans. She's the mother of my boy."

Soon Nonc's UPS van is grinding toward the top of the Lake Charles Bridge. The bridge cuts the city in two, and it has this weird way of making you forget. Nonc goes over it like ten times a day—parts for the petrochemical plants, drops at the riverboat casinos, a million foam coolers of crawfish to the airport—though he never really thought about the power of the bridge till the hurricanes came. This morning, Nonc delivered sausage casings to the hog lots in Lacassine and Taser batteries to the Calcasieu jail, but once he starts climbing the bridge—suddenly there's no more pig squeal in his ears, and his clothes don't stink of louse powder and prison okra. There's just the clean smell of rice barges, oyster shale in the sun, and that sandwich spread of ocean, twenty miles south.

For the bridge to work, there's only one thing you got to not think about, and that's how this lady from New Orleans tossed her kids off last week. She lined those tots up for the old heave-ho, and when the deed was done and it was her turn to splash, she chickened. The bridge is no stranger to jumpers, and Nonc has driven past exhaust-blackened wreaths and *we miss you so-and-so* messages spray-painted down the guardrail. What gets Nonc is that, in his experience, parents abandon you slowly, bit by bit, across your entire youth. Even after you get over being ditched, they keep calling to remind you. So the thought of casting off your children in one stroke is unnerving and new, and Nonc knows exactly how it will play out: they'll blame the hurricane and put that lady in a halfway house for a year—then she'll move to Vegas or something and live on dollar-ninety-nine prime rib.

Nonc coasts down the backside of the bridge before turning onto Lake Street, where the fat homes are, with their long docks and boathouses. Because the rich folks are still poshing it up wherever rich folks evacuate to, this is the last section of town to get service restored. Sections from downed oak trees have been rolled like old tires in the ditch, and Nonc's van lumbers over sprays of brick from fallen chimneys, making Geronimo's yellow boom box skip.

"Grow-grow," the boy shouts.

"Easy there, hot rod," Nonc says, forwarding through the CD tracks—there's Ernie and Bert singing "Elbow Room," and then there's "Batty-Bat," which the Dracula puppet does. He turns it up when Grover starts rapping the ABCs.

It took him a week to figure out the boy was trying to say *Grover*.

Nonc's had "custody" of him since the day after Katrina. New Orleans was being evacuated, buses coming in by the caravan, and the city was already overrun with tuffdicks from the offshore rigs. Nonc was making a FEMA delivery—which meant wading into a casino parking lot filled with thousands of people, looking for anyone wearing a tie. He emerged to find Geronimo in his van with a yellow boom box and a bag of clothes.

Marnie didn't even leave a note. Do you brush a toddler's teeth? What do you do when a boy stays awake all night, staring at the roof of the van? Nonc would give anything for a vocabulary sheet. What does *bway* mean? And the initials *M-O*? So far, Nonc's figured out a couple dozen words—*back, bed, mess, broke*—things like that. *Gla-gla* is chocolate milk. When Geronimo needs help, he says *up, up*. And then there's *eyeball*, which he says clear as a bell—why, what the hell for?

Relle taught the boy *hug* and *kiss*. You can say, "Baby kiss

van," and though you can tell he doesn't want to, he'll go like
a robot and put his lips on the dusty fender. Relle is always
saying, "Baby hug chair" and it kills her, it's so cute. Geronimo goes into this seek-and-destroy mode, and the next thing
you know, he's gotten to third base with the nearest barstool.
And it was Relle's idea that the boy should call him Nonc,
rather than Randall, his real name.

Nonc and Relle call him rascal, G, G-Ron, Nimo, things
like that, because he can't understand his full name, let alone
say it. That should tell you what kind of guy Nonc was back
when Marnie told him she was pregnant. "Geronimo," he
said in that fuck-it way, like someone jumping from a plane.
He didn't say it in a birth-certificate way, at least he thinks he
didn't. Marnie moved to New Orleans, had the boy there,
and once she figured out how to garnish Nonc's wages, there
wasn't much need to talk. Yet here they are, one mean delivery team—Nonc belted the boy's high chair to the jump seat,
and the changing station folds down from the rear doors. So
Nonc's surviving, it's been five weeks already, and Marnie's
vacation from parenthood can't last forever. Hurricane or no,
there are only so many places to hide in Lake Charles.

The utility crews have cut a primitive path down Lake
Street. The shrubs have been trimmed by sheets of flying
glass, and the trees are shot through with the cotton candy of
insulation. The weird thing isn't the destruction—you expect
to see the corpselike bloat of swamped mattresses or refrig-
erators that have exploded. What's unnerving is the way

clothes hang in the limbs of trees, making it look, out of the corner of your eye, like folks are up there watching you. It's spooky the way, instead of seeing yourself in the windows of passing houses, your reflection falls into their dark rooms.

Up ahead are a few City of Tulsa trucks and a command van. Some linemen are working their way down the street in a halo of sawdust and two-stroke smoke, while the electricians, T-shirts on their heads, sit in fold-up fishing chairs in the shade of a sailboat on its side. You can tell these guys have been living out of their rigs—milk crates of rations are everywhere, half-washed clothes flap from the outriggers of a boom truck. They're probably scavenging new frying pans every time one gets dirty, and crapping in five-gallon buckets. It's easy to live out of your vehicle, though. Once you accept your situation, your shit gets tight real quick.

The package he's delivering isn't some exotic engineering part or anything. When Nonc pulls the box off the shelf, the label reads *Amazon*. Nonc climbs down with it while Geronimo follows with the DIAD—it's his job to get the signatures. An electrician wearing a flipped-up welder's hood descends in a cherry picker to direct them toward a man sitting on the only surviving dock, reading blueprints.

He's an older guy, in his fifties probably, wearing a green boonie-rat hat and some serious binoculars, the kind with orange lenses. Nonc and the boy make their way over, Nonc calling out the address label, "Bob Vollman, City of Tulsa Utilities, care of Lake Charles, Louisiana."

"That would be me," Vollman says. "Thank God for Amazon—and UPS, of course." With a folding knife, he unwraps *Snyder's Guide to the Birds of the Gulf Wetlands.*

"People mostly shoot at birds around here," Nonc says.

Geronimo holds up the DIAD, and the engineer takes notice of him, pulls off his hat. With his hand, like a puppet, he makes the floppy hat talk like Yoda. "A signature is wanted, hmm?" the hat asks. "And here we have what, hmm, a child, a boy child, have we, yes?"

Geronimo nears the hat and stares into its folds as if trying to determine its intentions.

Yoda scrunches his face. "Serious, this one is, hmm. Much turmoil has he seen." The engineer glances at Nonc for confirmation. "All around is uncertainty." The puppet looks up and down the street, but Geronimo doesn't follow. "Broken are many things, yes, and not in their proper places." Vollman has the puppet take the stylus and, mumbling as if its mouth is too full to talk, sign the DIAD. That gets a laugh.

"Got a boy exactly his age," Vollman says. "Two kids off to college, and then along comes Henry."

"Cajuns call that lagniappe," Nonc says. "It means getting more than you were bargaining for."

"I tell you," Vollman says, tousling Geronimo's hair. "It sure is hard to leave them."

Nonc has tried to imagine that moment Marnie put the boy in the van—if only he could think up what she said to him when she left, maybe he'd know where she went, when she might be coming back for him.

"What did you tell him," Nonc asks, "you know, when you left?"

"Henry?"

"Yeah."

"I said, 'I'll be right back.' Kids this age, they don't understand time. They don't know what a month is. Plus, they don't remember. I made some mistakes, parent-wise, believe me. At this age, you got some wiggle room."

"This is all just temporary," Nonc says. "The boy's going back with his mama soon."

"The hurricane turned some lives upside down," Vollman says. "Obviously, you two are in some kind of situation, but seriously, the boy can't be running around in his jammies. Look at the glass and nails. He needs some boots and jeans, something."

The pajamas are actually a custom tracksuit that Relle made for the boy, but Nonc doesn't say anything.

Vollman lifts up his new field guide. "Amazon has tons of kid stuff."

At the sight of the book, Geronimo says, "Bird."

"That's right," Vollman says. "Let's check out a tweety bird." He lifts the binoculars and invites Geronimo to share, each peering through one of the lenses. Squinting, they do a sweep of the lake. "Saw a blue macaw this morning," Vollman says. "Not exactly Louisiana wildlife, but quite a sight. It was sitting on an upturned barge, right out there on the water, a big bell pepper in its beak."

"Macaw," the boy says.

"That's right," Vollman says.

"Big bird."

"That's right, she was one big bird."

Standing above them, Nonc, too, looks out on the water. With the outbound tide, all the refuse in the lake is dog-paddling back toward them, across three miles of brown chop. Shielding his eyes, Nonc makes out roof timbers, recycling bins, logged couch cushions and all the garage-filling crap a human could own. Out there slowly turning, as if from a logroller, is a black septic tank, and from the water, like a shark, a boat hull rises, flashes its keel and vanishes. Nonc had been picturing those kids tossed from the bridge dropping into blue lake water. He imagined their eyes open, their hands reaching for one another, and the knowledge that at least they had each other. But here it is, dark, entangling, a roil of propane tanks, plywood sheets and fifty-five-gallon drums.

Nonc takes the long way around the lake, past abandoned ice trucks with their bellies dripping, past livestock gone blind from drinking salt water, past a church whose marquee reads, "The Eye of the Storm Is the Peace of Christ." Here on the far side of the lake is the Southwest Louisiana Visitors' Center, which is where Relle works. Instead of handing out brochures for "The Cajun Riviera," Relle now spends her time drawing maps for relief workers to where towns like Gueydan and Grand Chenier used to be. Hurricane or no, the state is flush from gaming, so everybody still gets a souvenir bottle of Tabasco, a Sportsman's Paradise ball cap and a string of Mardi Gras beads draped on by a pretty girl. Relle is the pretty girl.

Through the window, Nonc can see her talking to some government types, guys with that carefree look that comes from being able to walk away. They're wearing like six strings of beads each, and they're all smiling and laughing, with Relle pausing at their punch lines to fan herself with a coupon book. Nonc flashes his lights at her, points across the street to a roadhouse that Marnie used to haunt back in the day. He flips across the street, hits his hazards and jams a straw into a juicy box. "Baby drink juice," Nonc tells the boy, and snags his cell. "Nonc be right back."

Geronimo lifts his arms and strains at his bouncy chair. "Bway," he says. "Bway."

"Look," Nonc says. "Nonc's got business."

Inside the roadhouse, he does a quick survey, then checks out a wall of beer mugs. If you hang out long enough, they put up a mug with your name on it. The wall's a regular "Who's Not Who" of South Louisiana, but no Marnie. The bartender looks like a tuffdick on leave from an oil rig. He asks, "What'll it be," and when Nonc says, "Nothing, thanks," the bartender raps the bar twice with his knuckle, which is what riverboat dealers do to point out a lack of gratuity.

All casual, Nonc asks, "You know a Marnie Broussard, ever see her come around?"

"You trying to make some kind of small talk?" the bartender asks. "You want a drink or what?"

"This girl," Nonc says. "She used to come in here, got dark hair, deep-set eyes."

The bartender drafts a beer, sets it in front of Nonc like it's the last one on earth. "Hurricane relief," he says. "On the house."

Nonc opens his phone, finds a weak signal and scrolls to the doctor's number. He doesn't really know what he's going to say to the guy, but he calls. Just when it seems like no one's going to answer, the phone picks up, but no one's there. And then Nonc can hear the valve in his father's trach tube clicking. Nonc hears that thing in his sleep. The history of that sound, of its wet, wheezy rhythm, is like a country song, it's "The Battle Hymn of the Republic."

If that doctor's right, Nonc's dad is going to die for sure this time. But the truth is, it's just an event. Life's full of events— they occur and you adjust, you roll and move on. But at some point, like when your girlfriend Marnie tells you she's pregnant, you realize that some events are actually developments. You realize there's a big plan out there you know nothing about, and a development is a first step in that new direction.

Somebody drops a kid in your lap—that's a development, you've just been clued in. Your ex–old lady disappears—you can't shrug that off. It's a serious development. Sometimes things seem like big-time developments—you get your wages garnished, your old man takes your car when he leaves town, you get evicted, your possessions get seized—but in time you adjust, you find a new way and you realize they didn't throw you off course, they didn't change you. They were just events. The truth is, the hurricane didn't change Nonc's life one bit. Neither will the death of his father. The tricky part, Nonc has figured out, is telling the difference between the two.

Nonc's just kind of sitting there, staring at the phone, when Relle walks into the bar. She always wears these sexy tracksuits—satiny, falling across her body—that she sews herself.

"Who you talking to?" she asks.

"It's my old man," he tells her.

Startled, she says, "I thought he was dying."

Nonc shrugs.

"Did you call him, or did he call you?" she asks, but she can see the answer on his face. "What did you tell him?"

"I don't know. What's there to say?"

"What's there to say? You hardly shut up about him."

"Me? You're the one who always brings him up. You never even met him."

"I don't need to meet him." She reaches for the phone. "I know all about him."

Nonc knows he shouldn't hand it over—in Relle, there is a cold, truthful streak—but he does.

Just to be sure, she asks Nonc, "You're positive he can't talk, right?" When Nonc nods, she smiles. It's the smile she flashes when a dude lowers his head to receive a string of beads. "Mr. Richard," she says into the phone. "I'm Cherelle. I'm a friend of Randall's, and I'm going to tell you a story. Once upon a time, there was a man who lived only for himself. He used up his family, making the most of them the way you'd make the most of a single square of toilet paper. He stole his son's car, and finally, he was gone, which is the happy ending. What could he possibly want now?"

When she hurts his father for him, Nonc feels a shiver of fear and satisfaction. Still, he says, "Ouch, did I mention he's fucking dying?"

She flips the phone shut. "Where's the G-Man?" she asks.

"He's chillin' in the rig. I can't believe you just said that shit. You were talking to my dad, you know, not yours."

Relle takes ahold of the beer, has a drink. "He had his chance."

Nonc takes a drink, too. "You think they'll cremate him?"

"Who's *they*?" she asks.

"You know, California."

"Like the state government? No way, sunshine. That shit's expensive. You're going to have to go all the way out there and bring him back. You got to have a funeral, it's the law."

"You know what I'd love to do?" Nonc asks. "I'd love to

take his ashes and scatter them on my mother's lawn. Wouldn't that freak her shit out?"

"I think your only chance is to go out to California, and when they lift the sheet, when you have to identify him, you say it's not your dad. Then it's the government's dime."

Nonc takes a hard look at Relle. "Where do you get this shit?" he asks her. "This isn't about money." He can tell she wants to say something smart about that, about how Marnie garnishes his wages, but Relle checks herself.

By way of sympathy, she says, "You'll never see that car again."

"I know," he says. It was only a Toyota, but those things run forever.

Then she pulls out a photograph and slides it to him. It's a blurry image of a woman on a table.

"You checking morgues now?" Nonc asks.

"No," she says. "FEMA's got a cadaver book you can flip through."

"Sorry to break it, but this isn't Marnie."

"Did you look at it? Five foot four, bottle blond, bit of fetal-alcohol to the eyes."

"Don't say shit like that."

"Did Marnie have a C-section?"

"How should I know?" he asks.

"Look, I don't want this to be her," Relle says. "Nobody wants nobody dead. I mean, that little boy needs a mom big-time."

"Marnie's not dead," Nonc says. "She's on a little vacation from parenthood, that's all. Actually, this is just like her, pulling something like this."

Relle shrugs. "Then why not go to Beaumont and see? If it's not her, great. Nothing's changed. If it is her, nothing's changed, except now you can plan, now you can take steps."

Nonc slides the picture back. "You don't know Marnie. She's not the kind to drown in a Quick Mart in Texas. She's going to come out of this hurricane better than ever."

"Lighter, at least," Relle says.

"She probably got some FEMA money and is living it up. When that's gone, she'll be back."

"Who ditches their kid in the good times and comes back in the bad?"

Nonc doesn't have an answer for that.

Relle opens her purse and digs inside. "Why don't you want to find her?" she asks.

Nonc takes one more drink and sets the beer aside. "I'm looking just as hard as you."

From her purse, Relle removes a big Q-tip, sealed in plastic. "I almost forgot," she says.

"Forgot what?"

"Open wide," she tells him.

"What for?"

"Just open up," she says, removing the wrapper. When Nonc does, she jabs the thing in his mouth, right in his gums, and twirls it.

"What the hell was that?"

"It's a swab."

"A swab of what?"

Relle takes a slug of beer and puts the swab in a plastic tube. "We better check on the little man," she says. "'Cause I have to roll."

Outside, crunching through the bottle caps and shale of the parking lot, they can hear Geronimo in the van. He's saying, "Up, up." When Nonc sticks his head inside, he can see the boy has managed to get the lid off one of the foam coolers. There are crawfish running around everywhere, and Geronimo, in terror, is dancing in place.

"Whoa," Relle says. "Party for one."

She moves to climb inside, but Nonc tells her, "It's okay. I got this."

"You pissed off?"

"No," he says. "We'll talk about it tonight."

"At A.A.?"

The boy is trying to climb the cords of his bouncy chair.

"Where the hell else?" Nonc says. "Look, I gotta take care of this."

But instead of leaving, Relle steps inside the van. "He is so adorable," she says. "One day we're going to have a little boy just like him." Then she sticks a swab in his mouth.

"What the fuck are you doing?"

"It's just a test," she says, then scrambles out of the van. "FEMA does it for free, to reconnect family members."

Nonc comes after her. "Are you crazy?" he asks. "This is my boy. Right here, he's mine."

"You don't know that," she says, and then, in her tracksuit, she bolts across the frontage road.

When Nonc climbs in the van, the crawfish are all clicking their pinchers, and he realizes Geronimo has the hiccups, which he gets when he freaks.

"Up, up," the boy says. He's kicking his legs and straining the cords of the bouncy chair.

It gets Nonc to see him like that. "Hey, hot rod," he says. "Don't be scared of those guys. Nonc's here, okay. Nonc will protect you."

He unhooks the cords, and the boy latches on. He's totally shaking, snot all over his face. Even though he's not dirty, Nonc takes him into the back of the van for a diaper change. That always soothes him. "Relax, relax," Nonc whispers, and lays him back on his changing pad. The boy's looking around for the crawfish, eyes going this way and that.

"Nonc's back, okay. Nonc always comes back." But there's no way to explain it to the kid. Right now, when he's afraid, he thinks fear lasts forever, that it is everything.

Nonc shimmies off Geronimo's pants, then unfastens the diaper. He tosses the thing away, even though it's perfectly fine, not wet or anything. Geronimo starts to chill when Nonc slides a fresh diaper under him. Nonc keeps saying *hush,* and when he asks the boy to lift his legs, Geronimo quietly obeys, holding them up and keeping them there. That's when Nonc does his favorite part. Nonc takes the baby powder and raises it high. Very lightly, he lets it snow down. The stuff is cool and sweet-smelling. He shakes the thing, and his son's eyes follow the dusty white powder as it slowly floats down. The boy can watch it forever.

The UPS yard is almost empty, its skeleton crew of drivers out on the road. Nonc docks the van so they can clean and fuel it before heading out again. Geronimo grabs the hose, and as Nonc sweeps the crawfish out onto the pavement, the boy sprays them into the storm drain. He seems to relish the way they skitter against the beam of water, but when they've all finally disappeared, when they've slipped through the grate for good, he looks lost.

UPS lets Nonc keep all his food and milk in the refrigerated cargo bay, so he can bootstrap up a few PB&J sandwiches and reload the sippy cups between runs. UPS is the coolest company that way—they let Nonc take the van at night, the way a cop brings home a squad car, and they look the other way about Geronimo riding shotgun. As long as you don't fuck up and get your name in the paper, Brown is on your side. One driver got drunk and ran his van into a ditch. UPS just towed it out, no questions. Got him some counseling, sent him back on the road.

Nonc downloads a new manifest to the DIAD, which diagrams the optimal route—right away, he sees that one of the stops is his own address, or his old one, the place on Kirkman Avenue he was evicted from. He heads there first. On his street, a pair of white oaks have blown down, letting a new light fall on the fourplex, so that he almost doesn't recognize it when he pulls up. All four doors have been kicked in, and on the porch, some crows are taking turns poking their heads in a cereal box.

When he came home last year to find the door padlocked, the sheriff's tag said all his possessions would be auctioned to pay the back rent. But Nonc enters to see his old TV on its stand, his couch blooming with mold, his table and chair dusted with broken glass. The rest of the stuff isn't his—the dishes on the floor, the broken picture frames, the bicycle on its back by the door. The mixture of his possessions with a stranger's isn't as weird as the fact that these things used to mean something to him. When did he find time to sit on this couch? Did he once know the names of TV shows? He feels like the person who owned that couch is just as much of a stranger as the person whose family photos litter the floor.

That's when Nonc looks at the package and sees that it is addressed to himself, Randall Richard, from his father. Nonc picks up a piece of glass and slits open the box. Inside is a note, one of his father's unmistakable notes: "Aside from killing me, California has been okay. These are my effects. They asked what I wanted done with them, and I didn't know."

Nonc turns the note over to see if there's more, but there isn't. Inside are his father's clothes, his pants, shirt, belt and

ball cap. Nonc's pretty okay with the man's death, but the notion that he'll never get dressed again, that he's to die in a
gown, seems strange and impossible. There's also a wallet.
Tooled into the leather is "Nonc," short for *n'oncle*, a Cajun
term for *uncle* that's used for close family friends. It's what he
called his father when he was a boy, before he started calling
him Harlan. It occurs to Nonc that he never called his father
Dad, and now, weirdly, neither does his own son.

Inside the wallet are a Costco membership card, some
cash and a handwritten list of Internet casinos with ID numbers and passwords. There is a California driver's license with
an address in L.A. that Nonc could map with his DIAD, and
there's an ancient laminated doctor's note stating that he is a
mute. Nonc picks up a key chain, a large one with all manner
of car keys, Toyota, Ford, Hyundai. One of the keys is for a
boat, a Grady-White, which are the best. And there's a packet
of white hankies, which his father used to clean his trach tube.
All this stuff is just sitting on Nonc's lap. He feels like he's ri-
fling through it, like his dad might walk in at any moment and
catch him. He feels like his father died long ago, and these are
relics. He brushes it all onto the couch, the keys, the cash, the
LSU ball cap. He stands and takes a last look around. He tries
to separate the different owners of all this stuff, tries to put
them together. He tries to close the door behind him, but it is
broken.

———

To get a break from Geronimo, Nonc and Relle attend A.A. meetings at the Presbyterian church, where an old maw-maw provides free child care. For two hours a night, they get to drink coffee and listen to other people's problems. Tonight Nonc arrives first, and after dropping off the boy, he grabs a piece of king cake and sits in the half-empty circle. Churches are always acting like they have something incredible going on—white envelopes for your money, toddlers in three-piece suits, cops in gloves directing Sunday traffic—but their basements are all the same: folding chairs, old appliances, bins of dead folks' clothes.

The regulars start arriving. Even though it's "anonymous," Lake Charles isn't such a big town, and Nonc has knocked on just about every door. Linda Tasso shows up, the oldest daughter of the mayor. She manages to find a new rock bottom every week, goes on and on about it. Jim Arceneaux brings this giant truck-stop thermos of iced tea. He used to run a reptile zoo out by the interstate, snakes and gators galore; he sobered up when they slapped him with animal cruelty charges after they caught him adopting too many kittens and puppies from the pound. Some folks from New Orleans show up—you can spot them right away, that look of wearing someone else's clothes, those faraway eyes.

Finally, Relle strolls in—she's got a chocolate and maroon tracksuit on, and she takes a chair across the circle from Nonc. She slouches in her seat, which pulls the fabric of her pants tight enough that you can see the shadow of her pussy. The girl has really taken a shine to A.A. meetings, and not just because it's the only time they're free of the boy. She seems to love the idea that normal-looking people, people with careers and houses, are actually, according to their own testimony, weak and susceptible. Relle was the one pretty girl in high school who was never popular, so she loves standing in their group at break, being among the chitchat, bumming cigarettes, laughing when they start to laugh. And then there's that moment when the break is over and everyone heads back inside for the second hour, that moment when she takes Nonc's hand and leads him into the van.

She's even become a talker at the meetings. She loves to discuss the state of their relationship, out loud, in front of witnesses. Tonight she starts right in. One of the evacuees from New Orleans stands up. "My name is James B.," he says, "and I am an alcoholic," and then Relle is off and running. But Nonc's still staring at James B., who's wearing a brandnew Chuck E. Cheese T-shirt, and the crispness of the white makes the rest of him look battered, like some shit has truly befallen him.

"My boyfriend," Relle says, and looks toward the ceiling, as if nobody knows who that might be. "My boyfriend's real strong, but so is his problem. There are struggles ahead, and he can't see them. A funeral's on the horizon, travel. I'm trying to help him. I'm offering my hand, but I'm afraid he's not going to take it."

Bill Maque, the guy who runs Game and Fish, says, "Tell

your boyfriend that he needs to find a meeting before he travels. Trust me, they need to be expecting him."

"A funeral," Linda Tasso volunteers, "send in the shrinks, that's a guaranteed spiral."

Nonc's job is to figure out what "problem" Relle is really talking about. Last night she said, "Nobody should have to handle two people's problems," which was code for the position Marnie had put them in, and hell or high water, that girl had to be found. But Nonc can't tell if tonight's problem has something to do with Marnie or the paternity test, both of which could result in major developments. Your baby's mama is dead? Your baby's not your baby? Those things are as irreversible as a kid thrown from a bridge, and if Nonc knows anything, it's that you want to minimize developments in life—a few are going to happen, sure, but you don't go looking for them, and you sure as shit don't cause them.

"I can't speak for your boyfriend," Nonc says, "but maybe he's thinking, thanks for the hand, but he's on top of it. Maybe he doesn't need any help right now."

Even though it's anonymous, everyone turns to look at Nonc. He can read their minds—*Dude*, they're thinking, *take the help.*

Astonished, Relle says, "You saying my boyfriend doesn't want my hand?"

"Take the hand," James B. calls out. He looks up. "Lord, help him take that hand." It's clear the man is imploring the Creator Himself, and it puts weird gravity in the room.

Nonc says, "I'm just saying maybe your boyfriend's doing okay. He's surviving, right? He's putting one foot in front of the other, he's making it."

Linda Tasso chimes in with a "One day at a time."

"Maybe that's what my boyfriend thinks," Relle says. "But he's stuck, and going nowhere is going backward. I'm making plans, you know. I'm trying to bring him with me."

"What makes you think you know what's best for him?"

"Because he's in my heart," Relle says. "And because I know him better than he knows himself."

Wearily, people turn to look at Nonc. They've had about enough of tonight's episode of the Cherelle Show, but Nonc doesn't care. "If this guy's in your heart," he says, "then so are all his mistakes, you know—so is his kid."

Relle leans forward in her chair. "I am making you," she says. She looks into Nonc's eyes. "Nobody ever made you, no one ever cared enough. Take my hand, let me make you."

That's when James B. points toward the rafters. "The roof is weak," he says, and everybody looks up. "Lord, let it be weak, let me find where."

There is a silence, and James B. stands. He really doesn't look very good.

"I used to plot out every single drink," he says. "I used to plot the liquor store, now you got to plot away from it, from the glow of it. Why would the Lord make a liquor store glow? Now you got to plot out a folding chair, a cup of coffee." He looks at his coffee like he's never seen coffee. "You got to plot a toilet, a bus, a single slice of pizza. Take the dogs off the chain."

Nervously, Jim Arceneaux says, "Okay, I think we've all been where James has been."

"Seize the knife from that table, you will need it," James B. says, and he's talking like a man from a Bible story, like he's one of the guys spelled out in the stained glass above.

Jim Arceneaux stands. Fake-laughing, he says, "Hey, no knives, please." He looks at Bill Maque like he should stand, too. "James B., we can hear your hurt," Jim says. He has a Bible. He opens his arms. "Would you like some personal fellowship?"

"Prepare for the dark," James B. says. "The water's at your feet, your knees, ribs. All day long I used to breathe for a drink. Close my eyes, and I'd still see the glow—Budweiser blue, Coors yellow. Take your knife to the ceiling, plot your way through the attic. Beware that insulation floats. A bottle you hid long ago. Take the dogs please take my dogs off the chain. In that small space, insulation will swarm you. You got to plot the roof. Please let it be weak. Cut till you see the glow, in the dark water look for the glowing. Make yourself small, scrape through. Lord unhook the chain off the porch or else they do drown."

After the break, Nonc has Cherelle's legs high, and he's inside her. The van smells of baby wipes and crawfish. From the chapel comes the sound of scales on the organ. The notes are aimless and mechanical, someone trying and trying to do better. Relle's thing is that she looks right at you when you're doing it, she never unlocks her eyes. It's kind of unnerving, but Relle says she can't help it, and she reminds Nonc that she comes every time. She reminds him how well their bodies fit, the fold of his arms around her shoulders, the way her legs figure-four his waist. Sometimes, though, Nonc gets the distinct feeling she's trying not to come, like she doesn't want to let go of something. Maybe it's more like she's trying to delay it, be in control of it as long as she can. Nonc can feel her fight what's building, and when she finally gives in, when she lets herself be swept, that's when she closes her eyes.

The result is that, with her glaring at him, Nonc tends to close his own eyes, and that puts him in his own world. Then it's easy for his mind to wander. It's easy to start thinking about James B. and what happened to those people in New Orleans. He'd been imagining Marnie freeloading a ride to town to drop off Geronimo in some kind of vacation from parenting. But it's clear some shit went down in N.O. to Marnie, to the boy.

Relle reaches down, grabs his hips and stops him. Sometimes, when she's in a bad mood, she'll stop him and make him put on a condom right in the middle. But she doesn't seem mad.

"You heard what I said in there, right?" she asks. "I'm trying to put myself in your heart."

"You're already there."

"Then I need you to act," she says. "Act that way."

"Okay, I'll go to Beaumont—I'll go see if it's her."

Relle reaches into her bag. "It's not her. I called after lunch. Turns out it was some other dead girl." She pulls out a powder-blue debit card from FEMA. "I'm acting," she says. "I'm making a future for us. The thing is, as decisions need to be made, as options materialize, I need to know you're with me."

Nonc's seen a thousand of these cards, all the evacuees have them. The trouble is they don't help you survive, because there's nothing for sale—the only thing they'll buy is your way out of Louisiana. "Where'd you get this?" he asks.

"There's five grand on it," she says. "It's a small-business grant. They're giving 'em away."

"Small business?"

Relle reaches into her bag and pulls out a brochure for "Nonc's Outfitters." On it are images of bird dogs and ducks, along with a scan of Nonc's high school photo and a Google map on the back to some property her father owns to the south. "Not bad, huh?" she asks. "I made it on the computer at work. All those hunting dogs and shit? I pulled those pictures off the NRA website. We spend the money on a four-by-four, and there you have it, there's our business. Maybe we'll build a hunting lodge someday. Or whatever, we can spend the money on whatever."

Nonc could remind her that he doesn't know anything about duck hunting, and neither does she. He could mention that her father raised greyhounds, not bloodhounds, that this is technically a crime, that his wages are already garnished. But it's his picture he can't stop thinking about. In it, his smile is a mix of optimism and relief, as if now that high school is over, the hard part is done. It's the sucker's look that people had on their faces when they got off the buses from Katrina, when they didn't know Rita was on the way.

"At the Visitors' Center," Relle says, "I get all these calls looking for hunting guides. I'm supposed to take turns recommending the guys on the list. And then it hits me. The answer is right there."

"This kind of shit doesn't bother you?" he asks.

"What?" Relle asks. "The hunters are stockbrokers and shit. We just drive them out there. They've got fancy rifles and gold-plated whistles."

"Shotguns," Nonc tells her. "You hunt birds with shotguns. And you know what I'm talking about."

"You wanna know what bothers me?" she asks. "I'm bothered by living with crazy people for my room and board. I'm bothered by having to go to A.A. to get a date with you."

He looks at the map to the property Relle's father owns. The guy used to run a racing kennel there. The whole thing was a fiasco, and everybody knows, though nobody will say, that there are dogs buried everywhere. Whenever Nonc feels bad about having his loser dad skip town, he just thinks of Relle and what it's like to have him stay. The truth is that Relle's not about schemes and money but about wiping her slate. For someone who grew up the way she did, Relle's the best possible version of herself.

"Just as long as you know how fucked up this is," he says.

"Please," she says. "I mailed this brochure to four people today—they're sending in their deposits. One of them lives in Hollywood."

She massages him, pulls him inside again, though he can tell she's got the sex cordoned off, like there's a velvet rope between her and what's happening below. Then she's looking at him, a narrowed, questioning gaze. It's not an angry look— he's just being read. He closes his eyes, sees a roadhouse he and Marnie used to go to, the place where they met, actually. It was called the Triple Crown, out on Highway 90. He recalls this one night they went out—hadn't known each other too long—and no, Marnie said, she didn't feel like drinking that night. That was okay with Nonc, he understood, but he had a feeling, and looking back, what seemed like an insignificant event was a major development. He wouldn't know for a month, but that was the day Marnie knew she was pregnant. Developments can happen right in front of you like that, you don't even see them.

When it's time, they pick up Geronimo in the annex.

At the door, they pause. Through the little window, they can see the maw-maws inside, arms folded as they confer with one another. Relle says, "These ladies give me the creeps."

"Just don't talk to them," Nonc tells her.

"I don't get old ladies," she says. "Who are they, what do they want from you?"

Nonc feels the same way. Old women look all innocent and goody-two-shoes, but then they level some all-knowing eyes on your ass. Plus, they look alike—Nonc can't even be sure if these are the same old ladies as last week.

Inside, Geronimo is sitting in a small plastic chair. He's wearing a smock, tied at the waist, and he's real serious about some clay that he's rolling out. He doesn't even notice when they enter. Nonc stares at the boy, his round forehead and long eyelashes. When Geronimo reaches up to rub his ear, Nonc knows he's sleepy. "Come to Nonc," he calls out, and crouches to receive him.

But the boy doesn't move.

The maw-maws walk to Geronimo. One takes his hand. "Such a sweet child," she says.

"Unbearably sweet," the other adds as she pulls the smock over his head.

When they bring him to Nonc, he can see they've given the boy a haircut, and they've applied a thick cream to his sunburned face. He's in a hand-me-down set of coveralls from the auxiliary.

"You give him a bath?" Nonc asks.

"We cleaned him up a little," one says, then adds, "Geronimo is such a special name."

"Synonymous with resilience and determination."

"In the Apache language, Geronimo means *fiercely loyal.*"

"One of the books we read together was *The Last Palomino.*"

The women go on and on about all the books they read and activities they did, enunciating everything like they're hosting an event, like Geronimo's a grand guest and Nonc and Relle are being introduced to him for the first time.

One of them takes a drawing of some yellow swirly lines and pins it to the boy's coveralls. The drawing is captioned "Macaw." "A disaster can be a trying time," she says.

"Especially for a child," the other adds. She holds out a brown paper bag, its top neatly rolled up. "Here are the child's pajamas."

Nonc can feel Relle wince. "Those aren't pajamas," he says. "That's a custom tracksuit, with piping and everything. It's tailor-made with fabric from—"

"Morocco," Relle says.

"From Morocco."

There is a pause. In it, the old ladies give Nonc that look.

"You were right to come here," one of them says. "Geronimo is always welcome here. All of you are. What a perfect age he is."

"A difficult age to be separated from a parent."

"Such a trauma that can be."

"Maybe I'm the boy's parent," Relle says. "Did you think of that? Do you know that I'm not her?"

———

Outside, it's dark. Nonc fires up the van and heads to Relle's halfway house. He doesn't prowl roadhouses or cruise Charity looking for Marnie. He steps on the gas to blow out the mosquitoes, and they go.

As soon as they arrive, Dr. Gaby opens the door, which means that Nonc won't be sleeping on clean sheets with Relle and Geronimo, that there will be no hot shower and toilet in the A.M. When Geronimo sees Dr. Gaby, he runs and leaps up onto her wheelchair, which makes Nonc cringe because Relle has told him that Dr. Gaby uses a piss bag, that you'd never know it, but it's under her clothes.

Dr. Gaby throws Nonc a dubious look. "You cut his hair," she says.

Relle says, "How do you know I didn't give him a haircut?"

Dr. Gaby doesn't respond to this. She turns the boy's face right and left, inspecting the sunburn. "It's better," she says, and throws Nonc a look of true distaste. Then she goes through her routine: She takes the boy's earlobe and peers inside. She runs a finger along his teeth. With a thumb, she pulls down his eyelid to inspect the white of the eye. She's not a real doctor—she was a psychiatrist before she retired because of her condition.

"Haircut itch?" she asks Geronimo.

Geronimo rubs his neck. "Itchy," he says.

Dr. Gaby blows the stubble off his neck, then wheels an about-face and rolls inside.

Nonc and Relle follow. It's not really right to call it a half-way house. There are four residents with permanent problems, and they live here permanently. Once you come to this place, you don't go anywhere. Relle doesn't have any training, so her job is more like babysitting, and you can believe she has a rule for everything.

Then, in the wake of Katrina, the dream team arrived. They got off a bus from the Superdome holding hands, eight adult men. Dr. Gaby thinks they have entrenched autism, but she doesn't know for sure—they came from an unknown facility without files, medical records, case histories or full names. Wherever they were housed, they were housed together, accustomed to staying up to ungodly hours, and damned if they don't get their nightly video. Tonight, as Nonc and Relle pass, they are in the living room, drinking diet sodas in the blue glow of a Robin Williams movie.

"They give me the willies," Relle says.

Nonc looks at their uncomprehending faces, at the sodas in their thick hands.

"So pathetic," she adds. "Can you imagine being like that, stuck watching whichever TV show is played for you, living in whatever town the bus plops you in?"

In the kitchen, racks of cookies are cooling, and the smell is overpowering. The counters are custom-made for a wheelchair, so they're just the right height for a little boy. Geronimo, on Dr. Gaby's lap, sits before a large mixing bowl. Dr. Gaby places an egg in Geronimo's hand, then wraps hers around his. Together, they crack an egg on the rim. Dr. Gaby then splits the egg, letting the yolk flop into the bowl. Without a word, she hands the next egg to Geronimo. He taps it on the rim, then hands it to Dr. Gaby, who splits it.

Relle grabs a cookie. "God, oatmeal," she says with her mouth full. "Someday our kids are gonna live on cookies."

To Relle, Dr. Gaby says, "Those are for the volunteers. And tomorrow's list is on the fridge." Then she turns toward Nonc. "You've gathered that your girlfriend's not too touchy-feely. I must say, though: give the girl a list, and have mercy, she can procure."

Nonc asks, "So nobody's come forward to claim the dream team?" He knows he shouldn't call them that. It's Relle's term, and she only calls them the dream team to get under Dr. Gaby's skin.

"Hundreds of thousands of people are displaced," she says. "I know your famous position that the hurricane is no skin off your nose, but for the rest of us, it's a different matter."

"What if nobody ever comes to get them?" Nonc asks.

"What if," Dr. Gaby says, and shrugs. "And before we get too chatty, I can't let you stay tonight, Randall. I know it happens, and I can't control what goes on when I'm not here, but these people, they're vulnerable right now, they need stability. Plus, I need to think of the child."

"Don't you worry about the boy," Nonc says. "He gets taken care of just fine."

"I don't want to imagine," Dr. Gaby says, "where this child spends his nights. But I'm talking about the boy's well-being in this facility. I don't know these men's backgrounds, what they're capable of. Telling right from wrong, that's a luxury of the able-minded. I'd have to take a host of precautions to have that boy safely sleep here." Dr. Gaby lets Geronimo dip a finger in the batter. "Where *do* you sleep?" she asks him.

Geronimo lights up. "Van," he says. "Baby kiss van."

"That's a sentence," Dr. Gaby says. "I don't want to know what it means, but he's talking in sentences already."

"I taught him that," Relle says.

"We sleep in a fat house by Prien Lake," Nonc says.

Dr. Gaby throws him a look that says, *I bet.*

"Oh, God," Relle says to Nonc, "I totally have to show you something." She takes off upstairs.

"So, how's parenthood treating you?" Dr. Gaby asks Nonc. "What have you learned from fatherhood so far?"

"I don't know," Nonc tells her.

She gives him a look.

"You trying to make me uncomfortable? Just go ahead and tell me something I'm doing wrong. I got the boy his shots, okay? Just like you told me."

"Dr. Benson, at the clinic?"

Nonc nods.

"That's good, Randall. That's a step. Have you ever seen a child with rubella? My Lord, and this is when it happens, after a disaster. Classic distribution potential."

Nonc takes a cookie. "If these guys could be dangerous, what about you, what about your safety?"

"Oh, that's not a concern," she says. "There is something I'm concerned about, though. In life, a lot of important decisions are made for us."

It's clear to Nonc that she's about to give a speech, like the one she gave a couple weeks ago about child development. The truth is that he's discovered, at the age of twenty-six, he loves being lectured. Never before has someone spoken to him, at length, with the sole purpose of making him better.

"I wouldn't have chosen to live in Lake Charles," Dr. Gaby says. "My marriage didn't work out as I would have wished. My illness, I didn't choose that. Similar things must be true for you, right? You're adaptive, though, very flexible. It's one of your attributes. But when it comes to things like that boy, you can't ever bend. You have to choose him—then you have to be one hundred percent. Don't think of it as making a choice but obeying one. Determine what you want, and be obedient to that. You can't stay here tonight because I've chosen these people, and nothing will let me compromise that. You've got to create family, Randall. You choose them and you never let go. Blood, it doesn't mean anything. Your kin, and I know of them—you don't owe them anything. Cherelle, she's talking like that little boy isn't yours, that there's a test that will say that. Do you think that matters to a little boy? Do you think these men are my kin? I'm not even positive of their names. But I chose them, Randall. And I don't let go."

There's a look on Dr. Gaby's face that says she has more to administer, but Relle comes downstairs with a painting of a duck. It's floating above the water, breast high, wings out, ready to land. It makes you wince to look at it—you can just feel the trigger that's about to be pulled.

"What the hell is that?" Nonc asks.

"I got this at the Salvation Army," Relle says. "It's for the lodge. Our hunting lodge."

On the south side of Prien Lake, out at the end of the point, is the foundation of a house that was blown away by Hurricane Audrey fifty years ago. The footings are brick, and the cement is mixed with lime shale, which glows eerily in the moonlight. Nonc used to park his van out there nights, pull right up like he was home from the office and string his hammock from the van to a lone fireplace stack. Now Nonc has the pick of the litter: Rita's storm surge floated all these houses out into the channel, where the tides broke them up.

In the dark, Nonc approaches a cement slab in the headlights. He muscles the van up onto the foundation, parking in the living room. Then he and Geronimo begin their bedtime routine. They stand on the cool of ceramic kitchen tiles, the wind from the lake rattling their clothes as they brush their teeth and stare out at the green-and-red channel markers of the shipping lanes and, farther off, the blinking derricks of oil platforms. There is a solitary toilet, the structure's only survivor, but when Nonc cautiously lifts the lid, it has already been fouled. Nonc pisses in the bedroom, then fastens a new diaper on the boy. When he grenades the old one into the marsh grass, the frogs go quiet.

The cargo racks fold up, the foam mat unrolls, and a father and son bed down for the night. Geronimo is on his back, looking up at the dome light. Nonc is on his side, looking at a boy whose breathing is untroubled for all he's been through, though there's a lack of shine in his eyes, as if the little light in him might someday go out. His breath is clean and perfect, though, sweet-smelling. While the boy might not look much like Nonc, there's a knit to his brow, one suggesting an uncertainty and reproof that is unmistakably Harlan's. And those deep brown eyes, streaked with wheat, are pure Marnie.

"Where's Mama?" Nonc asks him.

The boy looks at the light. "Eyeball," he says. He says it with clarity and certainty but not emotion.

"Eyeball?" Nonc says.

"Narc," the boy says.

"Nonc?"

"Eyeball," the boy says.

Nonc sees that there's clay gunked under the boy's fingernails. Nonc takes a hand and, with a pen cap, uses a half-moon motion to scrape them clean, one nail at a time. Geronimo shifts his eyes and, with a blank relaxation, watches his father work. The boy's nails are soft and smooth, perfect somehow. Dr. Gaby said you can tell when a kid's had poor nutrition by the streaks on his fingernails—Geronimo's nails were proof that Marnie had fed him well. Nonc had visited the boy once in New Orleans. Under Marnie's ever-suspicious eye, Nonc ate pudding with the boy and played along with games like "I'm Going to Grab Your Sunglasses and Throw Them on the Ground and There's Nothing You Can Do About It." But Nonc had to admit he had one eye on the apartment, looking to see how Marnie was spending the money. He never really *saw* the boy, how perfect he was, how utterly unspoiled. Nonc knows that someday, after Marnie takes the boy back and he grows older, he won't remember these moments, the way they showered early at the Red Cross, foraged for their morning pizza, roamed the countryside together in a brown panel van. *It's probably a good thing*, Nonc tells himself. *Developmentally, it's got to be good for him.* He strokes the boy's hair.

There's a ring—California—and Geronimo eyes the phone with great apprehension. Nonc takes the call, it's a woman's voice.

"I'm calling on behalf of Harlan Richard. Is this Randall Richard?"

"It's *Ree-shard*," he says.

"You may not be aware of this," she says. "But your father has lost the use of his vocal cords. He's asked me to read a note."

"Are you a nurse?" Randall asks.

"Nurse's aide."

"Is he dying?"

"They don't exactly write that on the chart," she says. "But this is hospice."

"Nobody leaves hospice, right?"

"I wouldn't say that."

"How long have you known my father?"

"I just came on shift," she says, then begins reading the note in a clipped, mechanical voice. " 'I know I haven't given you much, Randall. I haven't always had much to give. It's funny. All the things I have to say to you are all the things you already know. I have some things to transfer to you. You may find them useful. The doc says—' "

"Put him on," Nonc tells her.

"It may take some getting used to," she says. "But he's lost the ability to speak."

"Please," he says. "Hand him the phone."

When Nonc hears the wheeze and click, he says, "Here's your grandson," and hands the phone to Geronimo. "It's your grandpa," he tells the boy, but the boy just sits there, the blue buttons of the keypad casting a glow on his cheek. He doesn't even say *eyeball*. *Grandpa* is a word, Nonc realizes, that the boy has probably never heard. Nonc whispers, "It's Grover."

"Grow grow?" the boy asks. "Grow grow?" Then he starts mumbling his way through the entire Grover ABC song. His eyes stare blankly into space as he singsongs, and it occurs to

Nonc that the boy may never have seen the *Sesame Street* characters, just heard their voices on that one endless CD.

After a while, Nonc takes the phone back. "You got to talk to your grandson—that's not too shabby, huh? Not every grandpa gets that. Look, Dad, you should know there are no grudges here. There's no blame in me. I want you to tell yourself you did your best—then let things go. When the time comes, don't be looking over your shoulder, okay?"

Nonc closes the phone and pulls the cargo door shut. Then he kicks his leg out from under the sheet and leaves it exposed to lure mosquitoes away from his son, and before the timer on the dome light has extinguished the glow, Geronimo is snoring his baby-fat snore, and they are out.

The next morning is a blur of Brown know-how. After saddling up some sippy cups and sandwiches, they swing east through Welsh, Iowa, Lacassine, where the newly emptied hog lots speak of the sausage plant's return to glory. There is a shipment at Chennault airport, then they turn toward Calcasieu Parish jail, passing the equipment dealers and the boys' home, and finally turning off where the bail bond trailers line the road.

The Calcasieu jail is operating at triple capacity with all the prisoners from New Orleans, and in the parking lot, the evacuated families of evacuated prisoners have set up camp outside the perimeter fence, which is serving as a temporary visitation room. In the bare sun, a line of parents and wives lock fingers in the fencing, while on the other side, under guard, the inmates keep their distance and do what inmates always seem to do: affirm and reassure, make the future seem doable. Prisoner, visitor and officer alike are surviving off Red Cross kits, so everyone has the same Scope breath, the same hotel soap smell, the same ring of aluminum around their armpits. Nonc has delivered everything from video games to wedding tuxedos to this jail, but today, as he wheels a hand truck around folks strewn on the sidewalk, he brings quick cuffs, stab vests, and a box from a company called SlamTec.

Waiting in line for security, Nonc leans against those boxes and checks out an inmate tracking station the jail has set up. For the hell of it, maybe—he can't put it into words—he walks up and says he needs to see Marnie Broussard, that he's her brother, Dallas. The guard fingers through stacks of tracking sheets, makes a call on the radio. "If they've got her," she says, "they'll bring her out." Nonc finishes his delivery, buys a soda, then waits in the van with Geronimo, reading the newspaper while that one CD loops. There is an article about the lady who threw her kids off the bridge. It says there's no record of the kids, no birth certificates or anything; she probably had them at home, in the projects, then never took them to school or even a doctor. The weird thing is that she claims not to remember their names. For the life of her, she just can't come up with them. Nonc wonders if that's possible, that there can be no record somebody ever existed. Maybe if your life is screwed up enough, maybe if you're living way out on the edge.

Finally, through the windshield, he sees Marnie led out, hands up against the bright light. All kinds of people have been shuffling around in different-colored jumpsuits, but when he sees her in one, it's a shocker.

"Lo and behold," Nonc tells his son, then steps down from the van and crosses the lot.

When Nonc, too, clasps the fence, Marnie shakes her head at the sight of him. "I should have known," she says. "My brother would never come see me."

"What the hell are you doing here?" Nonc asks. "I've been looking for you."

"How's my boy?" she asks.

"He's fine," Nonc says. "So, what happened to you?"

"This is all a mistake, this is going to get cleared up."

"What did you do?"

"Nothing, I said it's a mistake."

"Did you try to scam FEMA or something?"

Marnie holds up a hand. "Hey, step off. You know what it's like in here? Half of New Orleans is in here. There's no showers, I'm sleeping on a cafeteria table. Men and women are together in here, Randall, fags and rapists. They sent our asses to Jena State Medium for a while." She stares at him to let that sink in. "There were some freaky bitches out there."

Beside them, a convict father is trying to reassure his wife and daughter, who, Nonc realizes, are listening with great trepidation to Marnie.

"What is happening?" Nonc asks.

"Look," Marnie says. "I was with this guy, and I didn't know what he was into. And they caught me up in that. I'd be out right now except for the backlog, there's like a thousand cases before me. I haven't even been arraigned."

"Arraigned for what?"

"I told you, nothing. I didn't do anything."

"I'm here every day, Marnie. You could have let me know. I could have used your help."

"You're doing fine, and I'll be out before you know it. He's a good kid, no instructions necessary."

"Oh, yeah," Nonc says. "Tell me what *bway* means."

She laughs. "Are you serious? What do you think it means?"

"I have no idea."

"It's the magic word, Randall. *Bway* is *please*."

"The boy says *eyeball*—what's that mean?" Nonc asks.

"He says *eyeball*?" she asks. "Why would he say that?"

Nonc shakes his head. "What about the initials *M-O*?"

"Jesus, Randall, are you shitting me? Try reading to him. I left a book called *Elmo's Big Vacation*."

"He said the word *narc*."

"You better fucking believe it," she says.

Nonc can feel a vibration in the cyclone fence. He turns

and looks past the hands of other visitors. In the distance, a team of trusties is using a backhoe to straighten sections of the fence leaned over from Rita.

Nonc asks, "You think it's best for him to see you like this?"

"He's here? You got my boy and you been keeping him from me?"

"I've got some questions, Marnie, and I got to know the answers."

"Don't be a prick," she says. "Where is he?"

Nonc just stares at her.

"You're a prick," Marnie says. "The only thing I did wrong was let Allen use my phone. That's it, I swear. He was into some shit, and I didn't know about it." She keeps trying to put her hands in her pockets, but she doesn't have any pockets.

Nonc and Marnie didn't date but two months, though he remembers clearly a gaze she'd sometimes get that he thought spoke of possibility. She gets that look now, only it's obvious that she wasn't looking toward the future but away from the past.

"Look, they think I was the person who delivered the stuff. Like I got all night to be driving eight balls of speed around. I've got a kid. I got responsibilities. I never even touched an eight ball." Marnie covers her eyes as if to shield herself from some great absurdity. "Jesus Christ, Allen is so stupid. I should have stuck with you," she says, and then laughs a miserable, self-reproaching laugh that says that would be the only way to make her life more wretched.

Nonc thinks of James B. and the way he shook. Of the way James B. couldn't believe God would make a liquor store glow.

"I got a question," Nonc says. "And no games, okay? Is Geronimo his real name?"

"What are you talking about?"

"I'm asking what's the boy's birth name?"

"Are you kidding?" she asks. "You named him."

"I never saw a certificate or anything."

"Where do you come up with this shit?"

"I was just thinking about that woman," he tells Marnie. "You know, the one who threw her kids off the bridge. She's probably in here. Hell, you probably know her."

"Oh my God," Marnie says, laughing away pain. "You fucking prick."

"What?"

"I can't believe you. You asshole. I love that boy more than you will ever know."

"What'd I say?"

"I know what you're getting at, and you're a prick for it. Just go ahead and say it. Say what you're thinking."

Nonc backs away. He backs toward the van, where he takes up the boy, strokes his hair. Nonc puts the drawing of the macaw in his hand, says, "Give this to Mama." They start to walk across the lot, but before long, the boy breaks into a run. Nonc holds up, keeps his distance. He watches his boy clasp the fence. He can see Marnie start crying, wiping the tears with shaky fingers. It's a pure thing, it's anguish. It's not a woman who thinks she's seeing her boy in a week, it's the opposite of that, and it's suddenly clear to Nonc that he's going to have that boy a long time.

Chuck E. Cheese is filled with body odor and booth campers, yet there's no place else to go. The little light inside Geronimo is dim, so Nonc puts him on all the rides, making a slow loop of the playroom. The ghostly thing, the thing Nonc can't get out of his head as he drops token after token into the hoppers, is that he doesn't know who put the boy in his van. It didn't really sink in until he was driving away from the jail, but the thought of a stranger's hands, it makes the pizza burn in his stomach.

Nonc kneels down to Geronimo—perfect cheeks, wide-set teeth, eyes bayou black—going like one mile an hour on a chuck-wagon ride. "Who brought you to me?" he asks the boy.

Nonc lifts his hand and passes it through the boy's gaze, but Geronimo will not track it. It's as if by not focusing, he doesn't see the place where his mother constantly isn't. Nonc touches the child on the earlobe, looks in his eyes. If the kid would just cry, Nonc would know what to do. When a kid cries, you give him an affectionate shake and then swat him on the butt.

Nonc pours some tokens into the ride, then calls Relle.

When she answers, he says, "Are you serious about this outfit-ter thing, about making that work? Because I need to know—no bullshit."

"What's wrong?" she asks. "Did something happen?"

"Tell me this lodge thing is for real, tell me that's going to happen. Raising my son in the back of a van, this has got to end."

"Of course it can happen, if you want it to. You've seen the geese out there. It's ducks galore. We get a vehicle, then we turn the kennel into a lodge, and the next thing you know, we have a chef and a sauna. Before you know it, people are coming for their honeymoons."

"I can get a four-by-four, but if this is some move of yours—"

"People are sending their deposits," she says. "And when have I not been on your side? I'm the only one in the world on your side."

Nonc watches Geronimo for a moment, slowly spinning in a teacup. "No more talk of DNA tests, okay? He's my son, that's final. And I don't want to hear about Marnie ever again."

"You're right," Relle says, "I shouldn't have done that test. That kid's your blood, it's obvious. The thing about blood is that your kid's always going to be yours, no matter what happens to you, no matter where you go."

"That's more like it," Nonc says. "I'm going to make a call, and you need to pack."

"What about the boy?"

"From now on, we do everything right."

Nonc wipes his face with water from a red plastic cup. He puts his wet hand on the shoulder of the boy, then dials California. When his father answers, Nonc says, "Get somebody. We need to talk."

In a minute, an orderly is on the phone. "*Hola,*" he says. "Enrique *aquí.*"

"Enrique," Nonc says. "Can you help me talk to my father?"

"Hey," Enrique answers. "You the guy who had his girlfriend call? Because I heard about that. That business is cold-blooded."

"That was somebody else," Nonc says.

"Good, good," Enrique says, "'cause your old man cracks me up. My dad, he was one crusty hombre, you know. Your dad reminds me of him."

"How's he doing?"

"He's dead," Enrique says.

"He's dead?"

"Yeah, died last year. Wait, are you talking about my dad or yours? I thought you were asking about my old man."

"You fucking with me?" Nonc asks.

Enrique doesn't answer. Nonc hears him call out, "It's your boy, he wants to know how you doing." Then he tells Nonc, "We gotta wait while he types."

"What's he got, a laptop?"

"The hospice ward is Wi-Fi," Enrique says. "On the computer he can talk, you know." Then he reads slowly as Harlan types: " 'Saw the hurricane on the TV. All okay?' "

Nonc's not sure who *all* is supposed to be, but he says, "Yeah, tell him a lot of folks are missing, but we made it through."

Enrique repeats this, then reads again. " 'Very hard on a boy. I was six when Audrey struck. They said that's what stunted my growth. That year after Audrey.' "

Nonc's heard all the old-timers talk about Audrey, the storm surge pushing in twenty miles, right to the ballsack of Lake Charles, how there was no warning, how the alligators slept under the trees, waiting for the bodies to rot out of the branches. But Harlan has never mentioned it.

" 'If I'd have stayed in Lake Charles,' " Enrique reads, " 'the storm would have taken me. That's where I should have been. That's how a Cajun's supposed to go.' "

"Tell him I got his package," Nonc says.

Enrique passes this along, then responds, " 'The numbers in my wallet are Internet poker accounts—that's my bank. No taxes, no traces. Wire cash in, wire it out.' "

"Ask him," Nonc says, "does he have a four-by-four?"

"Hey," Enrique says, "how about some small talk. You guys are acting like next of kin instead of family."

"What's his answer? Does he?"

Enrique asks, then reads the response, " 'What'd you name the boy?' "

"Geronimo," Nonc says.

"You named your kid Geronimo? That's fierce. You're going to have a fierce kid. Names are destiny that way. My real name is Maximillian."

Nonc says, "Ask him is it an SUV or pickup, you know, what's the mileage?"

Enrique asks, then comes back. "'I got a few cars— whatever they're worth, they're yours. I was gonna leave 'em for the lepers.'"

That's a phrase Nonc hasn't heard since he was a kid, back when people used to leave old furniture out on the docks for the supply vessel to Carville Island, where the leprosarium was. Harlan would joke that you never really owned anything, the lepers just let you borrow it a while. Harlan hasn't laughed since he lost his vocal cords—all that remains is a widening of the eyes, a thinning of the lips—but Nonc remembers him laughing with affection at the fate of the lepers, as if they were the closest to the Cajuns on the evolutionary tree.

"He doesn't sound like he's dying," Nonc says. "You think he's dying?"

"You ask him," Enrique says. "He wants to talk to you."

"What?"

"He's been practicing his talking."

"On the computer?"

"No, *talking* talking. You can't understand him, but you get what he's trying to say."

Nonc steadies the phone, speculates on what his father

wants to talk about—battles he ran from, how he'll be re-
membered, where he should be buried. But when Harlan
comes on the phone, when Nonc hears a hoarse, wet crackle
from deep in the esophagus, he can tell it's about the boy.
Nonc imagines his father's mouth open, like the door to one
of those roofless houses, and though the sound is nothing
Nonc can make out, he knows it's about a grandson, a hurricane and the year ahead.

Nonc drives to his old house, where he grabs the keys and the
cash and the wallet off the couch. Amid the junk on the floor,
Nonc notices a small pair of binoculars, like you might take
to a football game, and all the way to Dr. Gaby's, the boy
stares at the world through a single lens. When Nonc pulls up
and parks on the grass, the dream team is assembled in folding chairs on the porch, with Relle slowly reading them the
entire membership roster of the Louisiana Psychological Association. She reads a name, studies their faces for a reaction,
then reads it again before moving on. Geronimo races from
the van and joins them in an empty seat.

The day has become stagnant, baked over with clouds,
and all of them listen expectantly to Relle's voice as if she is
calling *their* names, as if at any moment, they will be chosen
to join the ranks of the known.

Nonc walks up the wheelchair ramp. Relle stands and

drops the printout on her chair. "I thought you'd never get here," she says. "Mississippi Psychological Association is next."

"Are you ready?" he asks.

"Are we really going?" As if to test reality, she adds, "I mean, what about your job? Won't you get fired?"

"Maybe," he says. "Maybe they'll blame it on the hurricane."

She gives him a measured, appraising gaze. "Okay," she says.

Inside, they find Dr. Gaby in the kitchen, folding an assembly line of sandwiches into plastic wrap. Geronimo fetches a mixing bowl from the cupboard, waits expectantly by it.

As if she knows why Nonc is there, Dr. Gaby doesn't turn to face him. She asks Relle, "Any response from the list?"

"They don't even know your name," Relle says.

"They don't have to know any names," Dr. Gaby answers. "Just recognize them."

Nonc speaks up. "We're going to California," he tells her.

"When are you leaving?" Dr. Gaby asks.

"Right now."

"And how are you getting there?"

"The van."

"You're taking your work truck to California—they're okay with that?"

Nonc shrugs, but Dr. Gaby doesn't see this. She's carefully

placing each sandwich in the center of a plastic square. She folds one side, then the other, then twists the ends together.

"You can't take the boy," she says. "Not in a stolen van. You don't even have a car seat."

"I know," Nonc says. "That's why I'm here."

She wheels around to look at him.

"Dr. Gaby," he says. "I did what you said, I chose. I chose, and I'm going to be the right kind of father. All my dad's bullshit, all that he did to people, there's a chance to make something good of that. I'm only asking for a week. It's not in the boy's interest to take him. I knew that's how you'd think about it, what's in his interest."

Relle says, "We're going to bring back a four-by-four."

Dr. Gaby asks, "Do you know what you're getting into? You'll have to have a death certificate, out-of-state registration, insurance, and that's just for a title transfer. God forbid there's probate."

Nonc says, "We're going to get there before he dies."

Dr. Gaby turns to Relle. "Is she going to drive this vehicle back? What if it's a stick shift? Will she drive the van?"

"This is about more than a four-by-four," Nonc says.

Relle says, "Quit trying to undermine this. We haven't even got out the door."

Dr. Gaby hands Relle the sandwich platter. "Please, will you pass out lunch?"

Instead, Relle goes upstairs to finish packing.

"Helping with the child, that's not the issue," Dr. Gaby

says. "I have a heart for the boy. The issue is this: name one person who left Louisiana and came back."

"Me," Nonc says. "I'm coming back."

"Are you listening to yourself? You don't commit to a child by leaving him."

"It's only a week," he says.

Dr. Gaby thinks about this. She wheels to the fridge for milk, then pours Geronimo a Dixie cup of vitamin D. "You know my philosophy on these matters, right? You understand that if you leave this boy with me, I'll have to do what's best for him. That's what will make the decisions."

"That's exactly what I want," Nonc says. "That's why I'm here."

"Did you find the mother?"

"She's in the Calcasieu Parish jail, ma'am."

Dr. Gaby takes a breath and looks at the boy. "Can you give me a contact out there? If your cell phone breaks or loses service, is there someone I can get ahold of?"

"No," he says.

"And can you tell me exactly when you'll be back?"

"I'm figuring a week. Two days out, two days back, two days for the paperwork. A day for unknowns."

"I'm sorry I have to be like this, Randall. Can we agree on an exact time of your return?"

Nonc looks at her with sudden distrust. "Well, the situation is fluid. There are unknowns. I suppose no is the answer, if you're being exact."

"I'm going to have to make a note of that, okay, that you can only guess at your return?"

Nonc lowers his brow in a look of betrayal.

"Randall," Dr. Gaby says. "Do you know what you're doing? You don't have to go, you know. You have a job, I can help you. Do you want me to choose you? I will. I'll do that."

"Come on, Dr. Gaby," Nonc says. "It's just a week."

Dr. Gaby sets a blank sheet of paper on the counter, then searches for a pencil. "You'll have to write me a note giving me guardianship. If there's an emergency or a medical decision has to be made, I'll need that."

"Temporary guardianship."

"Of course," she says. "Temporary."

Quietly, Dr. Gaby pulls out a small cooler for their trip. While Nonc writes the note, she puts sandwiches and diet sodas inside, with some blue ice to keep them cold. The words come easy for him, but when he's done and tries to read them, his mind can't put them together.

"You must watch her," Dr. Gaby says, handing him the cooler. "I've always believed Cherelle's capable of goodness, though honestly, I haven't seen much sign of it."

When they head outside, they can see Cherelle is crossing the lawn. In a waddle, like she is pregnant with it, Relle carries her heavy-ass sewing machine toward the van.

"What are you doing?" Nonc calls to her. "We're going to be right back."

Grunting, Relle says, "I don't go anywhere without my sewing machine."

Dr. Gaby looks up at Nonc. It's the look the old ladies at the church gave him.

"What?" he asks.

She keeps looking at him. "Nothing," she says.

Nonc goes to the van to get Geronimo's yellow boom box and the rest of his stuff, which is still in the same bag Marnie used. It feels like there should be a bunch of things Nonc has to do to prepare for the trip, but really, there isn't. He comes back and sets the gear on the porch. Geronimo is sitting on the ramp with his feet hanging off the side, holding up the binoculars. He's only looking through one lens, so Nonc can look through the other.

"Big bird," Geronimo says to him.

Nonc lowers himself to the boy. "Nonc's got to go," he tells him. "But he'll be right back. Nonc always comes back, remember that." Then he takes his DIAD and hands it to Geronimo. "This thing has a GPS chip in it. No matter where you go or what happens to you, I can find you with this thing. If anything goes wrong, I'll talk to my friends at UPS, and this is how I'll track you down." Nonc kisses the boy on the forehead. "You remember that Nonc's your real father," he says. "And that he'll be right back."

Before he can say goodbye to Dr. Gaby, she wheels inside.

When Nonc climbs in the van, Relle is already sitting shotgun. She unhooks the bouncy chair that hangs between the seats, then pulls out lots of material she's downloaded from the Internet. One printout is called "The L.A. Apartment Hunter's Bible."

"What?" she says when he looks at it. "You can't sleep in a van in L.A."

Things are going okay, Nonc thinks as he fires up the rig. This part went easier than he'd figured. Nonc was afraid that saying goodbye to Geronimo would flatten him, that the boy would fall apart, and then he would fall apart and everything would start off wrong. But things are working out. "We got to make some time," he says as they pull out of the drive. Nonc gives a last wave out the window—the dream team observes him without judgment, without response; his boy looks back at him with one eye. Through those binoculars, Nonc thinks, he must be magnified, he must be the boy's entire field of view.

They turn onto Lake Street, and the plan is in motion. For once, instead of things happening to Nonc, Nonc is making things happen, and that is a new feeling, a good one. The plan is going to take his best, he knows that. It's going to take everything he's got.

Relle starts changing the presets on the van's radio. "Some people say New York is the fashion capital," she tells him. "But really, it's L.A."

Nonc is thinking about the one time he went with Relle to her father's property. He kept visualizing where all the dogs were buried. He could imagine a bubble of greyhounds below his feet wherever he walked. But he's got to change that kind of thinking. They have those A-frame lodges that come in a kit, you set them up anywhere you want. He's got to be visualizing that kind of thing.

"You know who would make a good chef," he says. "Donny Trousseau's brother. That guy can cook anything."

"Yeah, that guy's great," Relle says. She opens the cooler and takes out two sodas. Then she grabs the sandwiches. "I have eaten a thousand of these," she says, and throws them onto the road.

Nonc watches them tumble in the rearview mirror. He suddenly remembers that he was going to make a vocabulary sheet for Dr. Gaby. "Aw, shit," he says. "I was going to write down instructions for the boy."

"Don't worry," she says. "Dr. Gaby's a pro."

"I suppose you're right."

"Of course I'm right," she says. They hit the on-ramp for the I-210 bridge. "And you got to relax a bit, okay? Ease up on yourself. Your dad's not going to mess with you—he's almost dead. And it doesn't matter if we're a day late coming back or even a week. What's Dr. Gaby going to do, roll the boy up in a carpet and put him on the curb? No, she loves him. So if something comes up, everything will be okay. If I got to make a pit stop in Denver, everything will be okay."

"You got to make a pit stop in Denver?"

She takes his hand. "See, you're not relaxing."

Climbing the Lake Charles Bridge, Nonc can see the muscles and elbows of the petrochemical plants, their vent stacks blowing off maroon-blue flame. Below are the driven edges of a brown tide, and everywhere is the open abdomen of Louisiana. At the top of the bridge, there is no sign of what happened here, not a sippy cup in the breakdown lane, not a little shoe. Nonc looks out on the city. It looks like one of those end-times Bible paintings where everything is large and impressive, but when you look close, in all the corners, some major shit is befalling people. Nonc shifts into fourth, and even doing that feels like a development, like it's the first step in a plot so big you can't imagine. The smallest thing now feels like a development, a turn signal. You kiss your son on the crown of his head, and no doubt, no denying, that's a serious development. You turn the ignition and drop the van in gear, and you know this is no ordinary event. You crest the Lake Charles Bridge, headed west with the wind in your eyes, and even flipping down your sunglasses feels charged with forever.

Interesting Facts

Interesting fact: Toucan cereal bedspread to my plunge and deliver.

It's okay if you can't make sense of that. I've tried and tried, but I can't grasp it, either. The most vital things we hide even from ourselves.

The topic of dead wives actually came up not too long ago. My husband and I talked about it while walking home from a literary reading. It was San Francisco, which means winter rains, and we'd just attended a reading from a local writer's short-story collection. The local writer was twenty-something and sexy. Her arms were taut, her black hair shimmered. And just so you're clear, I'm going to discuss the breasts of every woman who crosses my path. Neither hidden nor flaunted behind white satin, her breasts were utterly, excruciatingly normal, and I hated her for that. The story she read was about a man who decides to date again after losing his wife. It's always an aneurysm, a car accident or the long battle with cancer. Cancer is the worst way for a fictional wife to die. Anyway, the man in the story waits an appropriate amount of time after his wife's loss—sixteen months!—before deciding to date again. After so much grief, he is exuberant and endearing in his pursuit of a woman. The first chick he talks to is totally game. The man, after all this waiting, is positively frisky, and the sex is, like, wow. The fortysomething widower nails the twentysomething gal on the upturned hull of his fiberglass kayak. And there's even a moral, subtle and implied: when love blossoms, it's all the richer when a man has discovered, firsthand, the painful fragility of life. Well, secondhand.

Applause, Q&A, more applause.

Like I said, it was raining. We had just left the Booksmith on Haight Street. The sidewalk was littered with wet panhandlers. Bastards that we were, we never gave.

"What'd you think of the story?" my husband asked.

I could tell he liked it. He likes all stories.

I said, "I sympathized with the dead wife."

To which my husband, the biggest lunkhead ever to win a Pulitzer Prize, said: "But . . . she wasn't even a character."

This was a year after my diagnosis, surgery, chemo and the various interventions, injections, indignities and treatments. When I got sick, our youngest child turned herself into a horse: silent and untamable, our Horse-child now only whinnies and neighs. Before that, though, she went through a phase we called Interesting Facts. "Interesting fact," she would announce, and then share a wonder with us: A killer whale has never killed a person in the wild. Insects are high in protein. Hummingbirds have feelings and are often sad.

So here are some of my interesting facts. Lupron, aside from ceasing ovulation, is used to chemically castrate sexual predators. Vinblastine interrupts cell division. It is a poisonous alkaloid made from the purple blossoms of the periwinkle plant. Tamoxifen makes your hips creak. My eyebrows fell out a year after finishing chemo. And long after your tits are taken, their phantoms remain. They get cold, they ache when you exercise, they feel wet after you shower, and you can towel like a crazy woman, but still they drip.

Before my husband won a Pulitzer, we had a kind of deal. I would adore him, even though he packed on a few pounds. And he would adore me, even though I had a double mastectomy. Who else would want us? Who else, indeed. Now his readings are packed with young Dorothy Parkers who crowd around my man. The worst part is that the novel he wrote is set in North Korea, so he gets invited to all these functions filled with Korean socialites and Korean donors and Korean activists and Korean writers and various pillars of the Korean community.

Did I leave out the words *beautiful* and *female*?

You're so sensitive to the Korean experience, the beautiful female Korean socialite says to my husband.

Oh, he's good about it. He always says, *And this is my lovely wife.*

Ignoring me, the beautiful female Korean socialite adds, *You must visit our book club.*

If I could simply press a button every time one of them said that.

But I'm just tired. These are the places my mind goes when I'm tired. We're four blocks from home, where our children are just old enough not to need a sitter. On these nights our eleven-year-old son draws comics of Mongolian invasions and the Civil Rights Movement—his history teacher allows him to write his reports graphically. (San Francisco!) Our daughter, at nine, is a master baker. Hair pulled into a ponytail, she is flour-dusted and kneading away. The Horse-child, who is only seven, does dressage. She is the horse who needs no rider.

But talk of my children is for another story. I can barely gaze upon them now. Their little outlines, cut like black cameos, are too much to consider.

My husband and I walk in the rain. We don't hold hands. I still feel the itch of vinblastine in my nail beds, one of the places, it turns out, that the body stores toxins. Have you ever had the urge to peel back your fingernails and scratch underneath, to just wrench until the nails snap back so you can go scratch, scratch, scratch?

I flex my fingers, rub my nails against the studs on my leather belt.

I knew better, but still I asked him: "How long would you wait?"

"Wait for what?"

"Until after I was gone. How many months before you went and got some of that twentysomething kayak sex?"

I shouldn't say shit like this, I know. He doesn't know a teaspoon of the crazy in my head.

He thought a moment. "Legally," he said, "I'd probably need to have a death certificate. Otherwise it would be like bigamy or something. So I'd have to wait for the autopsy and a burial and the slow wheels of bureaucracy to issue the paperwork. I bet we're talking twelve to sixteen weeks."

"Getting a death certificate," I say. "That has got to be a hassle. But wait—you know a guy at city hall. Keith Whatshisname."

"Yeah, Keith," he says. "I bet Keith could get me proof of death in no time. The dude owes me. A guy like Keith could walk that death certificate around by hand, getting everyone to sign off in, I don't know, seven to fourteen days."

"That's your answer, seven to fourteen days?"

"Give or take, of course. There are variables. Things that would be out of Keith's control. If he moved too fast or pushed too hard—a guy could get in trouble. He could even get fired."

"Poor Keith. Now I feel for *him*, at the mercy of the universe and all. And all he wanted to do was help a grieving buddy get laid."

My husband eyes me with concern.

We turn in to Frank's Liquors to buy some condoms, even

though our house is overflowing with them. It's his subtle way of saying, *For the love of God, give up some sex.*

My husband hates all condoms, but there's a brand he hates less than others. I cannot take birth-control pills because my cancer was estrogen-receptive. My husband does not believe what the doctors say: that even though Tamoxifen mimics menopause, you can still get pregnant. My husband is forty-six. I am forty-five. He does not think that, in my forties, after cancer, chemotherapy and chemically induced menopause, I can get pregnant again, but sisters, I know my womb. It's proven.

"You think there'd be an autopsy?" I ask as he scans the display case. "I can't stand the thought of being cut up like that."

He looks at me. "We're just joking, right? Processing your anxiety with humor and whimsical talk therapy?"

"Of course."

He nods. "Sure, I suppose. You're young and healthy. They'd want to open you up and determine what struck you down."

A small, citrusy *ha* escapes. I know better than to let these out.

He says, "Plus, if I'm dating again in seven to fourteen days—"

"Give or take."

"Yes, give or take. Then people would want to rule out foul play."

"You deserve a clean slate," I say. "No one would want the death taint of a first wife to foul a new relationship. That's not fair to the new girl."

"I don't think this game is therapeutic anymore," he says, and selects his condoms.

Interesting fact: Tamoxifen carries a dreaded class-D birth-defect risk.

Interesting fact: My husband refuses to get a vasectomy.

He makes his purchase from an old woman. Her saggy old-lady breasts flop around under her dress. The cash register drawer rolls out to bump them.

My friends say that one day I'll feel lucky. That I will have been spared this saggy fate. After my bilateral, I chose not to reconstruct. So I have nothing, just two diagonal zipper lines where my boobs should be.

We turn south and head down Cole Street.

The condoms are wishful thinking. We both know I will go to sleep when we get home.

Interesting fact: I sleep twelve to thirteen hours a night.

Interesting fact: Taxotere turns your urine pink.

Interesting fact: Cytoxan is a blister agent related to mustard gas. When filtered from the blood, it scars the bladder, which is why I wake, hour after hour, night in and night out, to pee.

Can you see why it would be hard for me to tell wake from sleep, how the two could feel reversed? Do you hear me trying to tell you that I have trouble telling the difference?

"What about your Native American obligations?" I ask my husband. "Wouldn't you have to wait a bunch of moons or something?"

He is silent, and I cringe to think of what I just said.

"I'm sorry," I say. "I don't know what's wrong with me."

"You're just tired," he says.

The rain is more mistlike now. I hated the woman who read tonight. I hated the people who attended. I hated the failed wannabe writers in the crowd. I loathe all failed wannabe writers, especially me.

I ask, "Have you thought of never?"

"Never what?"

"That there's never another woman."

"Why are you talking like this?" he asks. "You haven't talked like this in a long time."

"You could just go without," I say. "You know, just soldier on."

"I really feel bad for what's going through your head," he said.

Interesting fact: Charles Manson used to live in our neighborhood at 636 Cole Street.

Manson's house looms ahead. I always stop and give it my attention. It's beige now, but long ago, when Manson used this place to recruit his murderous young girls, it was painted blue. I used this house as a location in my last novel, a book no one would publish. Where did all those years of writing go? Where does that book even reside? I gaze at the Manson house. I feel alive right now, though looking through the gauze of curtains into darkened inner rooms, I can't be sure. In researching my novel, I came across crime-scene photos of Sharon Tate, the most famous Manson stabbing victim. Her breasts are heavy and round, milk-laden since she is pregnant, with nipples that are wide and dark.

I look up at my husband. He is big and tall, built like a football player. Not the svelte receivers they put on booster calendars. But the clunky linebackers whose bellies hang below their jerseys.

"I need to know," I said. "Just tell me how long you'd wait?"

He puts his hand on my shoulder and holds my gaze. It is impossible to look away.

"You're not going anywhere," he says. "I won't let you leave without us. We do everything together, so if someone has to go, we go together. Our 777 will lose cabin pressure. Better yet, we'll be in the minivan when it happens. We're headed to Pacifica, hugging the turns on Devil's Slide, and then we go through the guardrail, all of us, you, me, the kids, the dog, even. There's no time for fear. There's no dwelling. We careen. We barrel down. We rocket toward the jagged shore." He squeezed my shoulder hard, almost too hard. "That's how it happens, understand? When it comes, it's all of us. We go together."

Something inside me melts. This kind of talk, it's what I live on.

———

My husband and kids came with me to the hospital for the
first chemo dose. Was that a year ago? Three? What is time to
you—a plucking harp string, the fucking *do-re-mi* of tuning
forks? There are twelve IV bays, and our little one doesn't like
any of the interesting facts on the chemo ward. This is the
day she stops speaking and turns into Horse-child, galloping
around the nursing station, expressing her desires with taps
of her hooves. Our son recognized a boy from his middle
school. I recognized him, too, from the talent show assembly.
The boy had performed an old-timey joke routine, complete
with some soft-shoe. Those days were gone. Here he was with
his mother, a hagged-out and battered woman beneath her
own IV tree. She must have been deep into her treatments,
but even I could tell she wasn't going to make it. I didn't talk
to her. Who would greet a dead woman, who would make
small talk with death itself? I didn't let my eyes drift to her,
even as our identical bags of Taxotere dripped angry into our
veins.

That's how people would later treat me; it's exactly the
way I'm treated today when I come home to find my husband
sitting on the couch with Megumi, a mom from the girls'
grade school. My husband and Megumi are talking in the
fog-dampened bay-window light. On the coffee table is
chicken katsu in a Pyrex dish. Megumi wears a top that's
trampoline-tight. She has a hand on my husband's shoulder.

Even though she's a mother of two, her breasts are positively teenybopper. They pop. Her tits do everything but chew bubble gum and make Hello Kitty hearts.

"Just what's going on here?" I ask them.

They brazenly, brazenly ignore me.

I got to know Megumi on playground benches, where we struck up conversations while watching our daughters swing. I loved her Shinjuku style, and she loved all things American vintage. We bonded over Tokidoki and Patsy Cline.

"I love your dress" is the first thing she said to me.

It was a rose-patterned myrtle with a halter neck.

"Interesting fact," I told her. "I'm from Florida, and Florida is ground zero for vintage wardrobe. Rich women retire there from New York and New Jersey. They bring along a lifetime of fabulous dresses, and then they die."

"This is something I like," she said in that slightly formal way she spoke. "No one in Tokyo would wear a dead woman's dress." Then she apologized, worried that she might have accidentally insulted me. "I have been saying the strangest things since moving to America," she admitted.

Our family was actually headed to Tokyo for the launch of my husband's book in Japanese. Over the weeks, Megumi used sticks in the sandbox to teach me kanji that would help me navigate the Narita airport, the Shinkansen and Marunouchi subway lines. She asked about my husband and his book. "Writers are quite revered in Japan," she told me.

"I'm a writer, too," I said.

She turned from the kanji to regard me anew.

"But no one will publish my books," I added.

Perhaps because of this admission, she later confided something in me. It was a cold and foggy afternoon. We were watching a father push his daughter high on a swing, admiring how he savored her delighted squeals in that weightless moment at the top of the arc.

"If my life was a novel," Megumi suddenly said, "I would have to leave my husband. This is a rule in literature, isn't it? That you must act on your heart. My husband is distant and unemotional," she declared. "I didn't know that until I came here. America has taught me this."

I was supposed to reassure her. I was supposed to remind her that her husband was logging long hours and that things would get better.

Instead, I asked, "But what about your kids?"

Megumi said nothing.

And now here I find her, sitting on my couch, hand on my husband's shoulder!

I'm the one who introduced them. Can you believe that? I'm the one who got her a copy of his novel in Japanese. I watch Megumi open her large dark eyes to take him in. And I know when my husband gives someone his full attention.

I can't make out what they are saying, but they are discussing more than fiction, I can tell you that.

Something else catches my eye—arrows. There are quivers of arrows everywhere—red feathers, yellow feathers, white.

In the kitchen is a casserole dish wrapped in aluminum foil. No, two casserole dishes.

I discover a hospital band on my wrist. Have I left it on as a badge of honor? Or a darkly ironic accessory? Is the bracelet some kind of message to myself?

Interesting fact: The kanji for *irrational*, I learned, is a combination of the elements *woman* and *death*.

There was an episode not long ago that must be placed in the waking-and-sleeping-reversed column. I was in the hospital. Nothing unusual there. The beautiful thing was the presence of my family—they were all around me as we stood beside some patient's bed. The room was filled with Starbucks cups, and there were my brother, my sisters and my parents, and so on, all of us chatting away like old times. The topic was war stories. My great-uncle talked about playing football in the dunes of North Africa after a tank battle with Rommel. My father told a sad story about trying to deliver a Vietcong baby near Cu Chi.

Then my brother looked stricken. He said, "I think it's happening."

We all turned toward the bed, and that's when I saw the dying woman. There was a wheeze as her breathing slowed.

She seemed to get lighter before our eyes. I'll admit I bore a resemblance to her. But only a little—that woman was all emaciated and droop-eyed and bald.

My sister asked, "Should we call the nurse?"

I pictured the crash cart bursting in, with its needles and paddles and intubation sleeve. It was none of my business, but: *Leave the poor woman be,* I thought. *Just let her go.*

We all looked to my father, a doctor who has seen death many times.

He is from Georgia. His eyes are old and wet, permanently pearlescent.

He turned to my mother, who was weeping. She shook her head.

Maybe you've heard of an out-of-body experience. Well, standing in that hospital room, I had an *in-the-body* experience, a profound sensation that I was leaving the real world and entering that strange woman, just as her eyes lost focus and her lips went slack. Right away, I felt the morphine inside her, the way it traced everything with halos of neon-tetra light. I entered the dark tunnel of morphine time, where the past, the present and the future became simultaneously visible. I was a girl again, riding a yellow bicycle. I will soon be in Golden Gate Park, watching archers shoot arrows through the fog. I see that all week long, my parents have been visiting this woman and reading her my favorite Nancy Drew books. Their yellow covers fill my vision. *The Hidden Staircase. The Whispering Statue. The Clue in the Diary.*

You know that between-pulse pause when, for a fraction, your heart is stopped? I feel the resonating bass note of this nothingness. Vision is just a black vibration, and your mind is only that bottom-of-the-pool feeling when your air is spent. I suddenly see the insides of this woman's body, something cancer teaches you to do. Here is a lumpy chain of dye-blue lymph nodes, there are the endometrial tendrils of a thirsty tumor. Everywhere are the calcified Pop Rocks of scatter-growth. Your best friend, Kitty, silently appears. She took leave of this world from cancer twelve years earlier. She lifts a finger to her lips. *Shh,* she says. Then it really hits you that you're trapped inside a dying woman. You're being buried alive. *Will be* turns to *is* turns to *was.* You can no longer make out the Republican red of your mother's St. John jacket. You can no longer hear the tremors of your sister's breathing. Then there's nothing but the *still,* the gathering, surrounding still of this woman you're in.

Then pop!—somehow, luckily, you make it out. You're free again, back in the land of Starbucks cups and pay-by-the-hour parking.

It was some serious brain-bending business, the illusion of being in that dead woman. But that's how powerful cancer is, that's how bad it can mess with your head. Even now you cannot shake that sense of time—how will you ever know again the difference between what's past and what's to come, let alone what is?

My husband and kids missed the entire nightmare. They are downstairs eating soup.

Interesting facts: The Geary Street Kaiser Permanente Hospital is where breasts are removed. The egg noodle wonton soup in their cafeteria is divine. The wontons are handmade, filled with steamed cabbage and white pepper. The Kaiser on Turk Street is chemo central. This basement cafeteria specializes in huge bowls of Vietnamese pho, made with beef ankles and topped with purple basil. Don't forget Sriracha. The Kaiser on Divisadero is for when the end is near. Their shio ramen with pork cheeks is simply heaven. Open all night.

My Vulcan mind-meld with death has strange effects on our family. Strangest of all is how I find it hard to look at my children. The thought of them moving forward in life without me, the person whose sole mission is to guide them—it's not tolerable. My arms tremble at how close they came to having their little spirits snuffed out. The idea of them making their way alone in this world makes me want to turn things into sticks, to wield a hatchet and make kindling of everything I see. I've never chopped a thing in my life, I'm not a competent person in general, so I would lift the blade in full knowledge that my aim would stray, that the evil and the innocent will fall together.

Interesting fact: My best friend, Kitty, died of cancer. Over the years, the doctors took her left leg, her breasts, her throat and her ovaries. In return, they gave her two free helpings of bone marrow. As the end came, I became afraid to go see her. What would I say? What does *goodbye* even mean? Finally, when she had only a few days left, I mustered the courage for a visit. To save money, I flew to Atlanta and then took a bus. But I got on the wrong one! I didn't realize this until I got to North Carolina. Kitty died in Florida.

My husband soldiers up. He gives me space and starts getting up early to make the kids' lunches and trek them off to school. The kids are rattled, too. They take to sleeping with their father in the big bed. With all those arms and legs, there's no room for yours truly. They're a pretty glum bunch, but I understand: it's not easy to almost lose someone.

I spend a lot of time in Golden Gate Park, where my senses are newly heightened. I can see a gull soaring past and know exactly where it will land. I develop an uncanny sense of what the weather will be. Just by gazing at a plant, I can tell its effects upon the human body.

Interesting fact: The blue cohosh plant grows in the botanical gardens just a short stroll into the park. Its berries are easily ground into a poultice, and from this can be extracted a violet oil that causes the uterus to contract. Coastal Miwok tribes used it to induce abortions.

All this is hard on my husband, but he does not start drinking again. I'm proud of him for that, though I would understand

if he did. It would be a sign of how wounding it was to nearly
lose me. If he hit the bourbon, I'd know how much he needed
me. What he does instead is buy a set of kettle bells. When the
kids are asleep, he descends into the basement and swings
these things around for hours, listening to podcasts about bow
hunting, Brazilian jiujitsu and Native American folklore.

He sheds some weight, which troubles me. The pounds
really start to fall off.

He gets the kids to music lessons, martial arts, dental ap-
pointments. The problem is school, where a cavalcade of
chatty moms loiter away their mornings. There's the
Thursday-morning coffee klatsch, the post-drop-off beignets
at Café Reverie, the book club at Zazie's. These moms are
single, or single enough. Meet Liddi, mother of twins, famous
in Cole Valley for inventing and marketing the dual-mat yoga
backpack. She's without an ounce of fat, but placed upon her
A-cup chest is a pair of perfectly pronounced, fully articu-
lated nipples. There's rocker mom Sabina, heavy into ink and
steampunk chic. Octopus tentacles beckon from Sabina's
cleavage. And don't forget Salima, a UCSF prof who's fool-
ing nobody by cloaking her D's under layers of fabric. Salima
will not speak of the husband—alive or dead—whom she left
in Lahore.

How are you getting by? they ask my husband.

Let us know if you need anything, they offer.

They give our kids lifts to birthday parties and away games.

Their ovens are on perpetual preheat. But it's Megumi who's always knocking. It's Megumi who gets inside the door.

Interesting facts: Chuck Norris tackles seventeen bad guys at once in *Missing in Action III*. Clint Eastwood takes up the gun again in *Unforgiven*. George Clooney is hauntingly vulnerable in *The Descendants*. Do you know why? Dead wives.

Interesting fact: One wife who didn't die was Lady Mary Wortley Montagu. My MFA thesis was a collection of linked stories on Lady Montagu's struggles to succeed as a writer despite her demanding children, famous husband and painful illness. I didn't have much to say about the subject. I just thought she was pretty amazing. Not a single person bothered to read my thesis, not even the female professor who directed it. "Write what you know," that's what my professor kept telling me. I never listened.

One afternoon, I wander deep into Golden Gate Park, beyond the pot dealers on Hippie Hill and the rust-colored conning tower of the de Young Museum. I pass even the buffalo pens. In the wide meadows near the Pacific Ocean, I discover, by chance, my husband and children at the archery range. What are they doing here? How long have they been coming? They have bows drawn and, without speaking, are solemnly shooting arrows, one after another, downrange into heavy bales. The Horse-child draws a recurve, while my daughter shoots Olympic and my son pulls a longbow with his lean and beautiful arms. My husband strains behind a compound, its pulleys and cams creaking under the weight. He has purchased hundreds of arrows, so they rarely pause to retrieve. When the sunset fog rolls in, they fire on faith into a blanket of white. When darkness falls, they place balloons on the targets so they can hear the pop of a well-placed arrow. I have acquired a keen sense of dark trajectory. I stand beside my husband, the power of a full draw bound in his shoulders. I whisper *release* when his aim is perfect. He obeys. I don't need to walk through the dark with him to see the arrows stacked up yellow in the bull's-eye.

Later, he doesn't read books to the children before bed. Instead, on our California king, they gather to hear him repeat a story he has heard podcast by Lakota Sioux storytellers. My husband never speaks of his Sioux blood. He has never even visited the reservation. All the people who would have connected him to that place were long ago taken by liquor, accidents, time-released mayhem and self-imposed exile.

The story he tells is of a ghost horse that was prized by braves riding into battle because the pony, already being dead, could not be shot from under them. This pony, afraid of nothing, reared high and counted its own coup. Only at the end of the clashes do the braves realize a ghost warrior had been riding bareback with them, guiding the horse's every move. In this way the braves learn the gallop of death without having to leave this life.

The Horse-child asks, "Why didn't the ghost horse just go to heaven?"

I realize it's the first time I've heard the Horse-child speak in—how long?

My daughter answers her. "The story's really about the ghost warrior."

The Horse-child asks, "Why doesn't the ghost warrior go to heaven, then?"

My daughter says, "Because ghosts have unfinished business. Everybody knows that."

My son asks, "Did Mom leave unfinished business?"

My husband tells them, "A mom's work is never done."

A health issue can be hard on a family. And it breaks my heart to hear them talk like I no longer exist. If I'm so dead, where's my grave, why isn't there an urn full of ashes on the mantel? No, this is just a sign that I've drifted too far from my family, that I need to pull my act together. If I want them to stop treating me like a ghost, I need to stop acting like one.

Interesting fact: In the TV movies, a ghost mom's job is to help her husband find a suitable replacement. It's an ancient trope—see Herodotus, Euripides and Virgil. For recent examples, consult CBS's *A Gifted Man*, NBC's *Awake,* and *Safe Haven,* now in heavy rotation on TCM. The TV ghost mom can see through the gold diggers and wicked stepmoms to find that heart-of-gold gal who can help those kiddos heal, who will clap at the piano recitals, provide much-needed cupcake pick-me-ups and say things like "Your mom would be proud."

I assure you that no such confectionary female exists. No new wife cares about the old wife's kids. They're just an unavoidable complication to the new wife's own family-to-be. That's what vasectomy reversals and Swiss boarding schools are for. If I were a ghost mom, my job would be to stab these rivals in the eyes, to dagger them all. Dagger, dagger, dagger.

The truth is, though, that you don't need to die to know what it's like to be a ghost. On the day my doctor called and gave me the diagnosis, we were at a party in New York. Our mission was to meet a young producer for *The Daily Show* who was considering a segment on my husband. She was tall and willowy in a too-tight black dress, and while her breasts may once have been perfect, she had dieted them down to nothing. Right away she greeted my husband with euro kisses, laughed at nothing, then showed him her throat. I was standing right there! Talk about invisible. Then my phone rang— Kaiser Permanente with the biopsy results. I tried to talk, but words didn't come out. I walked through things. I found myself in a bathroom, washing my face. Then I was twenty floors below, on Fifty-seventh Street. I swear I didn't take the elevator. I just appeared. Then I was on a bus in North Carolina, letting a hard-drinking preacher massage my shoulders while my friend was dying in Florida. Then it was my turn. I saw my own memorial: My parents' lawn is covered with cars. They must buy a freezer to store all the HoneyBaked hams that arrive. My family and friends gather next to the river that slowly makes its way past my parents' home. Here, people take turns telling stories.

My great-uncle tells a story about me as a little girl and my decision to wed the boy next door. My folks got a cake and flowers and had the judge down the street preside in robes over the ceremony. The whole neighborhood turned up, and everyone got a kick out of it. The next day brought the sobering moment when my folks had to tell me the marriage wasn't real.

My brother tells a story about my first Christmas home from college and how I brought a stack of canvases to show everyone the nudes I'd been letting the art-major boys paint of me.

My mother tries to tell a story. I can tell it will be the one about the Christmas poodle. But she is overcome. It scares the children, the way she slow-motion folds up, dropping to the ground like a garment bag. To distract them, my father decides on a canoe ride—that always was a treat for the kids. Tears run from their eyes as they don orange vests and shove off. Right away, the Horse-child screams that she is afraid of the water. She strikes notes of terror we didn't know existed. My son, in the bow, tries to hide his clutched breathing, and then I see the shuddering shoulders of my daughter. She swivels her head, looking everywhere, desperately, and I know she is looking for me. My father, stunned and bereft, is too inconsolable to lift the paddle. My father who performed more than fifteen hundred field surgeries near Da Nang, my father who didn't flinch when the power went out at Charity Hospital in New Orleans, my father—he slowly closes his pearl-grey eyes. They float there, not twenty feet from us, the boat too unsteady for them to comfort one another, and we onshore can only wrench at the impossibility of reaching them.

Back inside the New York party, I realized time had ceased to flow: my husband and the producer were laughing the exact same laugh, the lime zest of their breath still acrid in the air, and I saw this was in the future, too, all these chilly women with their iron-filing eyes and rice-paper hearts. They wanted something genuine, something real. They wanted what I had: a man who was willing to go off the cliff with you. They would come after him when he was weak, I suddenly understood, when I was no longer there to fend them off. This wasn't hysteria. It wasn't imagination. I was in the room with one of them. Here she was, perfect teeth forming a brittle smile, hips hollow as sake boxes.

"That story is too funny," the producer said. "Stop it right there. Save it for the segment!"

In a shrug of false modesty, my husband accidentally sloshed his soda water.

"Well," he said. "Only if you think it would be good for the show."

I put my hand on the producer's arm. She turned, startled, discovering me.

I used my grip to assess her soul—I felt the want of it, I calculated its lack, in the same way Lady Montagu mapped the microscopic world of smallpox pustules and Voltaire learned to weigh vapor.

You tell me who the fucking ghost is.

There is a knock at the door. It's Megumi!

My husband answers, and the two of them regard each other, almost sadly, for a moment.

They are clearly acknowledging the wrongness of whatever it is they're up to.

They head upstairs together, where I realize there are Costco-size boxes of condoms everywhere—under the sink, in the medicine cabinet, taped under the bedside table, hidden in the battery flap of a full-size talking Tigger doll!

Megumi and my husband enter our bedroom. Right away, the worst possible thing happens—they move right past these birth-control depots. They do not collect any condoms at all.

My kind of ghost mom would make it her job to stop hussies like Megumi from fucking grieving men, and if I were too late, it would be my job to go to Megumi late at night, to approach her as she slept on her shabby single-mom futon and, with my eyedropper, dribble one, two, three purple drops upon her lips, just enough to abort the baby he put inside her. In her belly, the fetus would clutch and clench and double up dead.

Megumi and my husband do not approach the bed. They move instead toward the armoire, beside which is a rolling rack of all the vintage dresses I could no longer wear once I lost my bustline. I moved them onto the rack but couldn't bear to roll them out of the room.

Megumi runs her fingers along these dresses.

She pauses only to eye a stack of my training bras on the dresser.

Interesting fact: While you can get used to being titless, the naked feeling of not wearing a bra is harder to shake. You just become accustomed to the hug of one. I recommend the A-cup bras from Target's teen section. Mine are decorated with multicolor peace signs.

Megumi selects a dress from the rack and studies it—it's an earthy pink Hepburn with a boat collar, white trim and pleated petticoat. At the Florida university where I met my husband, I was in his presence three different times before he finally noticed me. I was wearing that dress when he did. I wonder if he remembers it.

Megumi holds the dress to her body, studying herself in the mirror. Then she turns to my husband, draping the dress against her figure for his approval.

Interesting fact: The kanji for *figure* is a combination of the elements *next* and *woman*.

I study my own figure in the mirror.

Interesting fact: The loss of breasts doesn't flatten your chest—it leaves you concave and hollowed-looking. And something about the surgery pooches your tummy. My surgeon warned me of this. But who could picture it? Who would voluntarily conjure herself that way?

Megumi waits, my dress held against her. Then my husband reaches out. He has a faraway look in his eyes. With his fingertips, he tugs here and tapers there, adjusting the fall of fabric to the shape of her body. Finally, he nods. She accepts the dress, folding it in her arms.

I do not dagger her. I stand there and do nothing.

Interesting fact: My first novel that no one would publish was about Scottsdale trophy wives who form a vigilante group to patrol their gated community. It contains, among other things, a bobcat killing, a night-golfing tragedy, the illegal use of a golf ball–collecting machine and a sex scene involving a man and a woman wearing backpack-mounted soda pistols. It was called *The Beige Berets*.

Interesting fact: My second novel that no one would publish concerns two young girls who have rare powers of perception. One can read auras, while the other sees ghosts. To work the ghost angle, I had their father live in Charles Manson's old apartment. To make the girls more vulnerable, I decided to kill off their mother, so I gave her cancer. To ratchet up the tension, I had a sexual predator live next door named Mr. Roses. My husband came up with the name. In fact, my husband became quite enamored with this character. He was really helpful in developing Mr. Roses' backstory and generating his dialog. Then my husband stole this character and wrote a story from Mr. Roses' perspective called "Dark Meadow." I can't even say the name of this novel without getting angry.

My husband does not return to the novel he was working on before my cancer. After the kids are asleep, he instead calls up the website bigboobsalert. He regards this on slide-show mode, so ladies with monstrous chests appear and fade, one into the next. My husband has his hand lotion ready, but he doesn't masturbate. He stares at a nebulous place just past the computer screen. I contemplate these women. All I see in their saucerous nipples and pendulous breasts is the superpower of motherhood. Instead of offering come-hither looks to lonely men, these women should be feeding hungry babies, calling upon foundling wards and nursing the legion orphaned of the world. We should airdrop these bra-busters into tsunami zones, earthquake epicenters and the remote provinces of North Korea!

I kneel beside my husband, slouched in his ergonomic office chair. I align my vision with his, but I can't tell what he's looking at. Our faces are almost touching, and though he is lost and sad, I still feel his sweet energy. "Come to bed," I whisper, and he sort of wakes up. But he doesn't rise to face our bedroom. Instead, he opens a blank Word document and stares at it. Eventually, he types, "Toucan cereal."

"No!" I shout at him. "I'm the one who got cancer, I'm the one who was struck. That's my story. It belongs to me!"

Interesting fact: Cancer teaches you to see the insides of things. Do you see the *can* in *uncanny* or the *cer* in *concern*? When people want to make chitchat with you—even though, if they took the time, they could see that under your bandanna you have no hair—it's easier to just say to them, "Sorry, I have some uncanny concerns right now." If you're feeling feisty, try "I feel arcane and acerbic." Who hasn't felt that?

But sometimes you've got chemo brain and your balance is all woo-woo and your nails are itching like crazy and you don't want to talk to anybody. Be prepared for that.

Person 1: "Gosh, I haven't seen you in forever. How's it going?"

You: "Toucan cereal."

Person 2: "Hey, what's new? I'm so behind. I probably owe you like ten messages."

You: "Vulcan silencer." Smile blankly. Hold it.

———

Arrows boat-tail through the night. Raccoons rear, yellow-eyed, to watch them fly. In spring the surf sorrel, considered an aphrodisiac by the Miwok peoples, open their gate-folding leaves. I can't look at my children head-on. From afar I study them. I watch my husband shuttle them to school from a distance great enough that I almost can't tell my kids from other ones.

Even worse than cancer glommers are widower clingers. They approach my husband with their big sympathetic eyes and force him to say things like "We're managing" and "Keeping our heads above water." But he's no fool. He returns their casserole dishes to be refilled.

Our daughter takes on my voice. I study her as she admonishes her brother and the Horse-child to take their asthma medicine and do their silent reading before bed. When lice outbreaks arrive, she is the one who meticulously combs through their hair after my husband succumbs to frustration and salty talk.

I keep a hairy eyeball wide for Megumi. She doesn't come around, which makes me all the more suspicious. I wonder if my husband took some of that Pulitzer money and bought a "studio" in the neighborhood. You know, a place to hide your book royalties from the IRS and "get some serious work done." I flip through his key chain, but there is nothing new, just keys to the house, his Stanford office, the Honda Odyssey, five Kryptonite bike locks.

I use my powers of perception to scan the neighborhood for signs of this so-called writer's studio. I try to detect the effervescence of my husband's ever-present sparkling water, the shimmer of his condom wrappers or the snap of Megumi's bra strap. My feelers feel only the fog rolling in, extinguishing the waking world block by block, starting with the outer avenues.

Interesting fact: The Miwok believed the advancing fog could draw one into the next world.

Interesting fact: Accidentally slipping into the afterlife was a grave concern for them. To locate one another in the fog, they darkened their skin with pigment made from the ashes of poison oak fires. They marked their chests with the scent of Brewer's angelica. They developed signature calls by which they alone would be known.

For some reason, my family skips archery tonight. And there is no Native American story when the kids are put to bed. Even bigboobsalert has to wait. In his office, my husband calls up his document and continues stealing my story. I don't shout at him this time. He is a slow and expressive writer. Word choices play across his face. He drinks sparkling water, urinating into the plastic bottles when they're empty, and writes most of the night. I miss talking with him. I miss how nothing seemed like it really happened unless we told each other about it.

Interesting fact: My third, unfinished novel is about Buffalo Calf Road Woman, the Cheyenne warrior who struck the felling blow to Custer at Little Bighorn. I wrote about her life only because it amazed me.

My husband has my research spread before him: atlases of Native American tribes and field guides for botanicals and customs and mythology. I think this is good for him.

I'm there when he hits one last Command-S for the night.

I follow him upstairs. The children are sleeping in the big bed. He climbs in among their flopped limbs, and I want to join, but there is no room. My husband's head comes to rest upon the pillow. Yet his eyes remain open, growing large, adjusting focus, like he is trying to follow something as it disappears into the dark.

Interesting fact: My husband doesn't believe that dreams carry higher meanings.

Interesting fact: I had a dream once. In the dream, I stood naked in the darkness. A woman approached me. When she neared, I could see she was me. She said to me, or I guess I said to myself, "It's happening." Then she reached out and touched my left breast. I woke to find my breast warm and buzzing. I felt a lump in a position I would later learn was the superior lateral quadrant. In the morning, I stood in front of the mirror, but the lump was nowhere to be found. I told my husband about the dream. He said, "Spooky." I told him I was going to the doctor right away. "I wouldn't worry," he said. "It's probably nothing."

Eventually, my husband sleeps. An arm passes over one child and secures another. All the pillows have been stolen, then half-stolen back. The children thrum to his deep, slow breathing. I have something to tell him.

Interesting fact: My husband has a secret name, a Sioux name.

He's embarrassed by it. He doesn't like anyone to say it, as he feels he doesn't deserve it. But when I utter the Lakota words, he wakes from his sleep. He sees me, I can tell, his eyes slowly dial me in. He doesn't smile, but on his face is a kind of recognition.

Through the bay windows, troughs of fog surge down Frederick Street.

"I think it's happening," I say to him.

He nods, then he drifts off again. Later, this will only have been a dream.

I near the bed and regard my children. Here is my son, back grown strong from pulling the bow. Still I see his little-boy cheeks and long eyelashes. Still I see the boy who nursed all night, who loved to hug fire hydrants, who ran long-haired and shirtless along a slow-moving river in Florida. His hair is buzzed now, like his father's, and his pupils behind closed eyes track slowly, like he is dreaming of a life that unfolds at a less jolting pace.

My daughter's hair is the gravest shade of black. If anyone got the Native blood, it is her. Dark-skinned and fast afoot, she also has fierce, far-seeing eyes. She is the one who would enter the battle to save her brother, as Buffalo Calf Road Woman famously did. Tonight she sleeps clutching my iPhone, alarm set for dawn, and in the set of her jaw, I can feel the list of things she'll have to accomplish to get her siblings up and fed and off to school.

And then there is the Horse-child.

Interesting fact: My youngest's love of interesting facts was just a stage. When my illness turned her into a horse, she never said interesting facts again.

Interesting fact: Horses cannot utter human words or feel human emotions. They are resilient beasts, immune from the sadness of the human cargo they carry.

She is once again a little human, a member of a weak and vulnerable breed. Who will explain what she missed while she was a horse? Who will hold her and tell her who I was and what I went through? If only she had never been a horse, if only she could remain one a little longer. What I wouldn't give to hear her whinny and neigh her desires again, to see how delicately she tapped her hoof to receive a carrot or sugar cube. But it is over. She'll never again gallop on all fours or give herself a mane by drawing with markers down her back. It will just have been a stage she went through, preserved only in a story. And that, I suppose, is all I will have been, a story from when they were little.

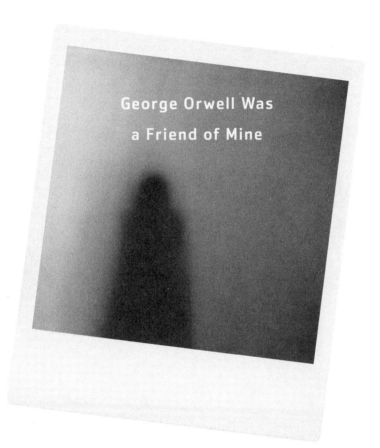

George Orwell Was

a Friend of Mine

In the morning, Prinz leaps onto the bed and stands on my chest, the handle of his leash in his mouth. For a little dog, he has large, wet eyes. I can smell his breath—*wurst*—and I realize I must have left a link of sausage on the cutting board. Though Prinz is capable of obedience, he succumbs to criminal tendencies. I am no longer a prison warden—I retired after the Wall fell—but I can tell a subversive personality when I see one. And it's the charming ones you have to look out for.

Prinz cocks his head and goes *pant-pant*.

"I do not forget this betrayal," I tell him, and take the leash in my hand.

At the front door, I help Prinz into his miniature jacket, which is made of leather and gives him the look of a tough little VoPo. It's November, so I button up, too. I know, the East German Volkspolizei haven't existed for eighteen years.

It's 2008, after all. But you can't change what a man and his dog look like in matching leather jackets.

Outside, the air is sharp. Crisp leaves blanket the dormant lawn. Prinz sees a red squirrel and barks like mad till I drop the lead and let him race off. I peek in the mail slot, where I find the new *Der Spiegel* and a letter, but it's not addressed in the handwriting of my wife, Gitte—or *ex-wife*, or whatever she's calling herself.

The letter is probably from an old inmate—my former prisoners are entering the period in life when they are "recovering their voices" and want to speak to me about what their time in my facility did to them. My address is public record, and I have nothing to hide. I welcome their letters but admit I only kind of skim them. It is a little like the rhetoric of *Anonyme Alkoholiker*—you understand that the steps are important for someone's sobriety, but who really wants to hear about it? I close the mail slot. Those old inmates would piss their pants if I ever wrote back and reminded them of the criminal actions they took that landed them in my facility, let alone the things they did once they found themselves inside—lying, snitching, begging, weeping and stooping to every possible indignity and deceit.

I set off after Prinz, crunching through the leaves, and I can tell what you're thinking: *Hans, what are you doing reading a liberal rag like* Der Spiegel? All I can say is that Gitte used to subscribe. She and I were storytellers. Swapping stories constituted our good times. That's what sustained our marriage until, I guess, stories weren't enough. While we cooked or gardened, I would tell stories from my day at the prison. They were glorious stories, worthy of retelling long after the prison was closed. Sometimes they were romantic, about young lovers who made terrible promises to each other before their interrogations. Often they were funny, like the color-blind prisoner who was always in a panic because he couldn't tell whether the security lights were flashing red or green. I withheld only the tragic stories from Gitte, because she'd had enough of tragedy already.

To my stories, she would always say, "Oh, Hans, that's awful. Where is your humanity?"

But she'd say it in that imploring way I took to mean, *Tell me more.*

Gitte tended not to leave the house. She was convinced—wrongly—that people looked at her a certain way because she was married to the warden of a Stasi prison. So she started a little business repairing cameras, Prakticas and Exaktas, mostly. All the East German models. She would read in the morning, and in the empty afternoon hours, with her fine tools and the bright light of a swing-arm magnifying lens, she would open up the camera bodies and tell her stories, which came from the pages of *Der Spiegel.* In her robe, she'd sip gimlets and relate all the anti-government articles she'd read about: surveillance programs, Bundeswehr in Afghanistan, Abu Ghraib, drones. As she spoke, she would smoke and gesture and drink until she couldn't make the tiny screws go in their tiny holes.

She had a big heart for the underdog and was not the type to give any thought to the difficult, thankless decisions authorities have to make in order to keep a society functioning properly. I had a duty to the larger picture. To her stories, I always pointed out the hard truths those leftie articles conveniently omitted.

At a certain point in the evening, when we had made it through another day, there'd be no more need for talk. I'd prepare her last drink of the night, a large icy vodka with a wedge of grapefruit. It would be just the two of us—gone would be her tales of American intervention, gone would be the ghosts of my aging former inmates. As she quietly drank, I'd watch her lips embrace the rim, her throat lifting as she swallowed.

When only ice remained, I'd take her upstairs and help her to bed, where she would recline in total peace, and there would be no strife in the world—gone would be her regret at having married the warden of a Stasi prison, gone would be the guilt she carried over her past affairs. Even the war would recede, and all she'd endured as a girl in its aftermath.

"The embers," she'd say at the edge of sleep. "Cup the embers."

Her eyes would grow heavy, her lips mumbling words that belonged to the first flashes of a dream, and I'd ask her,

"What are these embers you always speak of, where do you find them, can you feel their warmth?" But the liquor would have transported her already. I'd stroke her hair and run my hand along her shoulder. I believed she could perceive these gestures, that they reached the faraway place where the embers still glowed, even if her words and sentiments couldn't bridge the passage back. That's why, when her faint snoring came, I'd open her robe and slowly, tenderly begin making love to her.

Prinz sniffs something on the lawn. Looking closer, I see it is a small package wrapped in brown paper and twine. I halt. Narrowing my eyes, I pan the neighborhood, sweeping for a trace of the culprit who leaves them for me. This is the third package. I look up to the guard towers of Hohenschönhausen Prison. If only the prison were still open, if only I could check the surveillance footage from the perimeter wall, I might be able to identify the subversive who leaves me these gifts. But the cameras are gone, the facility long shut down.

The package I will deal with later.

With my boot, I scrape up a pile of leaves until it can no longer be seen.

Prinz and I walk down Lössauerstrasse. St. Martin's lanterns hang from people's balconies. Pumpkins line winterized walkways. All these homes were built for prison staff, including my own. While most of the guards have moved, some remain, and there's a nice mix of old families and new. There were rumors after Reunification, after East Germany was no more, that we should give up our housing, that we were the evil apparatus of a country on the wrong side of history and didn't deserve nice apartments in Berlin.

That was the rumor. No person ever said such a thing to my face.

Prinz and I turn the corner onto Genslerstrasse and stroll along the prison's outer wall. Above are barbed wire and the ceramic insulators where electric wires once hung. Neighbors used to throw books over the wall at night, perhaps hoping that inmates would find them. It shows you how little people around here understood the nature of the facility. These books, together with objects that were confiscated from incoming inmates, constituted our "lost and found" box, which I regularly brought home to Gitte. In this way, in even the most repressive days of the GDR, she read *1984* and listened to cassettes of the Rolling Stones.

She once danced to this music and then, in a jaded, smoky voice, said, "Mick Jagger understands me. He gets who I am."

I laughed. "Yes, you and the singer are practically friends."

"Jagger and I have history," she said. "We've shed the same tear." She smiled and tossed her head—the signal for me to fix her next drink. "But you're wrong," she added. "It's Orwell. He's the one I'm friends with."

Ahead, school buses are already lining up, their doors swinging open to release throngs of bored teenagers. You see, my prison, which was once the terror of every agitator and seditious traitor in the GDR, is now a memorial to which every angsty teen in Germany must be dragged once in his high school career. Here, they are taught about tyranny, totalitarianism and the terror of the Stasi's central torture prison. The tour guides forget to mention the fact that not a single inmate was ever abused here, let alone tortured. That is because, and here I am not joking despite the grand absurdity of it: the tours are led by the criminals who used to be prisoners here.

Prinz hops into a little planter by the prison's main entrance. He begins to circle, left then right, which means a crap is imminent. He is cute even when he shits—after his circle dance, he squats, rolls back his marble-black eyes and shivers up and down. Even the tree wells are part of the propaganda: each one is dedicated to the memory of a former inmate. Any weepy grandkid in Germany can, for ten thousand euros, buy one of these markers that will instantly turn a subversive grandfather into a martyred saint.

The plaque that Prinz squats over is for Klaus Wexler.

A group of idle teens ambles by, and whom should I see directing them but the curator himself. He is youngish and handsome, a tall intellectual from the university who will soon be bald before his time. Though he and I catch sight of each other many mornings, we have never spoken. The curator sees me, does a double take and calls his group to a halt.

He addresses the students: "And here is a commemoration

to the playwright Klaus Wexler, who was imprisoned here for two years. After his release, he was a broken man and never wrote again."

The teens stare at Prinz as he strains his bowels. Then they look to me, wondering whether this man in the leather overcoat will clean up his dog's waste. But they do not know Hans, a man who believes in order and stability, who knows firsthand that without rules, everything descends into chaos.

As if on cue, Prinz makes his contribution to the memorial.

I remove a dog-waste bag from my pocket. It is biodegradable.

As I collect the dog crap, I speak to Prinz. "Did you hear that?" I ask him. "This tree is a reminder of the life of the playwright Klaus Wexler." Then I pretend Prinz is talking to me. I cup my ear. "What's that you ask, little doggie? Who is Klaus Wexler, and why would a fine writer be in prison?"

The teens look at me like I'm crazy.

But I continue, answering Prinz's question. "He was a fine playwright, that can't be disputed, my little doggie. But as I recall, far from being a persecuted playwright, Herr Wexler was a pervert and a drug addict who embezzled money from the Deutscher Bühnenbund to print pornographic flyers inviting women to dress up like Secretary Honecker, so he could photograph himself having sexual intercourse with our nation's leader for the purposes of 'art.'"

The curator smiles. "That is an amusing story," he says. "I

hope sex and art were legal in the GDR. Or was there a special prison for the pursuit of pleasure? And if Klaus Wexler's crime was embezzlement, why did he not go through the criminal courts? Why did the Stasi bring him here, to a secret interrogation prison?"

Prinz gets frisky when he finishes his business. He scratches in the dirt and barks a sharp, taunting bark. This interests the empty-eyed students more than our conversation. "What your tour guide here doesn't mention," I say to them, "is that I used to be in charge of this prison. So Klaus Wexler was more than a brass plaque to me. He was a real person, and when he confessed his true crime, I was there to hear it. Note that your tour guide didn't dispute that the playwright was a sexual deviant, a drug addict and a thief. But what Klaus Wexler confessed to was much worse. It is something your tour guide probably doesn't want you to hear."

"On the contrary," the curator says. "This is a rare opportunity for us."

"This time of year was confession season," I say. "It starts when the first frost arrives. The cold takes up residence in the concrete walls and steel doors, and everyone knows that it is here to stay. Many inmates were arrested in summer demonstrations, and over their first few months, as they come to understand the true meaning of the word *solitude,* these new inmates regret the foolish ways they have transgressed against the state and they begin wanting to confess. But plotting against your country and its people, that is no small thing.

When an inmate signals he is ready to confess, that is when he would be sent down to the bottom of the prison, to the part they called the U-boat, for a good long while."

There is a young woman with stereo speakers in her ears—I cannot tell if she is listening to me or to popular music. I try to look into her eyes, but she holds up a cellular phone, pointing it at me like it will protect her from the truth I have to say.

"So the criminal *feels* like confessing," I tell her. "So what. He does not get to *choose*, like it is a *favor*. He must long for it. He must harvest a single-minded desire to do nothing on earth but reveal, *everything*, and this moment comes with no coronation. No, the criminal must place this confession on a tin plate, along with his hopes and sorrows and some cold potato peels, and this he must send through the muck-tray slot in his cell door like the rest of them."

Behind the phone, the girl's eyes go wide.

"The playwright," the curator says.

"Yes, the playwright," I say. "I went down to the U-boat personally. There Klaus Wexler admitted he had plotted to escape East Germany, that he had copied his manuscripts, and at a performance of his latest play in Austria, he intended to flee. Personally, I think it was wrong for the GDR to restrict the movements of its citizens. It was a good country, a free country, and if people wished to leave, they should have been allowed to. But those weren't the rules, and it wasn't for us to decide. A pilot must obey the laws of aerodynamics, a doctor the protocols of medicine."

Steam rises from the dog-waste bag. I twist its neck into a knot and point at the curator. "Here is what the playwright confessed to: weeping, he told the interrogators that he had made no provisions for his elderly parents, that they were poor and weak and had no one, that he was going to abandon them, cold and alone, to their hastened deaths. With my own ears, I heard him say he was lucky to have been reported and caught. That is the truth of your beloved playwright. And in this way we saved Wexler from the bigger crime: condemning his parents to a slow, isolated death of hunger and infirmity."

The curator asks me, "Did Herr Wexler make this confession in the water cell?"

"I was not Stasi, I was not an interrogator. I was a civil servant, a prison administrator, but there was no torture here, if that's what you're implying," I tell him. "Not one person can show a single scar or bruise or wound from his time here. Not a single photograph can be produced to prove that an inmate was injured in my prison."

"Was Klaus Wexler naked when he made this confession?" the curator asks. "And had he been in total darkness, standing in ice water, as he later claimed?"

"The water was collected from the rain gutters," I tell them and point toward the roof of the remand center. "It was stored in that tank. In the summer, the water was warm, and in the winter, it was cold. That was the only method to its temperature."

The students raise their heads to the roof, their breath visible in the November air.

Here I lift my little dog and hold him. "Neither officers nor lawyers nor judges make the laws," I say. "Still they must be followed."

The curator offers a slight bow and says, "Thank you for the educational discussion," before moving the high schoolers toward the museum's gift shop.

Prinz and I spend the afternoon creating a surveillance device. I rummage the garage until I find our old Polaroid camera and a spool of fishing line for the trip wire. Prinz is a loyal assistant. He sits on a stool beside me, and as long as he gets a goldfish cracker every few minutes, he follows everything I do with great interest.

But how to get the *pull* of a wire to *depress* a shutter button?

I try various mechanisms—the flange of a toilet handle, the scissor arm of a garlic press and the lever of a paper punch. None works. It gives you a lot of respect for the Stasi, who were the masters at such things. They made cameras out of cuckoo clocks, bow ties and tree stumps. Yes, the Stasi may have turned the lower levels of my prison into an all-night spook show. But you have to admit—they were ingenious.

Finally, I use a brake caliper from my daughter's old bicycle. This I attach to the camera's plastic frame with two small screws. Did I mention I have a daughter? She's wonderful, grown already and married. I see her every summer and every Christmas, like clockwork. I point the camera at Prinz and give the fishing line a test pull, causing the brake arm to rotate. When the lever depresses—flash!

"Now we will catch our mysterious package leaver," I tell Prinz.

Even though his tongue is bright orange, I reward his loyalty with a bonus goldfish.

But the square of film the old camera spits out must have been trapped in there for years. Prinz and I watch it develop: slowly, a grainy image of my wife appears. She is reclined against a white sheet, and she is without clothing. Her eyes appear seductive, her face is not softened by liquor, and I know right away that I did not take this picture.

When it's dark, I sneak outside and set up the camera, hiding it behind a pumpkin and stringing the trip wire through a scattering of leaves. Prinz contributes his urine. Then I return with the package and place it on the dining table with the others.

When the first package appeared a month ago, I assumed it was a mistake, that it had been left at the wrong address. It sat unopened as I waited for its rightful owner to claim it. But when the next package appeared, I knew it was no error. I opened the first one right away. Inside were the keys I'd worn on my hip for sixteen years. It was the prison's master set.

How had they left my possession? Who had sent them to me and why? I clipped them to my belt, where they belonged.

The next package deepened the mystery. Inside was an ashtray. It was heavy and made of lens-quality glass. It was a souvenir Gitte brought me from a state-sponsored photography conference she attended in Dresden. When light struck the ashtray, it glowed eerily, making the inmates nervous as they sat before my desk. One day, after it had sat on my desk for ten years, it vanished. We tore the prison apart, scouring every inch, the prisoners not resting for weeks. Broken, the ashtray could become a terrible weapon—heavy and sharp, it could gash the necks of a dozen guards. We searched the latrines, the rain gutters, the ashes in the furnace. We dumped cauldrons of mess-hall stew. Inmates hand-sifted thirty thousand shovels of snow. Frozen corpses in the morgue were stripped, and the plaster casts were broken off everyone in the prison infirmary. The ashtray was never seen again—until it appeared, hand-wrapped, on my lawn. I could almost smell the f6 cigarettes I used to smoke.

The latest package I unwrap slowly. The twine is tied tight, the paper crisply folded. The clear tape that secures the corners is tinged a bureaucratic yellow. Inside I discover a silver bracelet that I bought for Gitte on our twentieth wedding anniversary. Because of what happened to her parents, because we'll never know how long they might have stayed married, Gitte and I always said we'd be married fifty years. So I had the bracelet inscribed:

"Hans & Brigitte ~ Only Thirty More to Go."

It was too heavy for her wrist, she said. She wore it only to official functions.

I don't know why, but holding the bracelet, I start to weep. Prinz leaps onto the table to lick my tears.

Later that night, Prinz and I curl on the couch—from here I'll be able to see the flash of the Polaroid if our mysterious package leaver returns. A wind shuttles up the chimney's hollow throat. There is a dry crackle in the leaves outside. A flat white light enters through laced curtains, casting a web over the dog peeking from behind my knees. It is in this patterned light that I regard the Polaroid of my wife. Her body is no longer youthful, but she is beautiful. The photographer, I believe, agrees. He has captured the elegance of how her hair falls, the way her breasts roll sweetly to the side. She is prepared for him. Her legs are slightly parted, her eyes curious and wry. It hurts to know that as soon as he pushes the button that captures this image, she will beckon him. It hurts to know that he will not have to heave wide the deadweight of her thighs. She will do that for him. Still, he would know nothing of her secret embers.

It's late when my daughter calls. We're not due to speak until mid-December, when we make our Weihnachten plans.

"Papa," she says. "There is a video of you on the Internet."

"This is not possible," I tell her. "I give no interviews. Please tell me—how is your mother? Does she speak of me?"

"The video is crazy," she says. "You are insulting a famous writer. You are waving a bag of dog shit around."

"Is she there?" I ask. "Is she in the house with you?"

"Papa, you must listen to me. There is a film of your dog shitting on the memorial of Klaus Wexler, and you're talking to the dog and acting like the dog can talk to you. Papa, this man won the Georg-Büchner Literaturpreis. You call him a deviant and an addict. You admit he was stripped and frozen and made to weep for his lost parents in your prison."

"I have done nothing wrong," I say to her. "I have hurt no one. Will you tell your mother that for me? That I never did anything to hurt her, that I followed all the rules, that I was the one who looked the other way when bad things happened in our marriage."

.

The next morning, I walk Prinz on the far side of the street, and I catch myself looking in people's windows. I wonder whether their lawn decorations are sincere or props. The packages have me in a suspicious frame of mind. Even though the Stasi no longer gang-stalk their subjects, my gaze lingers on everyone. A man bends to tie his shoe. A woman in jogging clothes brushes her stomach. I see a gentleman my age, and I study him—will he touch his ear or, worse, clasp his hands behind his back? I can't help but look for meaning in parked cars, in their colors and models. There was a day when you could spot the cars of those who were watching you. You knew what it meant when a blue Moskvitch curbed its wheels or a pair of white Trabants was working both sides of the street.

We stop across from 66 Genslerstrasse, where the prison's main gates are located. A parade of kids files out of a bus, and you can tell they're Wessis. The kids from the West have a sense of ownership, like East Berlin is a new toy they're trying out. The Ossis, on the other hand, are wary and unsure, like they're trespassing in their own neighborhood. They smoke twice as much and cut their eyes at everything.

And into this tableau appears the curator, walkie-talkie in hand as he connects the school group with a guide, a woman in her sixties. He practically bounces across the street when he spots me. "Guten tag, Herr Warden," he says.

"I'm just Hans now," I tell him.

He looks at my face. "You've seen the video?"

"I'm aware of it," I say.

"You mustn't be upset. The girl who recorded it, she is young. Just look at the other videos she posted. A boy falling off a bicycle, a toenail-painting party, a cat attacking a bowl of fruit."

I nod.

"Please, Hans, join me for a coffee—my treat. I have something to discuss."

We cross the street together, but at the prison gates I stop.

"Is it the dog?" the curator asks. "I assure you he is welcome. Many returnees bring psychological dogs to help with the ordeal."

"What ordeal?"

The curator frowns. "Of returning."

"Prinz is not a psychological dog."

"Of course," he says.

I stand at the threshold. He looks at me expectantly. "When were you last on the premises?" he asks.

"October third, 1990," I say.

"Nineteen ninety? Yet you live a block away," he says. He looks at my belt. "You still carry the keys to the prison. Come, Hans, I assure you that everyone is welcome here. The memorial is open to all people who wish to remember."

He touches my shoulder and directs me into the yard. I pull Prinz close.

The yard is filled with jostling teenagers and Dutch tourists. Where the Stasi officers' social club was once located, there is a bookstore. The south wall's tiger cages have been turned into a café. We head there and, after ordering cappuccinos, sit in modern chairs behind large panels of aqua-tinted glass. The café walls are adorned with framed photographs, some of which once hung in my office, including one of me greeting Stasi head Erich Mielke during his inspection of the facility.

"There was a photograph in my office of me and my wife," I tell the curator. "If it is possible, I would like it returned. When the prison closed, I thought there would be an extra day to retrieve my personal effects, but that was not so."

"I know the image," the curator says. "The archivists have actually just restored your office. They are amazing. You should see how they painstakingly document each cell. They record every letter scratched into the walls, they lift each fingerprint trapped in the coats of paint, all in an effort to determine the prisoners who were remanded here and when. As you know, all the records were destroyed."

"I only ran the prison," I tell him. "I was an administrator. I staffed the shifts, handled transfers, ordered toilet paper. Safety concerned me, not interrogation. What happened in those cells, I know nothing about. The head of the Stasi was Grünwald—he ran the interrogations. And I would say the Stasi command rather looked down on us administrators— the Stasi had their own dining room and club and sauna. It was they who decided to destroy the records."

The curator says, "Meaning Grünwald told you to destroy the prisoner files, and your people did it."

"It took almost a year, yes."

A girl delivers our cappuccinos. She wears a white T-shirt with epaulettes silk-screened on the shoulders, along with a host of ridiculous medals on the chest and a name tag that reads "Stasi Prison Warden."

The curator sees the horror on my face. "Yes, I know," he says. "I wish it weren't so. But this shirt is the gift shop's biggest seller, and the memorial is losing money. We charge only modest entrance fees, and the tour guides, they are quite an expense. These people were damaged by their incarceration here, and we are their only means of support. Our plans are big—exhibits, archives—but for now it is about the bottom line, as they say."

The cappuccino, when I sip, tastes like marzipan.

"Your financial problem is a simple one," I say. "This is just an abandoned jailhouse. Who would pay to see that?"

"You do not give yourself credit," the curator says. "This is no ordinary jail. But I take your point. How to get young people interested in the past, that's the question. Just look at them." He indicates all the students in the café with us. "Look at how they stare at these phones. That is our biggest competition. On the tours, half of them are updating their Facebook pages, texting their friends, tweeting and so on. Some YouTube the entire tour but never seem to experience it. To think what the Stasi went through to spy on us. Even they couldn't dream of a world in which citizens voluntarily carried tracking devices, conducted self-surveillance and reported on themselves, morning, noon and night."

"All this information," I say. "Yet the world is more mysterious than ever."

The curator leans forward. "You find the world *mysterious?*"

There is a very satisfied look on his face.

I ask, "How can I help you today?"

"Yes, of course," he says. "Here is my proposal. I think you are the philosophical type, Hans. I believe you are a man of opinions. I propose that you lead a tour of Hohenschön-hausen, perhaps for a group of students. We would record this on video and save it as an important document. You could say whatever you like—share information, counter criticisms, shed light. Most important, you would tell the story of this place. When you and I are long gone, a story like this will keep speaking."

I can't help smiling. "And who would listen to this tale?"

"Students, scholars, historians. Without the records, stories are all we have."

Prinz whimpers once, looking up to the biscotti on our saucers.

"You are wrong about me," I say. "I am no philosopher. And I don't know any stories."

Even as I say this, my mind wanders to Gitte, wondering where she is right now and what she's doing. Is she with her photographer friend? Do they climb mountains of A.A. talk and descend into dark valleys of sober sex?

Prinz whimpers once more.

"Actually, I have a question about dogs," the curator says. He snaps off a piece of biscotti and holds it above Prinz. "May I?"

I nod. "*Männchen machen*, Prinz," I say.

Prinz rears onto his hind legs, front paws held high.

The curator drops the treat.

Tongue out, Prinz eyes the falling biscotti and snaps it from the air.

"Prinz, is it?" the curator asks. "That's a good name for a dog."

"My wife named him. He was a farewell gift to me."

"I'm sorry to hear that."

"Hear what?"

"That you and your wife parted."

I look at little Prinz, oblivious to the problems of the world.

"It is only temporary," I say.

The curator nods. "Concerning dogs," he says. "A former inmate told me he found it difficult to sleep because of barking dogs. Yet there is no kennel. Did the prison employ the use of dogs, Hans?"

"The dogs came at night," I tell him. "A dog handler named Günter, he would bring them in at sunset. He still lives in the neighborhood. Günter was a famous dog trainer at the Stasi academy in Golm. But one day a pack turned on him and attacked him—that's how he was demoted to prison duty. There were terrible tooth marks on one side of his face, and the wound gave him a lisp. He tried to hide his injuries with a beard. I believe he lost a couple of fingers, too, because he always wore heavy leather gloves. He'd show up at sunset, that angry pack dragging him, and with those enormous gloves, he'd salute. 'The dogs are quite aggwessive tonight,' he'd announce. One night, perhaps hoping to rise in our esteem, Günter hid some meat in the tiger cages. There was still a prisoner exercising in the cage when Günter released the dogs, shouting—"

"Please, please," the curator says. "You must save this story for the video."

Someone tries to hail the curator on his walkie-talkie, but he mutes it.

"I could go anywhere in the prison?" I ask. "I could say whatever I wished?"

"You would have total freedom," he says. "Of course, the video would have some contextual material. It would have to tell the viewer what kind of prison this was, what happened here, how many people died and so on. It's very standard."

"The death rate in Hohenschönhausen was no different than the national average."

"I'm sorry, this is not accurate," the curator says. "The numbers are much higher. They've been verified. They are not in dispute."

I stand and tug on Prinz's lead. "What took place here wasn't torture. You have to let go of that. What happened here happened to people's minds, not their bodies."

A strange smile crosses the curator's face. "Please," he says. "Let's not end on that note. Let us see if we can find that picture of yours."

We take our cappuccinos and cross the courtyard, Prinz happy for the new adventure. Making our way to the Administration Complex, we must pass the ridiculous "Memorial

Stone" placed in the middle of the exercise yard. The building we enter has metal filing cabinets lining its long corridors.
There are hundreds of them, empty. Thousands of inmate
dossiers, thousands of confessions, shredded. What did any
of it mean, now that nothing remains?

We climb a staircase I've climbed countless times, yet I'm
still surprised at where it delivers me: the warden's office. The
archivists have prepared it as an exhibit. On the door is a
placard in German, English, French and Chinese. It reads:
"Office of Warden Hans Bäcker, who for fifteen years ran the
prison with exacting precision. Not once was an inmate ever
late to a Stasi interrogation or torture session."

I turn to regard the curator. He only returns my gaze.

I step inside, and a thought strikes me, one I've never had
before: the room is the exact size and shape of an inmate's
cell. There are other placards, explaining the radios that
communicated with the guard towers and the system of flashing lights that kept track of occupied interrogation rooms.
The walls are nicotine-stained, except where the archivists
have opened three holes in the plaster. Around these holes,
they have drawn red circles, one near the radiator, one beside
my desk and one on the ceiling. They are labeled Mic1, Mic2
and Mic3. A placard reads: "Not even Warden Bäcker was
safe from Stasi surveillance. Three listening devices recorded
him at all times." I approach a microphone and touch it with
a fingertip. My eyes trace its wire until it disappears, headed

to wherever it was that Grünwald's men listened in. My after-school phone calls to Nina. The times Gitte rang up, lonely and guilt-ridden, half sauced in the early afternoon as she confessed to infidelities I didn't want to hear about.

I turn away. On my desk is the wooden "lost and found" box. Its label reads only: "Objects confiscated from inmates." There are some pieces of jewelry, a rubber ball, a transistor radio, a miniature Bible and so on. I find a tattered copy of *1984*. I open the book and read a little. Of course it is fiction, but the author gets a few things right—the control, the scrutiny, the feeling that nothing can be spontaneous, that the slightest move carries consequences for your future. It evokes a feeling I haven't experienced in a long time, a sense that, even though you have a great job and house, there is no safe place to turn.

The curator closes the door, and here is the portrait: Brigitte and Hans on the Augustusbrücke in Dresden, the two of us tossing bread to swans on the Elbe. I hung it here so it couldn't be seen when I had prison business, so that it was only when the door was closed, when I was alone, that I could spend time with the image of her. It's the kind of picture a man hangs so he can be reminded that, no matter what happens in the cells around him, this is the woman who loves him, who awaits him, whom, after Günter finally arrives with his angry dogs, he will soon embrace.

I reach to take the photograph from the wall.

The curator stops me. "I'm sorry," he says, and clasps his hands together. "This is now the property of the citizens of Germany."

All afternoon, I walk Prinz. He doesn't sniff from bush to bush like normal. He smells doorways and car tires and each seat in the bus shelter. I can tell he is searching for Gitte. Everywhere he sniffs for her, but there is no sign.

The wind is from the northwest. I turn up my collar. On the opposite side of the street, a man in an overcoat also strolls slowly along, and I have the illusion that he is pacing me. I let my mind drift to the churches where, at this time of day, Gitte meets with her fellow *alkoholikers*. She is probably working out her troubled history—surviving the bombing of Magdeburg, how her family lived like mice in the rubble as they faced the tanks, the typhus, the nuns and then the Soviets. Long ago, after we first met, she told a story of how her father, following the January bombing, went out with a wheelbarrow in search of something unburned—clothes or food or wood for a fire. He returned before dawn with an unexploded bomb that he wheeled into the abandoned depository where they'd sought shelter. She recalled in mythical terms how her father gathered the family around to watch him challenge the bomb to a fight.

Many times I tried to get her to explain the meaning of this. The topic was a delicate one, and I had to be careful—

the sickness was to take her mother, a Soviet work camp her father and the orphanages her sisters. Hers was that kind of tale. Of the night her father fought the bomb, she would say only that it was a happy memory, that she didn't remember being cold or hungry, that they were all together and that her father won the fight.

"He fought the bomb how?" I once asked her.

"He attacked it with a brick," she answered.

I never suffered in the war the way Gitte did. After Rostock was bombed and I was injured, my mother fled to the safety of Schwerin, near where my father was stationed. Of the bomb that set this in motion, I remember little. I was five years old, standing on the street next to a team of fire horses, their coats steaming in the cold after they'd raced through the city center. I was struck by a wall of light. All at once there was wind and grit, and because the bomb had landed in a fabrication shop, in all directions went a hail of iron filings. The metal was like lightning—I could feel the electricity in each sliver.

When Gitte first saw me shirtless, she reached to touch these pocked scars, her eyes flashing to mine with a certain recognition, like she had finally found someone who'd been through what she'd been through, who could understand, without her having to say the words, the events that had formed her. And because I was already in love with her, because I'd already forgotten who I was without her, I allowed her to believe this lie. Over the years, however, when she needed someone who had these powers of understanding, I proved incapable.

Prinz and I pass an after-work local on Bahnhofstrasse, where couples share plates of Buletten and lift cups of Federweisser, cloudy as sea glass. Here Prinz stops. But he doesn't eye the food. He stares across the street to the man in the overcoat.

Across the street, the man in the overcoat stops.

Facing us, he touches his nose, which is a Stasi hand signal for *halt surveillance.*

He crosses to us, and when he nears, I see it is Grünwald, and he is smiling. He still sports a Stasi colonel's mustache, but his teeth, I notice, have been bleached.

"There you are, Hans. Have you been hiding from me?"

I see the newspaper under his arm. "How's the job hunt?"

"One no longer uses the classifieds," he informs me. "It's all on the computer now, yet this new system conspires to keep us older people out of the market. Isn't this new country supposed to be fair? Isn't it supposed to value a person's merits? Yet all we encounter is discrimination. For excellence in interrogation, Mielke personally pinned the Black Shield to my chest. But will anyone employ me? The Gewerkschaft der Polizei has three hundred interrogation specialists, but will they even look at my application?"

I ask, "Are you hitting me up for a letter of recommendation?"

Grünwald taps me with the newspaper. It's as much affection as he's capable of.

"Hans trying to be funny—this is a bad sign," he says. "How are you holding up? Have you heard from her?"

"Soon, I believe. It has only been four months. She just needs to get herself cleaned up. There are some problems for her to work through. I only wish I knew where she was, how she's spending her days."

"You didn't Facebook her, did you?"

"I don't know how."

"This is for the best, trust me," he says. "You know, I have five thousand friends on this website, the maximum allowable. Can you guess our current topic of conversation, can you guess our new hero?"

"I suppose you mean the video?"

"Yes, it's you, Hans! Our new leading man."

Before I can admit that I was unable to locate the video on the Internet, he plays it for me on his phone. The video is short, and yes, the waving of the dog-shit bag produces an unfortunate effect. The interesting thing is that the girl has managed to write over the video with arrows and red lettering. For instance, an arrow points to my forehead, and the caption says, "Throbbing Vein." Others read "Crazy Eyes" and "Spittle." When I make my most salient point, the viewer cannot help but be drawn toward red wavy lines emanating from my mouth and the caption "Old Man Breath."

I look down at Prinz. He is looking up at me.

"Do not be dispirited, Hans," Grünwald says. "The video is a good thing. You are the only one telling the truth. All these former inmates make me sick. They have turned themselves into little celebrities, writing books, appearing on chatty talk shows, and believe me, they know what the TV people want to hear—horrible stories of torture and tales of secret cemeteries. I heard one say we had turned him into a living puppet. A puppet? What were we, then—Guantánamo Bay, a North Korean gulag?"

Two women are heading our way, looking at a map. Grünwald immediately engages them. His wife, like most Stasi wives, left him right after the Wall came down, and I admit I'd long felt superior that my marriage had survived.

"I'm afraid we're lost," one woman says. We can hear she is Austrian.

"How may we help?" Grünwald asks. Even though his hair is white, he parts it dramatically, allowing him the opportunity, which he takes now, to correct the fall of his hair with a sweep of his long, sleek fingers.

The other woman adds, "We're trying to get to the torture museum before it closes."

Grünwald winces. "Torture museum?" He turns to me. "Have you heard of such a thing?"

I shake my head.

"Who would make such a museum?" Grünwald asks. "Who would want to visit one?"

The first woman stands her ground. "It's in a prison," she says. "This is a famous place."

She lifts the map so we can see. Marked are Holocaust memorials, Nazi deportation camps, extermination sites, and right in the middle, our prison.

"Is this some kind of atrocity tourism?" Grünwald asks.

The second woman takes the map back.

"This is history," she says. "This is how respect is paid."

"If you don't know the past," her friend says, "you have to repeat it."

"We know the place you're looking for," I say.

Grünwald interrupts. "Yes, yes, I remember now the prison you seek," he says and points the wrong way. "To get there, you must take the M5 tram five stops. No, six. Six stops. Your historical prison is exactly six stops in that direction."

The women offer suspicious glances, but they turn and walk away.

When they're gone, Grünwald rakes his hair as if to rid himself of what just happened. "Come to the local tonight, Hans. Let your old friends buy you a beer. We'll celebrate your new fame. And let me tell you, there are a few ladies who join us that prefer the company of a GDR man. I'll introduce you. They like the type who lights the cigarettes and buys the drinks. They crave our authority, Hans. They desire a man who takes charge. What do you say? You can bring your pooch if you like. There is a blind man who brings his."

I can imagine what it's like to spend a night drinking with

Grünwald in his Stasi speakeasy—endless talk of the GDR days, when the beer was stronger, the orgasms were longer and the coins were cast from pure silver. By midnight, they'd be practically singing in Russian. And the thought of talking to a woman other than my wife makes me ill.

"The video has you upset, I can tell," Grünwald says. "Pay no mind to how the girl mocked you. You were an admirable and respected warden. People would know that if these lying inmates didn't hog the media. Has one of them ever told an interviewer, 'The prison was clean and well ventilated and my meals came right on time, three times a day'? Do they ever mention their access to a state-of-the-art prison hospital with a medical staff of twenty-eight? Remember the blizzard of '84, when all of Berlin went black? Only you kept the lights on, Hans. Hohenschönhausen Prison alone had heat and power, and that was because of you."

I see the Austrian women have stopped at the end of the block to reexamine their map. They cast doubtful looks our way.

"Grünwald," I say, "you forgot to mention why you were following me."

"Yes, yes. It's because you were speaking with the curator of that place. I have to tell you, Hans, you must be careful with him. He bankrolls the former inmates. He books their television appearances. You must tell me what it was he wanted."

"He wants me to make a video. He wants me to talk about the prison and tell our side of the story."

"Why would he want that?"

"First there is a question I must ask you."

"Of course, Hans. For you, anything."

I want to ask about those hidden bugs in my office, about the secret files they must have compiled, the calls they recorded, how right now, in that little mind of his, he must know every secret thing about Gitte and me.

Instead, I ask, "Have you been receiving any packages? Things from our prison days, neatly wrapped and delivered at night?"

He's intrigued. "Would you call these packages *gifts*?"

"They are things I once possessed. Sentimental things."

Prinz grows impatient and barks. From a bag in my pocket, I remove a goldfish, but Grünwald stops me. "It is affection that the little fellow craves," he says, and lifts Prinz from the ground. "It is by giving and denying that you condition his response." He scratches the dog's small ears. "So you have a prison curator who desires something from you. And you have possessions from your prison days that suddenly appear."

Grünwald smiles. It comes with a glimmer of menace and intrigue, his eyes narrowing, not without a hint of delight, as he imagines various scenarios unfolding before him. This is the look that earned him the Black Shield. It's easy to forget, even for me, that thousands of inmates once lived in fear of him, that people hanged themselves rather than spend an afternoon in his presence.

The following morning the curator delivers the portrait. I rise from the couch when he knocks, and even I can smell the old upholstery on me. He wears a suit, and the frame he holds is cloaked in a black hood, as if the portrait is awaiting some kind of debut.

"I have it," he says.

He lifts the dark fabric a moment, and there are Brigitte and Hans, man and wife.

"The archivists undertook an examination," the curator says. "They believe this is the work of the photographer Sibylle Bergemann."

"My wife once modeled for Sibylle, back when they both worked at Praktica Kamera Werke. Back when there was a Praktica Kamera Werke. Everyone was let go when the Wall came down. Three hundred people."

He extends the portrait. "The archivists believe the photo is quite rare, and of course, it is public property. Can we call this a long-term loan? A remote exhibition, perhaps?"

The curator is quite classy. He does not let his eyes wander to the interior of my home, appraising, as others have, the kind of housing many might wish for. He makes no mention of my wife, of the video he desires or of the fairly obvious trip wire strung across the lawn.

I decide that he can't be the one leaving packages. I don't even ask about it.

"Thank you," I say. I accept the portrait and shake his hand by way of farewell.

Inside, I set aside the picture, draped in dark fabric. For some reason, I cannot lift its veil.

Prinz and I share a sausage. Leaning against the sink, I eat with my fingers. Gitte liked a single slice of bread for breakfast—in the morning, it was all her hangovers would allow. On the counter is her old East German toaster. I plug it in and toast a slice, just for the smell. I open the freezer and there are the frosted vodka glasses, frozen facedown to the bottom of the icebox. I decide to clean myself up, to shave, at least, but in the bathroom, I only stare at the second sink, hers, unused and overbright under a circle of white bulbs.

We head away from the prison today, Prinz and I, away from the school buses and the 256 line and the M6 tram. On the sidewalk, the shadows are frosted, so Prinz zigzags in the sunlight, paying tribute to everything of interest with three . drops of urine. We pass through neighborhoods and business strips, and soon we find ourselves gazing into the front windows of a liquor store. This is where I bought her daily bottle. In long rows and neatly stacked towers, the displays showcase bottles of every variety—some clear, some caramel-colored, some the green of unripe citrus. I know the weight and cost of these bottles. In their clear faces and strong shoulders, I feel the physicality of my wife, her presence, the shape of her day:

Her awakening. A long, silent, eyes-closed soak in the tub. Toast and tea, shades drawn. Rousing some, she made for the hothouse, where, almost ceremoniously, she concentrated on bulbs and transplants, her hands mixing soil as if she had no concerns. Midday, recovery under way, she would peer into the housings of the cameras she fixed. Afternoon brought to life the distant settings of her *Der Spiegel* articles, but a restlessness was already building. I could see an absence rise in her eyes, a perennial unhappiness. It was only with the first gimlet that she would take leave of these problems, whatever they were. Shaker froth, lemon rind, the wine-red velvet of the hours—these were our evenings, the drink bringing her back to me and then slowly taking her to a place where she alone could go. In bed, I was left only with her vessel. But the body I embraced was tethered to her spirit—this I believed. When I spoke, I knew that far away she could hear my words. When I parted her legs and entered her, her head would occasionally roll from the pillow to face me. Eyes closed, she would align her face with mine, and I knew that wherever it was she had traveled, her eyes were open there. A version of me was also in this place, and Gitte's gaze, for the first time that day, was meeting mine. That's the great irony—that she needed liquor to transport her to a location where we could connect in a pure and unclouded way.

Her face in this faraway place was lit by embers. Their heat warmed us. For all my imagination, for all my powers of perception, I could never lay eyes on these embers. It was like looking across the lakes of Schwerin to the campfires of advancing Russian soldiers—with what intent they were drawn toward flame, only daybreak would reveal.

That night I wake from a dimly lit dream to discover Prinz standing on my chest. He does not bark, but the little dog is so rigid, his coat bristles. I follow his gaze from the couch to the curtains in time to see a shadow stir outside. The Polaroid flashes, and I rise.

On the lawn, I discover my daughter, clad in a heavy coat. "Nina?" I ask.

She looks toward me, startled. Something is in her hands.

"Nina, what's the meaning of this?" I ask.

"I'm sorry, Papa," she says, and sets a small package on the lawn. "We keep discovering these artifacts. Mama can't have them around."

"Your mother—is this where they're coming from?"

Nina says, "She says she will contact you when she reaches Step Nine."

"Step Nine?" I ask. "What does this mean, *Step Nine*? What step is she on now?"

My daughter glances toward the street, where a car is waiting. There is a figure inside.

"Is that your mother?" I ask. "Is that her in the car?"

My daughter takes a step backward. "Papa, I wish it weren't this way," she says. "She will write you a letter soon, when she's ready. For now, she's healing."

I step toward her. "Healing from what?" I ask. "Is this about the war? Or how those damned nuns treated her?"

She begins moving away. "I'm sorry, Papa," she says. "I must go."

I race to cut her off. "Is it her photographer friend? Does he put her up to this?"

She shakes her head, tries to move around me. But I don't let her.

"Do they talk their stupid sober talk together?" I demand. "Or did he dump her, is that what she's healing from?"

My daughter tries not to listen, but I know I'm onto something.

"The photographer was cruel to her, wasn't he? He left her, and now she has no one. Now she's completely alone, isn't she?"

"There's no photographer," my daughter says. "It's you. You're the one she recovers from."

"Me?"

"Don't you remember?" she asks. "Don't you recall anything?"

"The past, those days when we were a family—that's all I think about."

"What about the dairy wagons?" she asks. "Do you think about that?"

"What?"

Nina points toward the street where my wife idles. "I grew up with milk wagons driving down our street," she says. "No one told me there was no milk, that they were really dressed-up prison vans delivering new inmates. Protesters, students, teenagers. People soon to be stripped and violated, their possessions confiscated."

"But that wasn't us," I say. "I'm talking about family. You're talking about work. These were duties I had to perform."

"You gave me gloves!" This she practically spits at me. "I wore them everywhere, showing them off, their softness, their perfect fit! How could I know where they'd come from? Why would no one tell me they'd been taken from a girl just like me, a girl who went into that house of crimes?"

She turns and hurries away.

My daughter, practically running from me. My wife, driving the getaway car.

At the dining table, I stare at the Polaroid of my daughter bending to place the package on the lawn. Her gaze is cast warily toward the house where I'm fast asleep. Her own house, the house where she grew up.

"It was no house of crimes," I tell Prinz.

Then I lift the package. My little dog is filled with nervous energy. He stands on his stool, looking from me to the package and back, his eyes wet, tongue flashing in and out.

A prison is not a pretty place, this we know. Perhaps it would be easier on a wife and daughter if a man were a farmer or a folksinger. But someone must run the facilities, someone must undertake the unpleasant tasks. It's not like, with a father who'd been imprisoned by the Soviets, I could advance in the Party. It's not like, with a mother who'd nursed Germans and GIs alike, I was welcome at any universities, which I'd dreamed of attending. And Nina forgets that she went to the best schools because of my service.

I snip the twine, tear away the brown paper.

Inside the box is a pair of calfskin gloves. There is no story behind them—I simply discovered them in the "lost and found" box and thought they'd fit my daughter.

Also in the box is a pen. This object I remember well. This the curator would deeply desire. It was found in the possession of a dissident writer. You can probably guess her name, as she had been in a relationship with another famous dissident writer, a Russian, and this was the pen he had made in prison and, upon his freedom, given to her. The pen is heavy and pointed and fashioned from pot metal. The Russian prisoners were allowed the use of pens, and these they created for self-defense, the irony being that this one was used for novels.

I brought the pen home, and when Nina saw it, she loved

it, so I made it hers. She wrote all her school papers with it. Tell me, if there was something wrong with the pen—how was it that Nina received such high marks? If I was so terrible, how was it that Nina excelled in singing and dancing and scholastics, how did she star in three consecutive school plays?

"I wasn't such a bad father," I tell Prinz. "I was no horrible man."

I set aside the gloves and pen and ashtray and bracelet. It's the keys to the prison I take in my hand. Prinz sniffs them once. "I'm not a criminal," I tell him. I flip through the keys, one by one, pausing to conjure in my memory the image of each door they open.

I decide to make the video but to do it my way. It takes an entire day to prepare. To modify my appearance, I buy a new vest and a fashionable shirt, both very modern. Next I purchase a toupee, and I am surprised at how natural it looks. To top this off, I invest in a sporty cap. At an electronics shop, I am shown eyeglasses with a miniature camera mounted in the frames. It can record hours of footage, everything I look at, and is nearly invisible.

The next morning, across from 66 Genslerstrasse, Prinz and I watch as the school buses arrive. Eventually, we spot a smaller bus, older, a bus from the countryside. One by one, Ossi high school students emerge. They all wear similar jackets, as if they are in some sort of Blaskapelle group.

Prinz and I approach. We find the driver sitting on a memorial planter, smoking.

"Visiting from Gera?" I ask.

"Zwickau," the driver says.

"How long do these tours take?" I ask.

"Fifty-five minutes," he says.

Despite looking generally worn-down by life, he is clean-shaven and wears a wedding ring.

"I need someone to watch my dog for fifty-five minutes," I say, and show him a twenty-euro note. "You must wait regardless, yes?"

He looks at the dog and nods. He takes the money.

"There's only one duty," I say, removing a bag of goldfish from my pocket. "The dog must receive one of these treats every three minutes."

The driver takes the orange treats and shakes his head. "Berlin" is all he says.

I kneel down to Prinz. "I must make this journey alone," I tell him.

His eyes flick back and forth, looking into mine. I know what he means to say.

I purchase a ticket and wait in the maintenance yard with a dozen teens from Zwickau, the children of auto factory workers. Across their matching maroon jackets are embroidered music notes of gold. A guide approaches, a man in his forties. His hair stabs in different directions from some type of styling, and he looks mildly hungover. What a libertine life—a fat salary for giving an occasional tour to high school kids. I bet he spends his days smoking hemp and listening to Volksmusik. But he veers toward a group of Wessi kids who I can tell at a distance are from Frankfurt—loud and entitled banker-babies with test scores that have already gotten them into colleges in California.

A woman steps up to us. "I am Berta," she says. She is a modest woman with short hair and stoically sad eyes that make her look Ukrainian. Berta surveys the students, then expressionlessly examines me. I always believed women should have their own prison. There were no problems, mind you. Perhaps I am simply old-fashioned. Grünwald pointed out that the degree of inmate isolation meant each person basically had an individual prison. I think he just liked interrogating women.

Berta wastes no time. She begins walking us to the cell wing, and we follow. "I arrived at the Hohenschönhausen remand prison in a vehicle disguised as a delivery van. It pulled up here," she says, indicating a patch of asphalt near the receiving door. "There was once a structure here, so that when you exited the van, nothing of the prison could be seen. I'd been driven around for hours, so I suspected I was far outside of Berlin. The first rule of Hohenschönhausen was that no prisoner had contact with another. For the next two years, I saw no one but my jailers and interrogators. Warning lights were used to make sure no prisoner accidentally encountered another. When I stepped out of the van, a light was shining red, which meant another prisoner was being moved through the cell wing. Right away, I had to crouch in a stress position."

I laugh a little, remembering the poor color-blind prisoner. Everyone looks at me.

Through the steel door and into the yellowed hallway we go. Right away, I am struck by the smell of the place, that Hohenschönhausen Prison smell—a mix of ammonia, battleship paint, sound-deadening panels and electricity coursing through the security wires. It feels deeply wrong to be escorted by an inmate. I recall a prisoner who came to believe that Hohenschönhausen was not a prison but a movie set. When she didn't like what you said, she would call out, "Cut!" When she didn't feel right about the direction things were heading, she'd start repeating, "Take it from the top!"

We rise through the caged staircase, but before we emerge into the second-floor cells, Berta stops us. The kids look up the steps to her.

"I always observe a moment here," Berta says, "to pay respect to the dead."

The students are from good working-class families. They bow their heads.

I gaze intently at Berta, to make sure my video footage is steady.

"What dead do you pay your respects to?" I ask her. "The dead in general?"

"I pause for those who did not make it out of this prison. They are not here to speak for themselves."

"The death rate here was no higher than in the rest of the GDR," I say.

"Actually," she says, "a young person was five times more likely to die in here."

"You're comparing the prisoners to normal people," I counter. "This facility housed criminals, subversives, depressives and suicidals. For this group, the death rate was the same, inside the prison or out."

Berta takes a moment to appraise me.

"Did you ever see any inmates die in here?" I ask. "Did you ever witness any of them suffer, for that matter?"

"I did not see inmates of any kind," she says. "I only speak for my own experience."

"Actually, as a tour guide, you have made yourself the voice of the entire prison."

"One of the unfortunate laws of atrocity," she says, "is that the ones who truly come to know its nature are never left to tell of it. Far from trying to speak for them, we mark their experience with silence."

I am itching to attack this word *atrocity*, but the students eye me with uncertainty, and I don't want to turn them against me. We observe the moment.

Moving slowly through the wing, Berta goes on and on about her treatment—the lights being forever on, the feeling of isolation, the lack of sleep. She holds up the blue slippers and baggy blue uniform prisoners had to wear. In the hall she makes us walk the prisoner walk: legs wide, hands high behind the back, head bent. She shows us the warning wire along the walls that, when pulled, would summon the immobilization squad.

As we pass through the east wing, a young man points at a door more heavily bolted than the others. The name on his coat is Matthias.

In a deep voice, Matthias asks, "What's behind this?"

"It is one of the isolation rooms," Berta says.

"That?" I ask. "That's a maintenance closet."

Matthias looks from Berta to me and back.

"It's of no importance," I say. "Mops were stored there, to clean up after incidents."

The boy points at the door's array of locks. "Then why all the security?" he asks.

"In here," I tell him, "the smallest item can become a weapon or tool of escape."

Berta tries to reclaim her authority. "All these rooms are for punishment," she says.

I flip through the keys on my master ring until I find the right one. In front of everyone, I unlock the door, and I can't tell you how satisfying it is to hear the snap of the action and the slap of the bolts when I pull them. For a moment, I listen to the sound ring through the ward. Then I open the door. Inside, there is a sink and a bucket and, on a shelf, a lone jug of cleaner.

I ask Berta, "Are you sure you're qualified to lecture on this prison?"

"What in your life," Berta asks, "qualified you to run this place? Do you have a degree in criminal justice? Did you write a book on prison administration?"

The students turn to me.

This question can easily be edited out of my video, so I do not respond.

"We kept plenty of cleaning fluid on hand," I tell them, "because of the intellectuals. You may have guessed that I once worked at this institution. In my opinion, intellectuals fared the worst. Questions of *why* and *how* plagued them. They endlessly bemoaned their fates and covered every surface of their cells with scribbling about absurdity and injustice. Of course, there was only one answer to their philosophical musings: they had conspired against their country, and now they had to pay. Give me a prison full of carpenters and butchers and plumbers—these people knew how to answer questions rather than ask them. They could follow rules and serve their time."

"During my time here," Berta says, "I was given not a moment with a pencil or paper or reading material of any kind."

Did she never stop fighting? Did she never settle into the routine enough to gain a privilege or two?

Then she moves on into Grünwald's territory—the Interrogation Wing.

We move down rows of identical interrogation rooms until we reach 124.

"This was my personal interrogation room," Berta says.

"For two years, no other prisoner was questioned here but me. I would be hooded and brought here for regular sessions in which I was hounded about my allegiances, associates and accomplices and crimes."

I ask Berta, "So what were your crimes?"

She stops and looks at me, right into the camera. "In 1985, my husband and I ran at the Berlin Wall with a window washer's ladder. It was early dawn, and we were near Potsdamer Platz. The location is now a shopping mall. We easily reached the top, straddled the wall and pulled up the ladder. But we were quite foolish. We had thought West Berlin would be on the other side. Instead, there were one hundred meters of barbed wire, sensors and Dobermans that patrolled the corridor along cable leads. Then there was another wall. We resolved to run for it. Shots were fired, and my husband was hit. The dogs took me down."

One girl fingers the cross around her neck. Embroidered on her jacket is the name Katja. "Why did you want to escape so bad?" she asks.

Berta and I glance at each other, reminded of how little the young people know about those days. In response, Berta lifts the peephole cover so students can take turns looking into a Stasi interrogation room.

"Allow me," I say. With a passkey, I open the door.

We regard a high-backed chair, a large desk and a little stool.

When a boy moves to enter, Berta stops him. "The tour does not go here," she says.

"This looks like a place for conversation," I say. "Not for torture."

Berta looks nervously at the stool. "This part of the tour is over," she says.

I appeal to the students. "How can talking be torture?"

Berta stares vacantly into the room. "When you haven't slept for days," she says, her voice subdued. "When they question you in shifts, saying you'll never see your family again, saying your father has lost his job and your sister was removed from college. When they tell you your husband is dead from his wounds, even though he lives, even though he's in the same prison with you for two years and you don't even know it. When they show you your death certificate, all filled out except for the date, and they do you the courtesy of asking your preference for the day you wish to expire. When you finally say you'll confess to whatever they like, and instead, they send you down to the U-boat."

Berta wipes her eyes and heads alone down the hall.

The students eye one another with uncertainty.

We follow Berta. I admit that no person should be shown her own death certificate. And no wife should be separated from her husband. Yes, the woman was a subversive criminal, but that doesn't mean I don't sympathize with what she endured in the wake of her defiance. However, when we catch up to her, the sadness in her eyes disappears. She enters high gear again, walking backward, citing various studies about torturers and victims. Then she goes into talk-show mode about mercy and empathy, throwing in a couple of public-service announcements on the topic of humanity. Passing the control rooms, she minimizes the inmates' crimes, insinuating that they were incarcerated for reading banned poetry, attending protest concerts and listening to Wessi radio broadcasts.

In the housing unit, Berta directs us to housing cell 124, which is standing open.

"I was 124," she says. "For two years, that was my only name. And this cage was my home." She does not enter, and neither do we. From a distance, she points out the reinforced door, the peephole, the muck-tray slot, the dripping ceiling and the wooden bunk. "You had to sleep on your back all night, spread-eagle," she tells the students. "All night the guards looked through the peephole, and if you were not sleeping in the proper position—punishment."

"What kind of punishment?" Katja asks.

"It varied over time," Berta tells her. "It could be as simple as your toilet privileges being revoked, which meant doing your business in a bucket. When I first arrived, it was gynecological exams."

"Please," I announce. "There was no such thing. There were rules to be followed. A guard would have been written up for such an infraction."

Berta ignores me, answering only the student. "A battery of female exams," she says. "Each day for my first three weeks. Twenty-one sessions with the speculum."

Katja crosses herself.

"This is a fabrication," I say. "Dr. Werner would never have submitted to this."

To the students, Berta says, "When we visit the U-boat, you will see there were worse punishments."

"The U-boat was never punishment," I say. "It was part of the interview regimen."

Berta ignores me. "Now to the medical wing," she says. "Where you can judge for yourself the nature of the health care."

I hold up my ticket stub. "I have paid my money," I say. "I am on this tour as well."

"Yes," Berta says, "and the tour is moving on."

"But we're not done here," I say, and step inside cell 124. "This is not so bad," I announce. "There are smaller rooms in the world. A person could stretch out here, even do some exercises."

"This feels roomy to you?" Berta asks.

"It is not the Kempinski Hotel," I say. "But it's certainly no cage."

"Have you felt the room this way?" Berta asks, and closes the door on me.

I hear it lock. When I try to open the door, there is no handle or mechanism to grab.

"What's the meaning of this?" I ask.

"Does the room still feel large?" Berta's voice is faint through the thick metal.

It is a strange experience to reach for a door and find nothing to grasp. I run my hands along the metal, but without any purchase, I can find no way to even rattle it.

I speak into the door. "Okay, you have made your point."

"Did I?" she asks. "Does the room feel different?"

I look over my shoulder at the wooden bunk and moldy concrete walls, at the open-throated cast-iron toilet. "The room is the same," I say. "Now open the door."

She does not answer.

I say, "If you will now open the door, please."

There is no response. I place my ear to the metal but hear nothing.

"Hello," I call. "Are you still there?"

"I know who you are," Berta says. "I remember you."

Now I'm the one who's silent.

"Do you recognize me?" she asks.

"This is not part of the tour," I call out. "I would like the door opened."

"I cannot open the door," she says. "I do not have a key."

I lower myself to my knees and look out through the muck-tray slot. I see the students' athletic shoes and Berta's ankles below the hem of her dress. She has a small tattoo of a butterfly. I reach through the slot and extend the ring of master keys. I hold them out for a long time, but they are not taken.

"First," says Berta, "I must know if you remember."

"I do not need to recall the past," I say. "I am certain of what it was."

"If this place was so innocent," she says, "how come they closed it down?"

"If this place was so horrible," I ask my guide, "how come you keep returning?"

"Part of my identity was stolen from me," she says. "I'm trying to get it back."

I have a good comeback line for this, but I will save it for the red letters on my video.

"This is not legal," I tell her. "I am not a criminal. You can't treat me like one."

The keys are taken from my hand. One thing about these cells is that the light switches are on the outside. I'm reminded of this when everything goes dark. Then I hear the footsteps of everyone walking away. I don't bother to bang and shout. Berta won't get that satisfaction from me. I stand and put my hand out into the dark. Even though I have these rooms memorized, I trip on something and almost go down. At last I find the wooden bunk. My video glasses are filming this black moment, but I don't know how to turn them off. How did this come to pass? What parade of indignities led to being locked alone in my own prison?

What I think about is Gitte's father, who somehow knew that his family was soon to be torn apart, and during one of their last beautiful moments together, he decided to take action. I wonder which moment was ours. I scan all the holidays and school events for such a time.

A family outing comes to me. We took our little blue Trabant up the hills and into the columbines overlooking Cottbus. Gitte had an old Praktica she wanted to test. Driving along, I pointed out many picnic spots. She rejected them all. Finally, she picked a location littered with trash and old tires. But when we parked and got out, I saw how the light fell through the trees, how if you faced just right, the backdrop was a wall of dappled granite. Gitte positioned her tripod and set the camera's timer. Then the three of us raced to pose upon a fallen log. I adjusted my epaulettes, Gitte teased her hair, Nina balanced on both our knees. The timer ticked. We stretched wide our camera smiles. We smiled and waited, the timer ticking. We looked at each other with our overwide smiles and rolled our eyes, and still the timer ticked. It was Nina who started laughing at how ridiculous we looked, and soon all of us were truly laughing. The timer never did go off, which made it all the more funny, and the picture was never taken. But this was the moment. Nina bouncing upon the two of us. Gitte, head back with laughter. Me in the middle of it all. This was the time to take up the brick, to raise it high and swing with everything into the face of the bomb.

Before long, I hear footsteps, a key in the lock. When the door opens, Berta regards me.

"I thought you forgot about me," I say.

Even backlit by bright light, I can tell by her look that forgetting me is not possible.

"Doing this was wrong of me," she says. "This is not who I am or what I believe in."

"The truth is that I don't remember you," I tell her. "I was responsible for a great number of inmates over many years. I'm sorry, but I don't recall."

"Of course," she says, and extends the keys. "I don't like possessing these."

"I wish I could remember," I tell her. "But perhaps that book is better left closed."

She nods. "If this is what you believe, then why not let it rest? I've seen you walking your little dog. Why not go home to him and forget about all this?"

I accept the keys. She returns to her tour. I decide to take her advice.

When I exit into the courtyard, I hear the students singing. They're in the central yard, circled around the Memorial Stone, and they are singing "Ins Wasser fällt ein Stein."

This is the video they will post of their visit.

Yes, I think, *Prinz has waited long enough.*

It's when I'm walking toward the main gate that I hear Berta directing the students toward the hospital wing. "And now for the house of horrors," she calls out. Her tone is indignant and angry. I stop walking, watch them file inside, and even from here, I can hear her indicate the rings in the walls where sick inmates were manacled and the waiting stations where wheelchairs were chained. Next she'll start again on those nonexistent exams and begin spewing the usual hogwash about how Dr. Werner healed the patients only enough to endure more interrogation.

This I cannot take, this is too much to stand.

I head in through the white-tiled corridor and find them standing around a lone examination table, where the students, wide-eyed, study the stirrups and their rotting leather straps. Berta seems surprised to see me, but she continues even more manically.

"In this way," she says, "Dr. Werner actually aided interrogators by letting them know how much abuse inmates could clinically withstand."

I cross my arms. Very calmly, I say, "It is time for reason to prevail. These lies must conclude."

Berta ignores this and takes the students into the surgical theater. They gasp when they see its condition. Berta testifies to all her experiences in the hospital. She rolls up her sleeves to reveal the white ridges of her canine-bite wounds. The way she talks, everything starts to seem sinister—the lead vest hanging on a peg, the yellowed hoses of a vaporizer, the rusty mechanical arm of a ceiling-mounted light.

I ask her, "Did you not, of your own free will, jump a wall into a pit of guard dogs?"

She doesn't respond. Instead, as if fleeing a monster, she shuttles the students into an empty pink-tiled room.

"Here," Berta says, "I will describe the most diabolical of all Stasi devices. It no longer exists because the Stasi were too afraid that anyone should discover it. While they left intact their torture rooms and pain-inflicting devices, the only remaining evidence of what I'm about to describe is this—four bolt holes in the floor."

The students circle around to view the holes.

"Mounted here was a machine to dose the inmates with radiation so they could be tracked with Geiger counters after their release."

"You can't be serious," I say. "This room was a dispensary. You can't fill their heads with such preposterous notions."

"But isn't it true?" Berta asks. "Do you deny that the Stasi marked suspects with radioactive dyes and tags?"

"It is difficult to discuss such a terrific lie," I tell her. "Yes, the Stasi was guilty of such things elsewhere, but I would know if it happened here. Who would concoct such a machine?"

"Who would invent a water torture room?" Berta asks. "Who would dream up a zero-light, stress-position isolation room?"

"Those rooms were a necessary element of the normal process of inmate questioning," I say. "Besides, no innocent person was ever subjected to it."

"No innocent person?" She looks right at me. "Why did you spend a year shredding thousands of inmate files if they only contained necessary answers to the normal questioning of the guilty?"

"You know the answer," I tell her. "In those files were sprinkled the names of the innocent—innocent interrogation officers, law-abiding field agents, patriotic informants and community collaborators."

"Where is the radiation machine, then?" she asks. "Why is it missing?"

"Because it never existed."

"Tell me, why did Rudolf Bahro, Jürgen Fuchs, Klaus Wexler and Gerulf Pannach all die of a rare blood cancer after being brought here?"

"When my daughter fell off her bicycle, I brought her here," I tell Berta. "Dr. Werner set the bone. He was the one who wrapped her little arm in wet plaster. He was patient and tender. He signed her cast—all the Stasi officers did. So there was no radiation machine. What you propose can't even be discussed. It is too outlandish."

"Inmates have testified to being brought to this room," Berta says. "They describe a device being pointed at their chests."

I wave my hands. "That's it," I declare. "This tour is officially over."

"No," Berta says. "The U-boat remains."

I have no desire to enter the U-boat just to demonstrate that this prison, however unsavory, was a necessary part of a functioning society. Plus, it is past the hour when Prinz and I usually share a sausage. It is nearly the time when he brings his lead to me. But I look at those four holes in the floor. Though I would rather end the video now and go about my day, the truth is that duty calls upon us to perform tasks we'd rather not.

I follow the students across the south yard and down the cellar stairs.

Underground, it is dark and smells of metal.

We see our breath by the light of bare bulbs.

The only sounds are the echoes of our footsteps as we pass zero-light chambers and padded rubber rooms. Berta is silent as she directs us, one by one, into a nearly black stress-position cell. You can barely make out the heavy wooden block of the contortion seat. I run my hands along its contours, the wood grain smooth and polished from human flesh.

One of the girls whispers a prayer.

Berta begins speaking as we move toward the water cells. "I'm not sure how long I was down here," she says. "The water cells act like time machines. You stand naked in the dark, ankle-deep in cold water, for how long—how many days, a week, two? Because you cannot endure the moments as they tick by, you travel to faraway places in your mind."

When Berta arrives at the end of the block, she swings a door wide to reveal a black interior. We are assaulted by the smell.

"This was the cell they put me in," she says.

At the sight of the water chamber, one of the girls, alarmed, sings "Amazing Grace."

Another girl, her voice high and clear, follows her in German with "Grosse Gnade."

And then they are all singing, echoing each other in two languages:

How sweet the sound,
  Wie süss der Klang,
That saved a wretch like me!
  Die einen armen Sünder wie mich errettete!
I once was lost,
  Ich war einst verloren,
But now am found,
  aber nun bin ich gefunden,
Was blind but now I see.
  War blind, aber nun sehe ich.

They inhale to start another round, and I call out, "Enough with the singing."

Berta turns to me. "What is the proper response?" she asks. "How should they respond to torture?"

"Stop it with the metaphors," I tell her. I unbutton my shirt cuffs. "You say you were in this very cell?"

The resolve in my voice changes the look on Berta's face.

I glance upward, visualizing where the rooftop water tank is positioned four stories above. I follow the old pipes along the ceiling to the cells. Then I flip through my keys until I find the one that opens the valve locks.

"What are you doing?" Berta asks.

It takes some effort, but I manage to work the key into the old lock. Then, with both hands, I grab the valve handle and struggle to crack it open. When I do, a blast of rusty water sprays into the cell. I close it and begin unbuttoning my vest.

"Unpleasant, yes," I say. "But I will show you this is not torture."

"I don't know what's going on," Berta says. "But there's no need for this. This place is a memorial now. Its capacity to do harm has been retired."

"I have a question for you," I say to Berta as I free the last button on my shirt.

I know by the students' faces that my scars have become visible.

"Please stop doing whatever it is you're about to do," Berta says.

"Just tell me," I say. "Was there nothing of value here? Was there not one good thing to come from your time in Hohenschönhausen?"

Berta studies me as I remove my shoes and socks and place them against the wall.

"There is one thing," she says. "If I tell you, will you stop?"

I pause to listen to her.

"The prison did something to me," she says. "It made something in me come to life. My husband and I, even though we were young, we could not manage to have children. We tried for years. Within a month of my release, however, I was pregnant. We have three kids now."

I imagine these children as I remove my hat, my false hair and my glasses.

"Your honesty is appreciated," I tell Berta. "Now I'm going to be honest with you. Your whole existence has become a little story that you tell to strangers. And I will show you how this story isn't true."

"My story? You mean my life, the thing I was living before the Stasi arrived? Or the story the interrogators wanted me to confess to? Or the story I live now, where everyone tells me to forget the past and move on, yet every single thing leads back to this place?"

"You're angry, I understand," I say. "But these things you say about radiation and torture and the dead—they're dangerous, they really hurt people. That's why I must show you the truth."

"And how will you do that?"

I remove my trousers and fold them neatly. Wearing only my undershorts, I step inside the cell.

"I'm going to close the door, and you're going to bolt it," I tell Berta. "Then you will open the valve."

"Have you truly no memory of me?" she asks. "Have you forgotten your little nickname for me? Or what you did when you found out I was afraid of the dogs? Or the question I asked you countless times? My memory of you is so clear. I recall sitting in your office one afternoon. You made me wait while you spoke on the phone to your child. How horribly wrong it was, I thought, that you were able to have one."

We gaze with strange wonder into each other's eyes.

"Now, if you will," I say.

When I pull the door shut, there is a new kind of dark.

"You will open the valve and leave it open," I shout to Berta. "And I will call out when the depth of the water constitutes torture."

I feel my heartbeat and the warmth of my breath in the tiny chamber.

The floor is wet, bracing with cold.

Through the door, I hear the muffled tones of a debate.

But I'm not concerned—I know what will happen. Running a prison teaches you a few things about human nature, and there's no better feeling than being right about people.

"Please stop this," she says through the door. "Please."

She goes on imploring me like this.

It is funny, but through the metal and the rubber, her voice is different. It's vulnerable. And that's all it takes, the sound of fear and pleading through thick rubber, and it comes back to me. I recall. We once had a conversation through this very door.

"A ring," I shout. "That's what you wanted. A ring is what you kept asking me about."

On the other side of the door is silence.

"Yes, a ring," I call out. "I will tell you the truth of this ring. It was something I gave to the daughter of a coworker at a party. She had received perfect marks in school, and your ring happened to be in my pocket. There was a butterfly on it, am I right? That must have been the day of your arrival. It was perhaps gone from your very first day."

There is silence on the other side of the door.

"Tell me," I call, "what did it mean to you, this ring?"

One moment later, I hear the screech of the old valve as it starts to turn.

When the icy blast of rusted water strikes me, it does not surprise. The bits of iron in my chest sing with it. My skin hardens, my teeth bite. Yet it's oddly not unexpected. I taste the zinc of metal rain gutters, breathe in the scent of fall leaves. Freezing bricks and cold mortar, that's what the water feels like, yet it's not necessarily bad, if such a thing is possible. It's essential somehow, familiar, like the prison itself.

And I believe that Berta is right about one thing, that such endurance could cause you to travel far away in your mind. I think of Gitte's journeys to a distant land where she need only cup a little ember to keep her warm. I suddenly feel it's possible to go where she went. Perhaps we might finally share that space together. My body starts to go numb, the cold becoming something other than cold. When I can no longer feel at all, I will start my journey. I wait for that moment, tasting rain that fell long ago on a nation called East Germany.

Dark Meadow

Normally, I garden when night falls, when the urges come. But I was up most of the night writing an article titled "Is Your Pornography Watching You?" I just posted it—under a pseudonym, of course—to a fairly influential IT security website, and it's going to get people talking. The article describes how a tracking beacon has made its way into child pornography files on the Web—every time a picture is copied, the beacon is copied, and every time the file is transferred, the beacon sends a signal. I'm the one who heard the signal.

I step from my small bungalow into the North Hollywood predawn dark. You can't hear a peep from the Ventura Freeway, and the first 737 won't lift from the Burbank airport for a little while yet. So I go to my roses, which line the chest-high fence around my yard.

The key to gardening at night is the headlamp. Don't go for the xenon or halogen or LED models. The ideal beam should be soft and pale—by its glow, you should struggle to make out the true nature of something. The proper light can cast no shadow.

The neighborhood is a mix of aging Ukrainians and young Latinos, of spent porn actors and newly arrived hipsters. I turn on my headlamp and inspect the dusky crimson buds of my tall Othellos. Then I check on the Applejacks, the Chorales, the Blue Skies and the Bourbons—there's a fascinating *National Geographic* article on the crossbreeding that produced the Bourbon. I spot a Marlowe on the cusp of perfection. Just before I touch it, someone approaches out of the darkness. In the faint glow of my lamp's beam, I can see it's Rhonza from down the street—she's out walking at all kinds of crazy hours.

As she strides by, she says, "I got my eye on you, you spooky-eye motherfucker."

A Marlowe is orange-red outside but opens pale pink. I clip the rose, trim its stem, then place it in a white bucket I've mounted to the fence. I leave roses for anyone in the neighborhood to take. I've got no great love of roses—the bushes were planted by the old lady who used to live here. "Missus Roses," everybody called her. Without *National Geographic,* I wouldn't have even figured out which rose varieties were which. But tending them is soothing. Besides, what kind of guy would I be if I let some old lady's roses die?

I pause to enjoy a carton of milk, a half-pint, the kind kids drink at school. I know most early risers are brewing coffee, but it's best to limit external stimulation. I toss a few more roses into the bucket, and here is where I see the Tiger's Mom staggering down the street toward me. She lives in the apartment complex next door and has two daughters, a music blog and a committed relationship with alcohol. She's out every night on the L.A. band scene, and it's true that her blog is well regarded, that she's famous for discovering breakout bands.

The Tiger's Mom stops right in front of me, her drunken eyes fixed on the bucket of roses. In her attempt to select one, her hand floats like a conjurer's, and though I'm standing right here, she seems not to see me. The Tiger's Mom selects two roses, one for each daughter, I assume.

The first jet of the day rises out of Burbank above us. It's five thirty A.M.

"You look like you could use a carton of milk," I tell her.

"Mr. Roses," she says. "Jesus, don't creep up on people."

She takes her roses and ambles toward her apartment's stucco courtyard, trimmed with dwarf palms and painted Hotel California pink.

The Tiger is the older daughter, a sixth-grader responsible enough at twelve to take care of her little sister. I see the Tiger riding her bike to school. She is her school's mascot—the tiger in question. Some mornings, she pedals past in her tiger costume, its oversize tiger head strapped to the rack on her bike. The Tiger doesn't activate. The Cub is the younger sister, a ten-year-old. Sometimes she walks to school on her own. The Cub often stops to examine the flowers in my bucket, but she never pulls one out.

I don't have a dungeon or an ankle monitor. I don't follow ice-cream trucks. I don't even have the Internet, which is God's gift to child sexual exploitation. You have to understand that I have never hurt anyone in my life and that I am the one who gets wounded in this story.

But I'll admit this now, because this is going to be a certain kind of story: the Cub activates.

In the morning, I take Laurel Canyon south to Studio City, where I partition a faulty array of servers—all serving porn, of course. Then in Encino, I hack in to the laptop of an Armenian dude who claimed his daughter password-protected the thing and then forgot the code. For lunch, I stop for Salvadoran on Lankershim Boulevard. I eat outside, under a Los Angeles sky that is blizzard white. The *pupusas* are good, but I stop here because there is a permanent rainbow overhead, caused by the mist of a car wash next door. Don't let anyone tell you there are no rainbows in L.A.

I used to eat next to my van to make sure it didn't get jacked. Ten years ago, when I started my computer-repair business, my van was a crash cart of parts and diagnostic equipment, but these days I do mostly tech security, and a wallet of thumb drives is my only set of tools. Porn is a huge security issue, especially child porn. One employee down-loading it can crash an entire network. Just glimpsing it can get you locked up, so nobody's studying the stuff, which is racked with malware and sinister code. Nobody but me, it seems. Seems like I was the only one in the world when the beacon sent the signal.

In the afternoon, I'm circling the Valley, kicking a few fire-walls and doing some general debugging, when I get a text for an old-fashioned repair job, and what the hell. In twenty min-utes, I'm knocking on a door in Van Nuys.

The guy answers, but he stands there, staring at me.

I say, "Someone messaged me about a problem with a hard drive?"

"A guy I know said you were *cool*," he tells me.

To the untrained eye, you'd think this was the type of guy you went to Northridge with, the kind whose baby fat, hipster beard and searing irony landed him in a crappy studio apart-ment like this. But I recognize his kind right away. There are those who are born, those who are made, and then there are ones like this guy, the kind who choose.

I can see the computer, a high-end desktop with a liquid-cooled multicore driving twin cinema displays. It's a standard movie/animation editing setup.

"The thing suddenly stopped," he says. "And it won't turn on. I tried everything."

"Did the screen flash or go blue?" I ask. "Did you see a cursor blink or hear a ticking noise?"

"I don't remember," he says, but he seems to make a decision about me and steps aside.

Inside, I give the computer a quick visual. There's a barcoded property sticker, probably from a studio lot. "If this is a work computer, just turn it in," I say. "Your boss will get it repaired."

"This guy I know, he said you fixed his computer for three hundred dollars, no questions." He holds up three one-hundred-dollar bills.

I pull on purple latex gloves and unplug the wireless router.

I drop the desktop's side panel, pull the fans, then attach an I/O cable and reboot. Soon I get the error codes and kernel logs, and while the system profiles, I insert a thumb drive that I've loaded with a few dozen pictures. I command the root system to search for data strings in these pictures, images that would look like nothing special to the average person—a photo of a shoulder, a table, a bedspread, a foot. But they're really innocent corners of pictures that depict adult sexual encounters with minors. Immediately, the search results appear, and together we see the screen fill with the flashing images of his child porn collection.

"All this stuff was on the computer when I got it," he says. "I was meaning to get rid of it."

"I'm sure."

Then he volunteers, "There are no boys on there."

"Wonderful," I say.

I do a quick inventory—it's all the usual fare. He's got the

Teensy Series, the Fawn Trilogy, Pale Ribbons and so on. A search like this is easy because the vast majority of child porn available to the average Joe consists of a few dozen image sets that are commonly traded back and forth or resold through zombie servers.

I stop on an image. "You see this girl here?"

He says nothing.

"What's your name?" I ask.

He pauses. "John."

"You see this girl, John?"

He nods.

"Her name's not really Sissy. And this guy here, in his socks. That's the girl's uncle. He's doing thirty-five in federal for the extended sexual abuse of a minor."

"Look," he says. He holds out the money, but I don't take it, not yet.

"You wanna know her real name?"

He shakes his head.

"Good," I say, "because she's all grown up now, and she has a court order—a blanket judgment against anyone found in possession of these images. That's how you find out her real name—after your arrest, you get a writ informing you that you owe her a hundred and forty thousand dollars."

I survey the rest of his directories, but it's all the standard business.

I ask him, "You know one thing child pornographers always get wrong?"

He eyes me suspiciously.

"The lighting," I tell him.

And here is an opportunity to test the thesis of my article. I swap thumb drives and search the computer's file formats for the signal, which is a simple ASCII string, 256 characters long. Right away, John's porn directories light up with the beacon. I sort the pictures by date and see that the first set he bought, over a year ago, was a legendary set of scanned Polaroids nicknamed Summer Poppies, which means that whoever is tracking these images has been doing so for a while.

John and I fall silent, staring at Poppie in her makeup and fake eyelashes, with the look on her face that made her famous. This is a series I find especially disturbing. I understand that humans are deeply corrupted and that over the course of life, each of us comes to understand the depth of our species' sexual depravity. But in Summer Poppies, the worst perversions are candy-coated with false innocence, with bunny slippers and lollipops and Snoopy bedspreads. Here, even pearls of semen hover and catch the light.

"There is a signal coming from this picture," I tell John. "It's like a Trojan horse. When you download the picture, you download the beacon. And when you connect to the Internet, the beacon goes *ping*."

"What are you talking about?" he asks.

"Here's the beauty of it," I tell him. "The beacon's not in the image but in the file format, as metadata, so you can alter the image, crop it, whatever, but the beacon is still there. No matter what you do to the picture, it can still call home, and that's how they know."

"Know what?"

"That the pictures are here, John. On your hard drive."

Then I notice an image that doesn't emit the signal. It's of a girl I haven't seen before. And she is a girl—not a teen, not a tween, but a child. She is alone, captured from the waist up, and she wears a small yellow T-shirt. There is nothing sexualized about the picture, not even a pigtail, and she's not on a set—there are no Hello Kitty curtains, no tripods or floodlights. No, this is a girl and she's in someone's kitchen and this is not a "shoot" but a normal day from her actual life, one that finds her standing next to a screen door, the diffused light from which casts a pale pattern across her skin. On her face is fear, and the wide-eyed uncertainty of what will happen next, laced with perhaps a glint of hope that she can spare herself in some way from the unknown bad thing that is about to begin. Then I see her arm is blurred, that it's lifting—to fend something off, to latch on to an adult for security, or is the arm lifting on its own, the way arms lift involuntarily when something horrible is encountered.

"Where did you get this picture?" I ask.

"I don't know," he says. "I traded for it. I forget."

"Do you know this girl?"

"Of course not," he says. "Look, I just want my computer fixed."

I understand that whether a child is hurt under the bright

lights of a highly produced shoot or atop the dingy linoleum of a family friend's home, the damage is the same. But the illusion is that the latter is happening right now, not long ago, that if the right series of actions were taken, taken by anyone, even someone like me, it could be stopped.

I copy the picture of the girl and eject my thumb drive.

"You've got a bad pin on a RAM card," I tell John. "It only fails in heavy data cascades. It's an easy fix, but don't bother. You need to pull those drives out of their bays and take them out back and break them with a hammer. The spindles must crack to ensure the data cannot be retrieved. Tell your boss the computer was stolen and then crack the drives. Understand?"

He nods, but I can tell it hasn't sunk in.

"And don't try to save those pictures. They know you have them."

"Who knows?" he asks.

I take the cash from his hand. "Who do you think?"

At home, I walk right past my rosebushes. Inside, I turn on all the lights and pace the small rooms. The image of that girl has me completely fucked up. Everywhere I look, there she is. I am racked by the little blur of her arm. It lifts, but there's nothing she can do to stop what will happen. Innocence is on that face, as well as knowledge of what's to come. And the arm lifts. The past, the present and the future all exist at once.

And the most fucked-up and wrong and horrible part is that I activate. It kills me to masturbate, to stand there at the bathroom sink and jerk off into the basin—when I close my eyes, I see her; when I open them, there in the mirror is myself—but it's the only thing that will make it stop.

I start crying while I do it, I really do, because she knows what's going to happen, she knows it can't be stopped, and even though you know what's ahead, it still comes as a surprise when, after a day of sailing, after the Skipper has doled out performance ribbons to your Sea Scouts troop, and you've been having fun and there's a sense of wonder and achievement after rounding the tip of Catalina Island, and despite all the times it has happened before, it takes you by surprise when the Skipper comes for you in the dark and you're taken down to the storage cabin, with the musty smell of sail canvas and the petroleum bite of foul-weather gear. Atop a mound of the other boys' dirty laundry is where he forces you face-down. The anchor chain pulls taut against the hull, and there is no light beyond the pale glow of the bilge-pump sensor, no sound beyond the scratch of his razor stubble against the back of your neck and the cinch of his hands as he grips the straps of your life vest.

For the next couple nights, I ignore my gardening and instead initialize my computer. Here is where I keep a library of images. The pictures activate, strongly, like a muscle capable of folding you in half. There is nothing erotic about them. They are actually quite troubling. But they activate. I view before-and-after pictures, hundreds at a time, just before and just after. It helps to modify the pictures, to make a big one into little ones—focusing on a small hand, defiant, clenching the sheets, or a hand open and limp, fully relented. A single look can tell an entire story, so I often crop pictures down to the eyes—eyes fallen, eyes without focus, eyes closed, the pinwheel of an eye that's seeing something far different than what's before it, or a single, daring upward glance.

When you view these pictures, the best way to handle what you must confront is to view a picture series backward: something awful is happening to a child, it becomes less bad, and less bad, then the child and the adult separate, and after talking a brief moment, they exit through different doors.

At my computer, I do not masturbate, because that ends the sessions too soon. I can only say that in pushing me to the edge, the pictures help me find center again. I feel purged somehow. For a couple of days, I'm just like everybody else.

I've read a couple of books on the topic. This One Doctor Lady writes that by watching the scenario, the victim revictimizes himself. This Other Doctor Guy's book says that emotional development is arrested at the time of abuse, which makes you incapable of a relationship beyond the level of an adolescent. There's only one thing I'm sure about: these experts have never been victimized—they have never even seen it. They couldn't stand a single image. Not for a minute, not for sixty measly seconds, could they direct their gaze at a video portraying the brutalization of an innocent.

A knock at the door wakes me. It is midday. Since I sleep fully clothed, I'm able to answer right away. By sleeping with your clothes on, you don't need to climb under the sheets. You don't need to disturb a perfectly made bed or even fold the bed back into the couch.

When I open the door, a police officer is standing there.

"Those are some pretty serious flowers," the cop says, nodding at the yard.

"They're from the lady who used to live here," I tell him.

"I'm Officer Hernandez," he says. "Jaime Hernandez. A colleague of mine, Sergeant Rengsdorff, said I might talk with you. He said you helped crack a couple laptops a while back, that you helped with a kiddie case."

I nod. "That's right. Denis. How is he?"

"Sergeant Rengsdorff retired last year. I took his place on the Crimes Against Minors task force."

His phone keeps vibrating with text messages, but he pays them no mind. I peg him as the cool cop who gives out his number to the troubled and at-risk, letting them know he's *there*.

Just then Rhonza comes walking by. "You finally busting

that creepshow?" she calls out. "Someone's been peeping in the neighborhood, and I knew it was him. I could see it in his fucked-up eyes."

The cop lifts his hand in a semi-salute that says, *I heard you, ma'am; thanks for the input.*

But Rhonza isn't done. "Look at him," she demands. "He got Rikki-Tikki-Tavi eyes."

When she's gone, Officer Hernandez offers a knowing smile.

"There's one in every neighborhood," he says, but he is now studying my eyes.

"Please," I say. "Come in."

He steps inside. "You just move in?" he asks, and I almost tell him I've been living here for seven years. Instead, I shut my mouth and watch him sweep his eyes along the empty white walls and blank refrigerator and neatly made foldout bed.

"You never really get settled," I tell him.

"When you do, it's time to move again," he says, staring at the bookcase that houses my *National Geographic* magazines, the rows and rows of yellow spines.

We stand at the kitchen counter. "Glass of water?" I ask. "Half-pint of milk?"

"That's a lot of magazines," he says. "I didn't know they still published that one."

"I have a lifetime subscription."

"What'd that set you back?" he asks hollowly, for he is really scrutinizing the contents of my fridge when I open it.

"I received it as a prize when I was a boy in the Sea Scouts. I was our troop's scout of the year, though I didn't do anything special to earn it. It was more of a consolation prize, really."

The cop returns his gaze to me. "Sea Scouts?"

"It's just like the Boy Scouts, but on water. You learn navigation and maritime skills. The troop I was in doesn't exist anymore. It disbanded after our troop leader took his life. He hiked up Topanga Canyon and hanged himself."

He watches me unfold the carton's spout.

"Sorry to hear that," he says. "I'm sure his legacy lives on."

I take a swig of milk. "Well, the magazines keep coming."

"Right," Officer Hernandez says. "I'm here because of an article on the Web. It basically says that a code can be placed in explicit imagery, that it can be tracked somehow. I can't claim to understand it. Denis, Sergeant Rengsdorff, he said you were the guy to talk to."

"I know the article," I tell him, and I explain the whole thing, about the signals and beacons, how the child pornographers seem to have no idea their files have been modified, which suggests that some agency, probably federal, has swapped the pornographers' source files for doctored ones. Rather than shutting them down, the feds are using them to build a database of viewers.

After I pour this information out, Hernandez stares at me a moment. Then he begins asking questions, all the right ones, about detection, distribution, how come I know so much. Then he asks me, "The guy who wrote this article, he signed his name 'Dark Meadow.' Does that mean something in computer talk?"

"Not that I know of."

"Here's what I don't understand," Officer Hernandez says. "If this signal, if this two-hundred-and-fifty-six-digit code is the key, how come this Dark Meadow guy didn't publish it with the article?"

"I don't know," I say. "Maybe revealing that would jeopardize a major federal investigation."

"But didn't writing the article do that?" he asks. "I mean, are we dealing with one of the good guys or one of the bad?"

"I don't understand the question."

"The question is simple. Is this guy trying to protect kids by alerting the authorities of a way to catch predators? Or is he trying to help pedophiles by warning them of a vulnerability?"

I still don't quite follow. "Information is information," I tell him.

Hernandez asks, "Do you know this Dark Meadow?"

I don't say anything.

"Maybe I will take that milk," he says.

When I open the fridge, he again peers inside. There's nothing of interest to see, just a few shelves stacked with neat rows of milk cartons.

"If I understand you right," he asks, "a person with this code could find all the child porn viewers in L.A."

"If you had the code," I say, "you could make a real-time Google map of them."

I hand him a carton. He shakes it to froth the milk inside.

"But who would you catch?" I ask. "I dig in to a half-dozen computers a day, and any number of them are loaded with porn. It comes in all varieties. So I run across this kind of stuff. And you must believe me—there is no pleasure in seeing it. In fact, it is quite painful to me. But you got to understand that most of these pictures are from ten, twenty years ago. The victims are grown, the offenders are old, probably sucking on oxygen bottles somewhere."

"Yeah?"

"You can't go back in time," I say. "You can't stop what's already happened. It can only be dealt with."

Hernandez takes a drink from his tiny carton. "You know they sell this stuff by the gallon."

"I like to take things in increments," I tell him.

"I got kids," he says. "So I'm on this task force for personal reasons. And I'm going to share my belief that there's no difference between the guy who rapes children and the guy who looks at pictures of children being raped. Most officers on the force think these guys should be hunted down and shot like dogs in the street. I haven't dwelled too much on that end of it. For me, it's the children, they're the ones I'm concerned about. And how long ago it was that they got hurt, that doesn't matter to me at all."

He regards me a moment, almost sadly.

"Personally, I don't think you're one of the bad guys," he says. "But you, whether you think you're a good guy or a bad guy—that's something you should be very concerned with. There's a way you can prove to yourself that you're not a bad guy. You can save us a lot of trouble and pass along that code."

He leaves his card.

I follow the cop outside and watch him drive away. From the porch, I can see the Tiger and the Cub have opened a lemonade stand. They've taken a table and two folding chairs into the parking lot and are sitting, waiting. They have some lemons, a sugar jar and a pitcher of ice water. The Cub's legs swing back and forth below the vinyl tablecloth. Nobody visits their lemonade stand, including me.

Come dark, I initialize my computer and crop images for a while. This is controlled, orderly work, and it soothes me. I take the images I've copied from people's hard drives, and then I crop out the erections and penetrations and grimaces. I don't need to tell you that I hate videos. You can't crop a video. And once it's in motion, it's impossible to control.

I call up the picture of the girl in the kitchen. First I crop her photo down to an image that shows only her eyes. Save. Then I frame the pattern of light that falls across her skin.

Save. I crop an image that is simply yellow—a square of her yellow shirt, nothing else. Save. And then the hand. I trim and trim, narrowing in until there is only blur. You wouldn't even know it was a hand. Then I destroy the original. In this way, I cripple the picture's power to hurt—it's not child pornography, it's not pornography, it's not even a child. I remove what racks you, what leaves you unable to raise yourself from the bottom of the boat.

Outside, I harvest a few flowers but soon find myself staring at my hand in the headlamp's beam, which is pale and even. The light is eclipse light, as when the moon is in transit across the face of the sun. There was a weekend when Skipper had us sail to Santa Cruz Island to witness an eclipse. On the voyage over, he showed us girlie magazines and told us jokes about sailors and sharks and faggots and priests. We anchored in Potato Harbor, then rowed in teams to the beach. As the eclipse began, the light slowly dimmed. Most of the boys stared upward with their stupid black glasses. Only I recognized the kind of light we were standing in. Suddenly, the Skipper had his hand on my shoulder.

Normally, his Merchant Marines ring flashed aqua, but here it glowed a royal blue.

How had he gotten close without my noticing?

"When most people think of light, they think *on* or *off*," the Skipper told me. "But the observant scout will see there's a hundred kinds of light. Just like there's a hundred kinds of water. Each with its own set of rules."

He produced a twelve-pack of beer—one for each scout in the troop.

We toasted the sun and the moon and their temporary union. It was my first taste.

"What happens in the eclipse stays in the eclipse," Skipper announced, and we cheered.

The way he said it was both funny and menacing, like when he'd tell a gay joke. We all knew what he thought of the gays.

The next day, the Tiger and the Cub are having a yard sale. They sit at a table covered with household goods. I drift over. The Tiger is wearing gym shorts and a jean jacket. The Cub has on a red hand-me-down hoodie.

When I approach the table, I ask, "Why aren't you guys in school?"

The Cub says, "It's Saturday, Mr. Roses."

This is the closest I've been to the Cub. There is no single trait that makes her activate—it's not the brown ringlets or baby-fat cheeks or exaggerated expressions. It's just the cusp she's on. I can see on her face a wide-eyed, trusting openness. She directs this look to a world that has yet to reveal its dark and unapologetic nature. Part of me wants to kill the person who manages to steal that look from her. And a loathsome, unfathomable part thinks it's only natural to be the thief.

When I let my gaze fall upon a power juicer, the Tiger says, "It's like new. We never even used it." And when I look at a waffle iron, the Cub forlornly lifts her eyebrows and says only, "Waffles."

"You guys trying to save up for something?" I ask.

"Just making ends meet," the Tiger says.

They are eating slices of frozen French toast straight from the box.

I look over at their apartment, door standing open. "Your mom sleeping?" I ask.

The Cub says, "She's on tour with a band."

"What band is this?" I ask.

"We forget," the Tiger says. "And we can't check Mom's blog. The Internet's not working."

"The cable, too," the Cub adds.

"Is your Internet working?" the Tiger asks.

"I don't have the Internet," I tell them.

The Tiger nods in sympathy. "Anyway," she says, "the band is going to be the next Nirvana."

"Do you know when your mother's coming back?" I ask. "Are you in contact with her?"

"Yeah," the Tiger says. "We texted her, and she texted back. She said we shouldn't worry about her, that she's just fine."

The Cub holds up a clock radio. "Five bucks," she says. "It beams the time on the ceiling."

"No, thanks," I say.

"The sad part," the Tiger says, "is that our place is filled with rock memorabilia."

"It's priceless," the Cub says.

"But we can't sell any of it," the Tiger says.

"Because it's priceless," the Cub says. Then she adds, "My dad is a rock star."

"Mine, too," the Tiger says. "But her dad is seriously famous. Like, sell-out-stadiums famous. He sends us a check every month, which is why we don't have to work."

I look at some of their things—a bathroom scale, a pop-up Polaroid camera, a lamp.

I try to remember how long it's been since I've laid eyes on their mother.

"You guys have any relatives looking after you?" I ask. "Some folks you can call?"

They shake their heads, and I nod at the situation.

"I always have to buy something at a yard sale," I tell them. "It's an addiction I have."

"What about a picture?" the Cub asks. From behind the table, she lifts a painting of a boat upon a moonlit velvet sea. The wooden frame is hand-carved and darkly stained. It's the kind of painting you see Mexican guys selling at stoplights on Sepulveda.

The Tiger says, "I think it's a clipper ship."

"It's actually a sloop," I tell her. "A Bermuda sloop, rigged to sail alone."

"You a sailor?" the Cub asks.

"I used to sail," I say. "I haven't in a long time. But it's easy to tell ships apart—you look at the sails and masts. It goes sloop, cutter, ketch, schooner, clipper."

The Tiger says, "Now you have to buy it."

"It is a fine painting," I say, and scratch my chin. "Probably worth more than I can afford."

The girls look at each other. "Make us an offer," the Tiger says.

I open my wallet and look inside. I pull out those three one-hundred-dollar bills.

"This is the best I can do," I tell them.

After darkness falls, I sit on my small porch and read the latest *National Geographic*. I don't want to be in the same room as my computer, and my heart's not into gardening tonight. There's an article about U.S. soldiers who defuse bombs in a distant land. First they must approach the bomb—this is nerve-racking because anything they inspect might contain explosive material. Once they become acquainted with the device, they try to break it down to its elements. They separate the power source from the trigger, then the trigger from the charge. When a device detonates, it's not like Hollywood, one soldier says. You wake up later and you can't really be sure what's real and what's the echo in your head. He says you can defuse a bomb in the real world, but the bomb in your head, that's forever.

Somehow, without my noticing it, the Tiger and the Cub
have appeared before me on the porch. When I lower my
magazine, there they are, the Tiger in her tiger-striped mascot suit, the Cub in pajamas patterned with rainbows and
unicorns.

The Tiger says, "Some guy was looking in our window."

"He was scary," the Cub says.

"We heard a noise," the Tiger says. "When we looked up,
there he was."

"I don't want to go back there," the Cub says.

"Everything's going to be fine," I tell them. "Come, let's
have a look."

We cross my yard, the parking lot and the courtyard to
their one-bedroom apartment.

Inside, the walls are covered with guitars, album covers
and cymbals autographed in black marker. The Tiger's Mom
has the bedroom, so the girls sleep on the floor in front of the
TV. The floors: there are heaps of dirty laundry, cardboard
boxes, bikes on their sides, and strips of masking tape worked
into the carpet to mark the mascot's dance steps.

"Where did you see him?" I ask.

They point at the window above a small breakfast table.

"I heard someone say there was a peeper in the neighborhood," I say.

"What's a peeper?" the Cub asks.

"He's a guy," I say. "He's a fellow who likes— What he
does is—"

"He looks in your windows," the Tiger says.

"Oh," the Cub says. "Why would he do that?"

The Tiger looks at me, wondering if she should explain, and I shake my head.

"Wait here," I tell them. Outside, I make my way to the back of the complex, squeezing between the trash bins and dryer vents as I traverse the apartment's rear wall. Here, I cup my hands to the glass and peer inside, observing the girls the way a pervert would. When the Cub looks in my direction, she screams and then the Tiger screams and then they realize it's only me.

I move to inspect the bedroom window. Below the window frame, the grass is trampled and someone has ejaculated many times onto the pink stucco. Nearing the glass, I gaze into the mother's bedroom. Here is the mattress where the Tiger's Mom sleeps off her hangovers, where—out cold, sheets balled, robe flopped open—she spends her days.

Inside, I tell the girls that some guy probably just looked in the wrong window. Still, we hang towels over both panes. The girls are happy to have a visitor. The Tiger shows me her tiger dance. She cages her eyes and moves seriously through a drill, like it is the fourth quarter and the home crowd is depending on her to spark a rally.

The Cub, too, performs for me. She begins to move about the apartment like a dolphin. Her elbows become fins. She puffs her cheeks and holds her breath. When she lifts her head, she's breaching the surface, and when her neck lowers, she's diving deep, and she is not running through soiled clothes, she is swimming in the open ocean. In this faraway sea, alcohol doesn't exist and neither do North Hollywood one-bedrooms. Here, men don't fuck groupies or masturbate while your mother dreams. I watch the Cub swim laps around me, her limber young body silently circling, wholly unaware of the designs the world has drafted for her.

When her eyes lift to mine, seeking my approval, I call a halt to this swimming and dancing business. I go to their fridge, papered with nightclub flyers. Inside, I find nothing, not even milk.

"You hungry, Mr. Roses?" the Cub asks.

The freezer, too, is empty. "What happened to the money I gave you for the painting?"

The Tiger says, "We had to pay a bill."

"What bill was this?"

The Tiger says, "A guy came by. He knows our mom, and it turns out there was a bill she forgot to pay."

"Wait here," I tell them, and then head to the 7-Eleven on the corner, where I buy whole-grain cereal, bananas, a gallon of milk and some dodgy-looking *taquitos*, but at least they are warm.

Behind the checkout counter are racks of dirty magazines. I turn from them. I feel like a good guy, a normal guy who has normal interactions with others. The Cub *is* a powerful force. She *activates*. But I feel strong and good. I deliver the groceries, and when I take leave of the girls, I stand on the front step and tell them to close the door and lock it.

"I want to hear it lock," I say.

They close the door on me, but instead of locking it, they say, "What are we going to do?"

"Read a book," I say through the wood. "Better yet, go to bed. Now lock the door."

They are quiet a moment. Then the deadbolt locks.

At home, I hang the boat painting where I can see it from my bed. I lie atop my covers, thinking about the guy who is sailing alone. All the lights in my apartment are off, but there's enough glow through the window to see the weight and size of the ocean rollers, to note how the rigging strains in the wind. The sailor is looking toward a dark horizon, so the viewer can't see his face, but it's easy to tell his story is an old one: a sailor has lost something far out at sea. Now he's heading back to claim it.

It's just a cheap painting, but for hours I wonder if the sailor can get the thing back, if he can find the place where he lost it. To do that, he has to sail back in time, to *before*. The journey is impossible, but he has his boat rigged right, and the rope is in his hands. The wind is up and he's bowfronting the waves. Most important, the sailor has made the decision. He has embarked.

I decide to text Officer Hernandez. It's the middle of the night. Using software to alias my SIM card data, I send him this message: 5c2758ba7d4f4dd90c5525b5aa6a09cb4305452 c121e5a5961c1f4fc451223fee2982285274b6e2ca36d2587f8 48b72517236ca950bf8934a6afada07976aaac098aeaf54e83 b70c4a00442bf548d7e307c5e1f93abfc0ef1d4777b69d9d9ea aa685947050483d8907f9516eb7f6870edbf52d7e7153e737a 80a60f2b5366eaf.

In the morning, I get a text for a computer consultation in Sun Valley. Shittier even than Pacoima, Chatsworth, Reseda and my own North Hollywood is Sun Valley. I take Tujunga north to La Tuna. I pull up in front of a defunct dog kennel sandwiched between a cement plant and a maintenance yard. There's a chain across the lot, so I park in the street.

I double-check the address. Then I text the number back: "Dog kennel?"

Right away, I get my answer: "Yes, DM14097. Just knock, we're home."

No one in the world has connected the real me with DM14097. I'm no longer that person. I no longer use screen names. I don't surf forums, chat rooms or P2P directories. I stopped using Tor, eDonkey and Fetch. I don't swap, barter, buy in or burn-request. I gave up the entire Internet. I have only my little library, and I'm chipping away at that.

I check my phone, but this person also knows how to alias his SIM data.

Just then he texts back: "btw, this is Dodger6636."

In the world I no longer inhabit, where people exist only online, fantasy and deed are indistinguishable. Yet there was one man known by his deeds. And that was Dodger6636, a legend in the realm. He must have outlasted them all.

I look at the abandoned dog kennel, taking note of the improvised satellite dishes on the roof and the aluminum foil covering the storefront windows. I get that feel, that kinetic conk inside when I'd receive a delivery from Dodger in my Fetch Dropbox: a puppy avatar would alert me by dancing across my computer window and then laying the bone in his mouth at the foot of my screen. When you got a delivery from Dodger, you knew it was special, it was some long-lost tidbit you'd never laid eyes on.

I step over the chain. Glass and gravel crunch as I cross the lot.

Dodger opens the door before I raise my hand to knock.

"Dark Meadow," he says, taking a good look at me. "You made it."

"Looks like you made it, too," I say.

He's older than me, a bit potbellied. He's had what were maybe some small skin cancers removed from his forehead and scalp. We've never met—I've never met anyone from that world—but he says, "I remember you well. You're different than I imagined, but tastes never change. Pictures only, if I recall. And you're a vintage guy, right, you like the classic stuff?"

One look into Dodger's eyes, and you can tell what kind he is: the kind that is born.

"Actually, I've embarked on a new life," I tell him.

"Certainly," he says. "I understand completely." He removes a thumb drive from his pocket. "You won't be needing this, then. But I'll give it to you for old times' sake. It's custom-loaded for you."

He holds out the thumb drive, and I take it, warm from his pants.

"You know how hard it is to find new vintage material?" he asks me. "What was it Wordsworth said, 'A springtime loss is autumn's gain'? Just remember that I made the effort, I walked the mile for you. It's encrypted, but the key is 'Dark Meadow.'"

When I close my fingers around the drive, Dodger beckons me in.

"You weren't easy to find," he tells me. "But we need you."

I follow Dodger through the empty waiting room into a hallway stacked with blinking server arrays; several box fans hum full speed to keep them cool. We enter what might have once been a dog-grooming area—there are stainless-steel counters and tables and sinks. The sinks are deep. One is filled with dirty coffee cups, and the other is ringed with beauty supplies. At one metal table, a man is editing video. He's got a couple of cinema screens and a mixing board.

Dodger addresses him, "Bert, this is Dark Meadow. He doesn't like video. It's only pictures for him."

Without turning from his screens, Bert says, "Old-school."

"Dark Meadow's the one who posted that article," Dodger says. "He's here to make sure our servers are clean."

The tables are tall and ringed with director's chairs. When we sit, Dodger says, "You don't know how glad I am to see you, old friend. Your article touched on a matter of grave concern for us. Can you lend us your expertise?"

"You've got a regular server farm in there," I say. "Do you have a T1 line?"

Dodger lifts his hands. "Our business requires it," he says, and he starts detailing all their hardware configurations.

I can feel there are other rooms down a short hall, maybe veterinary exam rooms or rooms filled with animal cages. When I glance over at Bert's screens, I see footage of a girl. She is naked except for her socks. She walks into the shot, facing away from the viewer, and she approaches a table. Bert backs the footage up so that she enters again, approaches the table again, and leaning forward slightly, she places her hands palm-down upon it.

"This should be no problem," I tell Dodger, even though I haven't completely heard him. Such is the absorbing power of video. "Let me grab my diagnostic drives from the van." I glance again at the screen.

Dodger catches me and smiles. "He said he didn't like videos," he tells Bert.

"I heard," Bert says.

"Who could blame you?" Dodger says. "She's special, brand-new. Look at her, knock-kneed and wobbly. She doesn't even know where to look. I have them leave their socks on. It's one of those touches."

On the screen, a naked man with pale skin enters. He approaches the girl from behind.

"She needs a name," Dodger says. "All the good ones have been used up—Dazzle, Sparkle, Crush, Taffy, Daphne, Tumble, Twist."

"What about Trample?" Bert asks.

"Go back to your editing," Dodger tells him, then says to me, "Bert has no sense of beauty, he appreciates nothing."

On the screen, the man nears the girl. He reaches around her and places his hands firmly atop hers, pinning them. Behind his large frame, she disappears, her little-girl self is gone, and I activate. It happens so fast that a shudder races through me and I feel my body jerk. The man's body hitches as he begins, and then she's gone, there's nothing of her left.

"Whoa," Dodger says when he sees my face. "Looks like we have a new fan. Bert, burn an extra copy of this, Dark Meadow here's an admirer."

Bert turns and gives me a sour look. He looks like he hasn't slept in a long time.

"You can't even see the girl," he says. "This is the part I'm editing *out*."

"What works is what works," Dodger says. "You said you

didn't like videos, but this does it for you, yes? Help us out, and I'll give her to you. Give our servers a sweep, and she is yours."

For the first time, I notice that the table in the video is stainless steel. And just as it dawns on me that I, too, am at a stainless-steel table, a girl walks into the room, right past me. She's carrying a bowl of cereal in both hands. The cereal's the kind with rainbow marshmallows and the bowl is filled to the brim, milk threatening to spill, so she's moving slowly, eyes glued to the rim. I see that her hair is wet, that she's wearing a bathrobe, and this is her, this is the girl on the screen, and I understand that when Dodger offered her to me, he was not talking about a video file.

My arms rise as if in self-defense, and I stand so fast that the director's chair is knocked to the ground. The girl turns to look at me, milk sloshing onto her hands. We lock eyes for a moment, and then I am running. I drop the thumb drive and run. I bump Bert's table, his monitors threatening to tip, and I almost take down a tower of servers as I race for my van.

At home, I drag my computer out front, and on the cement driveway, I start swinging a hammer. With the claw, I split the aluminum casing. I carve out the GPU and the optical drive and the RAM cards. I scrape all the circuitry off the motherboard. I pull the drives from their bays, and I think, *I am a bad guy, I am a broken guy*. I start to bang on the drives, actuator arms flying off, spindles cracking. "I am bad," I mutter to myself. "I am broken." I pound and I pound until there is nothing left but crumbs of plastic and aluminum meal. Of the hard drives themselves, the alloy discs knurl under the waffled face of the hammer into raw nuggets. Rhonza walks by. She casts a quick glance, but if she formulates an opinion, she keeps it to herself.

Hammer in hand, I rise and turn to look at my house. What kind of person lives here? I know there are those who are born. But what of those who are made? Do they also have a choice? Can they still choose?

I drive all day. I drive to the marina and park in its blindingly bright lot. I make my way along the floating docks, and things are familiar—ice being shoveled into plastic coolers, a charter captain hosing down saltwater tackle. But when I reach the slip where a sailboat named *Ketchfire* perpetually resides in my mind, I find nothing. There is only a rainbow sheen of spilled diesel on the water. Were there other boys? Was I the only one? My mind won't let me picture the Skipper except in snapshots: white-soled shoes, tanned forearms, grey stubble.

Just off La Cienega was a pizza joint Skipper used to take us to, and when I drive there, it is still open. In fact, it is still filled with boys—soccer teams, Little League, a brigade of boys in matching black karate uniforms. I drink diet root beer from a red plastic cup and stare at their faces. I study them as they hold pizza slices and tromp around in their cleats, and I don't care if people eyeball me. This is where, after our troop was formed and we sailed the *Ketchfire* for the first time, Skipper brought us for pizza and gave us our nicknames. Other boys got names like Nav and Crusher and Sparks and Cutter. Then he looked at me. He must have seen something in me. There must have been something *about* me. He said, "And you are Dark Meadow."

I head up Topanga Canyon, passing the Charlie Manson ranch and the lodge where Jim Morrison wrote "Roadhouse Blues." I suppose I should share the fact that there was another sound in the bottom of the boat. The Skipper had a camera, the old disposable kind. It used real film, and to advance the roll, he had to turn a plastic wheel three times—*scritch, scritch, scritch*. There would be a whine as the flash charged. He framed his pictures carefully, taking his time, and you never knew when that bright light would blind you.

I park at the Santa Ynez trailhead and walk up, above the dog park with its barrels of eco-bagged dog shit, above the footpaths where multicolored condom wrappers flutter in the thornbushes. Up here, tawny grass surrounds a giant coastal oak. According to the newspaper, this is where it happened. There is a stiff breeze. Looking west: a panorama of ocean. I study the ancient tree, with its burdened trunk and gnarled branches, and I wonder which limb Skipper Stevenson threw his rope over.

———

It is dark when I arrive home. The Tiger and the Cub are on my porch.

When I approach, the Tiger says, "There was someone outside our window again."

"We heard him," the Cub adds.

"Seriously," the Tiger says. "He was super-creepy."

"Was there really someone out there?" I ask.

They both go quiet.

"I don't want to go home," the Cub says, and the Tiger nods in agreement.

"Come on," I tell them, and open the door. Inside, I turn on all the lights and, in the kitchen, retrieve three milks.

The girls run around, inspecting everything. They race to my bedroom, where they discover only boxes of computer parts.

They come back, disappointed. "Where's your bed?" they ask. "Where do you sleep?"

I hand out milks and point at the foldout couch right in front of them.

The Cub, feeling kinship, says, "You sleep in the living room, too."

The Tiger asks, "Where's your dinner table?"

"I eat my sandwiches at the counter," I tell them.

"Don't you own a chair?" the Cub asks.

"It's on the porch," I answer. "You were just sitting in it."

"Where's the TV?" the Cub asks.

"Just drink your milk and go to bed, you two."

They are amped and squirmy, but they obey; slipping under the covers, they try to lie still.

The Tiger focuses on the Bermuda sloop.

She says, "I never really looked at this painting when it was on our wall."

I glance at the sailor, rigging in his hands. He has started his journey, the all-important one. He has decided his direction and charted a course. All he had to do was choose.

"Let's try to get some sleep, you two."

On the porch, I begin an article about Mars rovers, but I can't focus. Officer Hernandez keeps texting me, and so does Dodger. I don't often think back to the Sea Scout days, but the boy I used to be, he is everywhere tonight, his trusting face, his quiet hopefulness. Also in my head is the girl with her hands on the stainless-steel table. And Dodger's thumb drive, I keep hearing the satisfying click it would make sliding into my computer's USB port. My mind begins filling the lost drive with a thousand images. Already I miss my computer, its calm and order, how things would stop spinning if I could just boot it up. On the driveway, the crumbs of its carcass sparkle when a car passes.

When I figure the girls are asleep, I head inside.

They are awake.

"Turn the lights off," the Cub says. "I can't sleep with the lights on."

"Let's try them on a little longer," I say.

I sit on the side of the bed, where I unlace my shoes and

loosen my collar. Then I lie beside them—me atop the covers, them below.

The three of us stare at the ceiling.

The Cub asks, "Are you the son of Missus Roses?"

"She's just the lady I bought the house from."

"I want a nickname," the Cub says.

"Trust me," I tell her. "You don't."

Though the Tiger is between us, the energy of the Cub radiates to me. I feel her. Her unaverted gaze. The inquisitive lift to her brow. The dark hollow at the cuff of her pajama sleeve.

"Have you ever done anything bad?" I ask the girls.

The Cub stares into space. She says a slow "Yeah," like she's visualizing a graveyard of her bad ten-year-old decisions and the wasteland of their consequences.

"Everyone's done something bad," the Tiger says. "What about you?"

"I've done some bad things," I tell her. "But I've never hurt anyone. Not directly, not me doing the actual hurting."

"Did someone do something bad to you?" she asks. "Is that why you brought it up?"

"A long time ago, yes. Something bad happened to me."

The Tiger turns toward me, our faces not far apart. "Like what?" she asks.

"I suppose there are pictures of it," I say.

"Pictures?" she asks. "What do they look like?"

I shake my head. "They're out there somewhere," I tell the

Tiger. "But I haven't seen them. That's because I don't look at pictures of boys."

Narrowing her eyes, she tries to understand this.

She is the older one, so I tell her the truth.

"I look at pictures of girls."

The Tiger considers this. She says, "Some of the girls on the cheer squad, they trade pictures of boys on their phones. That's all they care about."

She begins to tell me all about it—her friends, their crushes, the perils of a forwarded pic.

"Will someone please turn out the lights?" the Cub pleads.

The Tiger begins to sing to the Cub. It's a song about a girl who goes alone into darkened woods. "'My girl, my girl,'" the Tiger sings, "'don't lie to me.'"

The Cub sings, "'Tell me, where did you sleep last night?'"

Together, they sing, "'In the pines, in the pines, where the sun don't ever shine.'"

"That's a pretty strange lullaby," I tell them.

They ignore me and finish the chorus together, "'I would shiver the whole night through.'"

The Tiger then throws me a look. "Tell that to Kurt Cobain," she says.

I stand awkwardly, because of my erection, and walk to the light switch.

I regard the girls a moment, their outlines under the covers, their small mouths as the Tiger leads the Cub through the final lyrics about going to where the cold wind blows. Perhaps I was too hasty with regard to the Tiger. Maybe I judged her too early. There is something about her. She does, in her own way, activate.

I turn out the lights.

Outside, I step across the yard into my rosebushes. Here, I lick my hand. I lick up and down, coating my palm and fingers. I position myself behind some Blue Skies and Bourbons, so I'm less visible from the street, and begin masturbating. It's not about pleasure but about security and stimulation control and self-management. I'm doing it for the girls. They need me to look out for them, I understand that now. I can be a force of good in their lives. I'm the one who heard the signal. I'm the one who knows the code. What Officer Hernandez doesn't get is that once something bad happens, it happens every minute of your life, and it can't be undone, not by a rescue or a raid or a rope or a hundred and forty thousand dollars. The time to act isn't after, it's before, it's now. And there is nothing beautiful about a pearl of semen tumbling toward a rose in the moonlight. It's just a duty. While the innocents sleep, it's just a thing that must be done.

Fortune Smiles

Every Friday, DJ met Sun-ho for lunch. The guy had been DJ's right-hand man in North Korea, and DJ owed him more than any man could pay. Since fast food was the only thing in Seoul that Sun-ho actually seemed to like, lunches were all DJ had to say thanks. Or maybe he was saying sorry. DJ didn't know what to call his debt to Sun-ho, though it was more than a super-size double-meal deal could articulate. Still, in the four months since they'd defected, they'd been to Bon-chon Chicken and Kyochon Chicken and Gimbap Cheonguk and half a dozen others. Today, they were to meet in Insa-dong for bulgogi burgers at a chain called Lotteria.

DJ set out from the male dormitory where he lived in the Gwanak District. The dorm was far from fancy, but it reminded him of home in all the right ways—unlocked doors, polished cement floors, a curfew and that feeling of being alone and together at the same time. Plus, he wasn't the only one with troubles. On the other bunks slept men who were battling alcohol, men who'd lost everything in the economic collapse and even a few unlucky bastards who'd been sent to Iraq to fight alongside the Americans. DJ understood that in South Korea, Americans were considered friends. He'd never really believed they were the enemy. After all, hadn't Americans invented scratch-off lottery tickets, crystal meth, hundred-dollar bills and, most important, the catalytic converter?

It was a cold February. Bundled in his heavy coat and scarf, DJ took the Blue line into central Seoul, then followed the Orange line north to Anguk Station. As soon as he exited the train, he heard echoing through the halls the unmistakable sound of an accordion playing "No Motherland Without You." People rushed in all directions in that unnervingly chaotic way Southerners moved. No one seemed to notice or recognize a North Korean song, let alone the great musical tribute to Kim Jong-il.

The surprising thing was that DJ had a pretty good hunch who was playing it. When he and Sun-ho finally made it to South Korea, they'd spent a couple months in a government transition facility called Hanawon. There he met a woman who was famous for defecting with her accordion. People said it had nearly drowned her while she was crossing the rushing autumn waters of the Tumen River. Her name was Mina, and she hadn't wanted to defect, she said, but her husband had disappeared, and she'd gone looking for him.

DJ started walking toward the melancholy sounds. The chords were triumphant and lonesome, a mix he hadn't heard since leaving home. Yet halfway to the Samil-daero exit, he realized the music was getting fainter, that he was heading the wrong way. The song stopped; he'd lost her. But the melody, the haunting way Mina had played it, stuck in his head. Aboveground, he wandered the neighborhoods, suddenly nostalgic for the North. The barren, snow-dusted mountains surrounding Seoul reminded him of the icy bluffs ringing Chongjin. The crooked tile roofs and bent aerial antennas of Bukchon Hanok Village felt familiar. Passing a church, he heard a huge congregation inside praising Yesu-Nim before falling quiet in prayer. Though he couldn't see the worshippers, DJ paused on the sidewalk, and here came a sound that was pure North Korea: the nearly silent shush of a thousand heads bowing in unison.

Soon his attention returned to Seoul's bewildering nature. Here were women in plastic surgery masks and little dogs wearing dresses. Passing a fitness center, DJ stared at rows of men running on treadmills. What force was driving them? What were they running from? Next came a cat café and a parlor where teenage girls danced with machines. At an empty shopping plaza, he watched an escalator endlessly cycle, the steps appearing, rising and disappearing as it carried no one up to nowhere.

In this state of mind, DJ arrived at Lotteria. Inside, he took a seat in a yellow booth. Through the glass, he observed the startling street life: a young woman with tattoos on her neck, a college boy wearing eyeliner, a fully grown and able-bodied man of military age sitting on the curb, doing nothing. The only normal thing DJ could see was Sun-ho, making his way slowly down the street. He had a bad hip and a sleepy leg that he dragged around. In the North, he was only as big as a thirteen-year-old. Here, he was the size of a child, though the intensity of his large, wide-set eyes kept anyone from mistaking him for one.

When Sun-ho entered, he offered DJ a subtle nod, and though he was no longer under DJ's command, he went right away to get their food, cutting to the front of the ordering line. Once there, he turned to examine the patrons he'd just skipped over. They looked down to their phones, pretending nothing had happened. Sun-ho studied them a moment, then shook his head. He had no patience for South Koreans, with their all-powerful sense of order and compliance. It was one thing to surrender to the rule of a murderous dictator, but what unseen forces did these Southerners obey?

"Ready to receive your order," a Lotteria worker said.

Sun-ho located his cigarettes and placed one in his mouth.

"Smoking is not permitted," the worker said. "Corporate policy."

Sun-ho pointed at the sign depicting all the food. He pointed at the bulgogi burger set, then held up two fingers.

"Would you like those burgers Shanghai-spicy?" the worker asked Sun-ho.

Sun-ho nodded and produced some government-issued meal coupons.

The worker shook his head. "We don't honor those," he said.

Sun-ho patted his pockets until he located his matches. "Do you believe in the divine spark?" he asked the worker.

Here was where Sun-ho's gruff Northern accent registered on the worker. The people in line also paused—the man in the golf sweater, a group of teens in school uniform.

"I don't understand," the worker said.

Sun-ho stared into the man's eyes. "Do you believe in the all-consuming flame of the Lord?" he asked. "Do you believe that only fire can burn away your sin?"

It was true that Sun-ho was not a large man, but make no mistake: he had served seven years of naval duty aboard a ten-man submarine; he'd run afoul of the Bowibu and made it through a winter in Camp 25. The man had walked the Arduous March in North Hamgyong Province through the worst of the famine. Sun-ho had survived the Purge of Chongjin.

The restaurant worker accepted the coupons and served the food in takeaway bags.

Sun-ho joined DJ in the booth, where he removed his dental plates and began unwrapping his burger.

"Where did you get that crazy talk?" DJ asked him. "You had *me* nervous."

"This is a discovery I made," Sun-ho said. "Christian talk, when said in a non-Christian way, scares these Southerners to death."

"You've been going to too many meetings."

"Far too many meetings," Sun-ho said, and took a bite.

When they first arrived at Incheon airport and surrendered to authorities, they didn't go free, as they'd expected. Instead, they spent eight weeks in Hanawon, where they were debriefed, interviewed, fingerprinted and subjected to a battery of physical and mental exams. All defectors ended up there. They took group classes about adjusting to life in South Korea—handling money, hygiene, being pleasant, avoiding crime. DJ and Sun-ho had lived pretty good lives in the North, so they weren't as stunned as other defectors. Still, one thing they learned in Hanawon surprised them: in the South, Dongjoo and Sun-ho weren't the most popular names for boys. Old-fashioned names might hinder their assimilation, they were told. The officials suggested Dongjoo adopt a hip nickname like DJ. Sun-ho left the room.

Even when they got out of Hanawon, they weren't free. Too many defectors had become alcoholic, homeless, suicidal or, worse, had redefected. So there were meetings—case officer meetings, support group meetings, Christian outreach meetings, weekly "Talk Out" sessions. On Saturday mornings, middle school children gave them English lessons. They were given bank accounts, housing allowances and a stack of food vouchers that no decent restaurant would accept. Luckily, this was the food they loved the most. So much flavor, so hot, and like magic, it appeared whenever you wanted it.

Together, they nodded in pleasure, savoring every bite.

"What do you think?" Sun-ho asked. "Would Willow have liked this burger?"

DJ was silent.

Sun-ho answered his own question. "Yes, I think she would have enjoyed this burger very much." With a french fry, he scraped Shanghai sauce drippings off the paper wrapper. "These fries, though," he continued, "they're too greasy for her. You remember Willow's skin, how perfect it was. So yes to the burger, but because of her complexion, she would avoid the fries."

Rumor had it that Sun-ho had slept with every widow in Chongjin. Yet all he talked about was Willow, how he'd nearly attained Willow, that with a little more time, Willow would have become his. And since their escape, Willow had somehow risen to the level of angel, as pure and inaccessible as Yesu-Nim Himself.

DJ knew better than to get Sun-ho going on Willow, but he couldn't help it. He asked, "What would Willow think of all the Namhan women you're sleeping with?"

"Preparing to sleep with," Sun-ho corrected. "You don't just jump on a Southern woman, my friend. You cultivate her. You must attend many meetings. And for the record, what I do with other women has no impact on Willow's purity."

DJ asked, "Are you telling these Southern women the juicy stories they crave?"

"The point of the meetings is to process your experience," Sun-ho said. "These women are volunteers; they care about our plight. The whole reason they're there is to listen."

"Ah, a celebrity defector in the making," DJ said.

They'd seen such defectors on ROK TV. Usually, they were beautiful young women who wept as they told the most harrowing stories—of starvation, separation, suffering and torture. Always a baby died. Always there was the moment when the dark shadow of rape fell across the story, and the interviewer let the silence linger before shifting to the desperate escape. All the average defectors, they weren't news. And never on TV was there a story of a man who escaped North Korea in a black Mercedes sedan with a driver who must sit on a briefcase filled with counterfeit lottery tickets in order to see over the wheel.

DJ asked, "Do these ladies drink white wine while you tell them about freezing winters and endless peril?"

"The winters were freezing."

"We had a propane heater."

"There was peril. People were shot. People disappeared."

"We paid protection money," DJ said. "You haven't told those ladies about the things we did in Chongjin, have you?"

"Of course not," Sun-ho said.

He licked the last streaks of sauce from his fingers and wadded up the wrapper.

"The famine was real."

DJ nodded. "The famine was real."

Sun-ho smiled. "Look," he said, "you're only going to meet hobos and crazies going to meetings in Gwanak. Come to Gangnam—all the ladies there are genuine do-gooders. They have absent husbands. Their kids have shipped off to Stanford. These are ladies with time on their hands, and trust me, they take care of themselves."

Sun-ho caught the teens in school uniform sneaking wary glances their way.

"What?" he called to their booth. "What the fuck are you looking at?"

The students feigned interest in their fries.

Sun-ho turned back to DJ. "When I was their age, I didn't sit around giving people stupid looks. When I was sixteen, life was hammer and sickle."

It was true. While DJ's path had been smoothly laid out for him, Sun-ho's had been one long scramble. DJ looked at the kids. Growing up in Pyongyang, he'd worn a school uniform, too, complete with a red scarf. Images of kids in uniform were everywhere recently. A ferry filled with such students had sunk, and DJ was newly aware of these uniformed kids drifting down the streets, huddling in the subway cars, killing time in fast-food booths. There was something ghostlike about them, the boys in their green-and-white ties, the girls with their slate-white scarves, their blazers the color of the cold, cold ocean. As the ferry slowly sank, the students were told to wait in their cabins, and there they passed the time until the ferry rolled under the waves.

"I almost forgot," Sun-ho said. "I brought gifts of good fortune."

He produced a handful of lottery tickets.

DJ took one. It was an instant ticket named Triple Jewel.

"What're you doing with these?" he asked.

Sun-ho shrugged. "I cash my government checks at a liquor store. On a whim, I bought some. I thought, why not try our luck with the Korean lottery?"

DJ held the card to the light. This was no cheap Chinese scratch-off. This was no forged Pai Gow Poker card that you printed off ten thousand at a run. This wasn't even Fortune Smiles, which was the finest lottery ticket they'd ever counterfeited.

"Look at this one," Sun-ho said. "This ticket's called 520. You win a pension from the Korean government. It pays out five million won a year for twenty years."

DJ retrieved his reading glasses, which the ophthalmologist at Hanawon had given him. He examined the 520 card. It was multi-layer, with dual win zones, holographic foil, confusion patterns and self-voiding strips. Looking closer, he saw micro-printing and perforation work. This was made on a very sophisticated machine, probably a series of machines, not the old Japanese press they'd managed to modify and keep running.

"Don't look so serious," Sun-ho said. "Scratch a few."

DJ watched Sun-ho use a car key to play a card, vigorously scraping away the grey vinyl topcoating. DJ recognized the mad energy in Sun-ho's eyes. In North Korea, crime was state-sanctioned; crime was an absolute necessity. If you dined at all, you dined on illegality. Here in Seoul, crime was a much different matter.

"Wait a minute," DJ said. "What are you doing with a car key?"

Sun-ho handed it over. It was a Toyota dealer's key, stamped for the year 2000. It would open and start any Toyota from that year.

"Where'd you get this?" DJ asked.

"I brought it with me," Sun-ho said. "I brought all our keys."

How, in the sudden mad scramble of their escape, had Sun-ho thought to bring the master keys? DJ handed it back. "Get rid of it," he said. "We don't have hard currency quotas to meet anymore. Those days are gone. And you don't need a 520 pension. We get deposits from the government now."

Sun-ho came around to the other side of the booth so the two men were shoulder to shoulder. Here he turned his wide, bulging eyes to DJ. The doctors at Hanawon said Sun-ho's eyes were the sign of a condition, a condition that had a name, but Sun-ho didn't want to know it. Most people were frightened of these eyes, but as DJ looked into them, he thought only that they were vulnerable and revealing.

"So I play the lottery," Sun-ho said. "So I'm friendly with a few Gangnam moms. So I borrow cars."

"You're borrowing cars?"

Sun-ho ignored this. "I'm trying to make the best of the situation we're in," he said. "I didn't choose to defect, if you'll remember."

DJ cast his eyes down. "I don't forget," he said.

"Good," Sun-ho said, and clapped DJ once on the back.

There was no word in the South for their relationship. Sun-ho was perhaps fifteen years older than DJ, yet he was more than an uncle. The term *comrades* no longer applied, though it never really captured the way they had each sacrificed to keep the other going. Even though Sun-ho called him *sajang* and, jokingly, *big boseu,* DJ had never acted like a boss. And there had never been an employee as cunning and steely-eyed as Sun-ho. Sun-ho was an assistant, a driver, a partner, an enforcer, a friend. Maybe there wasn't a name for their relationship in the North, either, but there they didn't need one.

"Besides, I'm not the one you should be worried about," Sun-ho said. "I only lost a country. But you, you're losing more than that. I guess you're worried you'll never fit in here. If you ask me, *DJ,* you're starting to fit in too well."

How to explain to Sun-ho that living in Seoul was bringing into focus not the South but the life he'd lived in the North? Where was the lottery ticket whose prize took the blood from your hands?

They heard a noise. It was the electronic-shutter sound of a cell phone taking a picture. They turned to look at the teens, who sat innocently, sipping their sodas.

Sun-ho rose and limped toward their booth.

"Let's just get out of here," DJ called after him.

"You want a picture of a North Korean?" Sun-ho asked them.

None looked up, though one girl let a nervous laugh escape.

"Here I am," he said. "Go ahead and take it. Take a Cho-sunin photo for your Internet pages."

"Come on," DJ said. "Let it go."

Sun-ho didn't let it go. He leaned in close and produced a maniacal, exaggerated smile. "I'm ready for my photograph," he said. "I'm smiling, I'm saying *kimchi*."

The students sat frozen.

"That's what I thought," Sun-ho said. "You are all passengers. And this whole fucked-up country is the ferry. You call us robots. You call us order-taking zombies. But we know what adversity is. We know what it is to survive, and I can tell you—not a single one of us would have drowned on that boat."

Maybe *blood* was too strong a word. Yes, DJ had lived a certain kind of life in North Korea. Perhaps there had been some privileges, but were his hands *bloody*? He'd never felt great about selling false hope, fake medicine and unsafe cars. And yes, the regime used the money he raised for sinister means. But it was only in the South that he'd started thinking about blood. It was only here that he heard others speak, something impossible in the North. In Hanawon, defectors told stories of eternal hunger, endless labor, random reprisals and punishments of the sort not seen since the Mongol invasions. There were tales of slavery and disappearances and prisons that sucked up entire families. There'd always been rumors, but here, DJ could gaze upon people from remote poverty-stricken provinces, places no one was allowed to visit. Here were their bodies, ropy and blackened. Here were their cored teeth, here was skin scaled from pellagra.

And then there was Google Maps. He'd become addicted to satellite photos of Pyongyang—the Mansudae Art Studio where his mother had been a painter and the Golden Lane bowling alley, where, in the shadow of the Juche Tower, he had been a teen champion. He gazed at the university where he'd taken courses in engineering, nostalgic for the way one bulb stayed lit after Pyongyang went black. This light cast its glow on the university's statue of Kim Il-sung. When he was a college student, DJ believed the formulas they memorized would one day be used to make their country great. They all did. So when the lights went out, the students drifted down from their darkened dorm floors to sit together at the feet of the Great Leader, reading and studying by his eternal light.

Of course, a different fate awaited. Upon graduation, the bottom half of DJ's class was given engineering positions. They actually got to design things. The top half, DJ's half, was recruited into foreign currency–generating units. One division manufactured counterfeit pharmaceuticals. Another ran a Pacific Rim insurance scheme. Others operated drug labs or repackaged cigarettes or distributed shark fins. DJ was sent to Chongjin to oversee a press that printed fake lottery tickets. Because of its success, he was also given command of a pan-Asian used-car operation. They imported eight hundred vehicles a month from Japan, removed their catalytic converters, stripped the airbags, rolled back the odometers and dumped them dirt-cheap in China.

It was hard to look at images of Chongjin. Even from space, you could see the toxic-waste dumps, the rusting steel-yards, the foothills riddled with an infinity of famine graves. The black specks dotting the main square were beggar kids, sleeping in the open. The tent city near the shipyards housed teams of guards shifting on and off prison vessels. And along the tracks west of town were the boxcars, packed with families, awaiting departure for the penal mines of Mantapsan and the Hwasong concentration camp.

It was Sun-ho who had protected him from all of this. From the moment DJ stepped off the train in Chongjin and was assaulted by *kotjebi* kids begging for food, Sun-ho was there to shoo them away. Sun-ho handled the drifters who swarmed their black sedan. Sun-ho kept the dockworkers in line and stood up to the ferry crews from Niigata. He faced down the Chinese lottery ticket peddlers in Yanbian and bribed the Bowibu. Even in the darkest days of '97, when humans were eating the paste off propaganda signs, Sun-ho arrived each morning with fish and rice, and DJ didn't have to ask where the food came from.

But what good was rethinking all this when North Korea was a place he'd never see again? It was Seoul he had to wrap his head around. And the longer they were here, the more it seemed their roles were reversing. It was Sun-ho who needed a guardian now.

DJ took Sun-ho's advice and went to a different meeting, but instead of heading for the glitz of Gangnam, he found a different meeting in Gwanak, one not far from a south-bank bus terminal. The new meeting was in a gritty urban church whose cross was fashioned from neon. When he approached, an alcohol-support group was on break. All the alcoholics were out front smoking and trading their jumpy energy. As the defectors filed past, DJ could read their minds: *My life may be a wreck, but at least I wasn't born in the North.*

Metal chairs ringed the basement. Above was a portrait of Yesu-Nim wearing a crown of thorns. When the meeting began, great tribute was paid to Him. Like everyone else, DJ bowed. There were no hot Gangnam moms running things— only Christian *ajummas*, serious in their demeanor.

The defectors went around the room introducing themselves, mentioning things like age, province of birth, date of defection. Then you had to say three things that were great

about life in the South. People listed the usual things: freedom, opportunity, the Internet and so on.

There was a young woman, quite poised, with the beauty
of some celebrity defectors, except she guarded her eyes.
Without her accordion, DJ almost didn't recognize her.

"I'm Mina," she said. "From North Hamgyong Province.
I was a schoolteacher until my troubles came." Perhaps because she was distracted or wasn't listening, she listed three
things that were great about life in the *North*. "I miss going to
karaoke and the hot springs with my friends. I miss my students most of all." She paused, then added, "This time of
year, the weather makes me think of deer. Before the famine,
my father raised them for their antlers. I loved their little
horns—how they felt like moss and smelled of cold stream
water."

The North was a land of thuggery, corruption, brutality
and murder. But Mina was right. There was beauty to be
found in Chongjin. Under the tufted rime of winter, even the
husks of old Soviet factories could be beautiful—gantry
cranes frozen under fat white clouds; abandoned zinc carts
crenellated with frost; rusted conveyor belts standing sentinel
over garbage-glinting icebergs drifting south from Vladivostok.

DJ studied Mina's bobbed hair, her elusive eyes. The only
place for karaoke in Chongjin was the Seamen's Club, a late-
night hangout for big shots and Party officials. And you had

to know people in the military to gain access to the Onpho hot springs. He wondered if her husband had held rank in the navy. There were only so many commissions, and that alone was a pretty good way to find yourself among the missing.

When it was his turn to speak, he didn't want to admit he was from Pyongyang.

"I defected from North Hamgyong Province" was all he said.

And what positive things could he list about life in the South, that he appreciated only burgers, Google Earth and the reading glasses they'd given him? He didn't want to fall into reverie about the North. He did miss Chongjin, the salty smell of fishing nets hung to dry, the jade-green waves of the East Sea. He missed traffic girls, pastel housing blocks and roaming calisthenics squads at dawn, none of which he'd ever see again. He missed women in rabbit-fur coats. He missed winter radishes, pulled cold from the dirt and wiped clean in the snow. He missed the power going out each evening, how a nightly blanket would be thrown over you and the person you were with, how the intimate conversations you'd held back all day would suddenly begin.

Mina's eyes found him. He realized everyone was looking at him.

"I appreciate democracy, freedom and the variety of television programming," he said, then added, "But I do miss how dark it used to get."

He received a few disappointed looks for this counterproductive commentary. At the end of the meeting, when Yesu-Nim was again worshipped, Mina slipped out, and DJ followed her. She walked down Bongcheon-ro, toward Boramae Park.

"I heard you playing the other day, in Anguk Station," he said when he caught up.

She gave him a look that was either suspicious or curious.

"You're very talented," he told her.

She didn't respond.

"Did you go to Mangyongdae or the conservatory?"

"I taught children propaganda songs all day," she said. "You need to know accordion to do that."

A squadron of obsolete fighter jets guarded the park entrance. They were mounted on grand pedestals, their nose cones pointing north. Mina turned in to the park and walked along a snow-flurried trail. "Your teachers didn't play the accordion?" she asked.

DJ shook his head.

"Where are you from?"

"Pyongyang."

"I thought I heard your accent," she said. "Maybe kids actually learned in Pyongyang. Where I'm from, it worked differently. Men came into my high school. They divided the girls into beautiful and not so beautiful. The beautiful girls were sent away. We got accordions. And that was that. How much you hated the accordion didn't matter at all."

DJ wanted to tell her he thought she was very beautiful, but he kept quiet. He wanted to ask her why she risked her life to defect with an instrument she hated, but he didn't.

They came to a group of women, bundled against the cold, doing some kind of slow-motion dance. They moved in unison, a hand taking forever to pass before the eyes, a foot lifting, seeming never to be set down. DJ and Mina exchanged a look. Then they walked on, to keep from laughing.

After a while, Mina said, "At Hanawon, you were with an older man. Was he your father?"

DJ hadn't seen his parents since he'd received his engineering degree. They were like the memory of a photograph to him, an image stared at so long that, before it was lost, it had begun to replace the real thing.

"That was Sun-ho," he said. "We worked together, generating foreign currency."

The look Mina gave him was clearly suspicious.

"It was nothing dangerous," DJ said. "Cars were stolen in Japan, shipped to Vladivostok, doctored in Chongjin, then hauled north by train, where the Chinese forged new documents. Other people got rich. We got to eat."

They started moving toward an outdoor ice rink. Groups of teens and couples skated counter-clockwise, some dancing to a kind of music DJ hadn't heard before.

DJ asked, "Does no one recognize the songs you play?"

"Only North Koreans," Mina said.

"You ever run across people you knew in the North?"

"A few."

"But not the one you're looking for."

She shook her head.

Soon they were leaning against the dasher boards, watching the skaters carve the ice. The music was loud, so you couldn't hear the best part—the blades scissoring the curves. The guy who was making the music wore headphones and fingerless gloves so that he could work a panel of knobs and turn records by hand.

"I'd like to hear you play sometime."

Mina looked toward the families skating ahead. "You can if you want," she said. "But you should know that when I play, I play for my husband."

DJ offered his best attempt at a smile.

A teen beside them was moving to the beat.

"What's the name of this music?" DJ asked him.

The teen stopped swaying when he heard DJ's accent. "You'd have to ask the DJ," he said.

DJ didn't understand.

"You're from the North, right?" the teen asked.

DJ nodded.

"Do you have DJs there? Do you know what I'm talking about?"

"DJs?"

"How to explain a DJ?" the teen asked himself. "The DJ, he's a kind of artist. He takes different kinds of music, you know, funky and strange and old-fashioned, even bad music,

music you wouldn't normally like. Then he mixes it all together. That mix, that's the DJ's brand, that's who he is."

On Friday, DJ went to meet Sun-ho at an American chain
called Burger King. As he opened the door, however, Sun-ho
came walking out with three Whopper meals in takeaway
bags.

"Who's the other meal for?" DJ asked.

"Come," Sun-ho said. "I need to show you something."

With his lurching step and slow foot drag, he led the way.

Two blocks later, they were standing before a 2002 Co-
rolla.

DJ knew his Toyotas. "The LE sedan," he said. "With the
upgrade."

"Go ahead," Sun-ho said. "Check it."

DJ bent low and inspected the tailpipe—sure enough, it
was notched. They did this to keep track of which cars they'd
modified. When he rose, he was smiling.

"I was walking down the street, and there it was," Sun-ho
said. "Imagine its journey—Niigata to Vladivostok to
Chongjin to Shenyang to Seoul to us."

He used a master key to open the driver's door, and the
two stepped inside.

Before closing the passenger door, DJ scraped a pile of
textbooks onto the curb. Out of habit, he flipped down the

visor, lifted the floor mat, opened the glove box. Their greatest source of wonder was the things you might find in a Japanese car—aside from food and money, they'd once found a bullhorn, an inflatable woman, a cooler containing a single eyeball. They'd even found a kitten once, living in the trunk off old apples.

The three meals sat between them. DJ looked from the extra bag to Sun-ho.

"I'll tell you who the extra burger's for," Sun-ho said. "First we need to make a stop."

They drove toward the university hospital in Sinchon-dong. Crossing Olympic, DJ realized that by taking the subway everywhere, he had never really seen the city. From the elevated causeway, here were Yeouido, the National Assembly buildings and the tourist boats lining the Hangang. Climbing the Seogang Bridge, he saw for the first time the Bamseom Islets, with great flocks of mallards and mandarins basking in the midday light.

At the hospital, Sun-ho parked across the entrance to the emergency room, blocking the ambulance ramp. "I'll be back soon enough," he said, slowly limping toward the ER doors.

DJ leaned to inspect the odometer, which registered a mere twenty-seven thousand kilometers. Then he rapped his knuckles where the passenger-side airbag should have been: hollow.

Soon enough, he saw two security guards escorting a man

from the hospital who gripped several dozen balloons. The guards tried to wrest the balloon strings from the man's hands, and when they couldn't, they pushed him to the ground.

By the time Sun-ho had made it back to the car, he was livid, barking insults toward the maternity ward as he set about stuffing *It's A Boy!* balloons into the backseat. "I would have given them their stupid money!" Sun-ho shouted. "Do they think fifty baby boys will be born in a single night? No, it's impossible, so why does the gift shop need all these balloons?"

DJ had no idea what Sun-ho was talking about, but he now knew whom the extra meal was for. "The burger will never get to her," DJ said. "You understand that, right?"

Sun-ho turned his anger toward DJ. "It doesn't matter if Willow gets the burger," he said. "What matters is that we sent it."

They headed north on Highway 1, toward the DMZ, with Sun-ho at the wheel. He drove like he was in North Korea, racing down empty roads a hundred meters wide with a free pass from the dictator himself.

"Yesu-Nim!" DJ shouted as the car floated across lanes of thick traffic.

He turned to see if they'd caused an accident, but there was only a wall of balloons.

When he turned back, Sun-ho was glaring at him.

"Yesu-Nim?" he asked, shaking his head.

"You have to be careful," DJ said. "This is the one car in South Korea that has no airbags."

They crossed the Imjingang and parked with a hundred tour buses at Dorasan Station. The air smelled of diesel and carnival food. They made their way through masses of tourists toward the observatory, where they approached a bank of binoculars. Together they beheld North Korea: Mount Songaksan, the Gaeseong Valley and the collective farms at Geumamgol, where several oxen were pulling something unseen through tall brown grass.

"Look at those peaceful meadows," Sun-ho said, dialing in the focus. "Doesn't it look like you could just walk home?"

DJ turned from the view to his friend. "Yeah," he said. "Except for the seven million land mines, you could take a nice stroll."

A group of high school boys approached and leaned their backs against the parapet. They were young and handsome and maybe were making fun of Sun-ho's balloons. In general, they seemed more interested in eating fried sweet-potato balls than gazing upon the North.

Sun-ho bristled at their arrival. He'd taken offense at teens in uniforms, and he seemed to take even more at students without them. He peered into his binoculars. "Imagine how stupid we must look to our countrymen," Sun-ho said. "Imagine what real Koreans think of our sequined ball caps and manga shirts and K-pop footwear."

When DJ panned the countryside, he saw only peasants in wintertime, laboring in heavy canvas coats. He saw packed-clay roads and corrugated metal roofs. No cars were visible, let alone freeways or hospitals or people contemplating South Korea.

"No launchings," they heard someone shout. "No launchings."

They turned to see the black-and-white helmets of border guards moving through the crowd. Working quickly, Sun-ho stuffed Willow's burger in a plastic shopping bag, hitched the handles together and secured a knot.

"No launchings," a soldier shouted.

Then Sun-ho let go. The balloons raced at great speed across the windswept fields. After clearing a stand of trees, the cargo rose high into North Korean air.

The soldiers arrived, barking. "Who launched that contraband?" they demanded.

DJ and Sun-ho were silent. The teens beside them were silent.

The soldiers stared at each face before moving down the observation line to question others. When they were gone, Sun-ho approached the boys. He spoke to the tallest one, who must have played basketball. "You're loyal," Sun-ho said. "I like that. You weren't afraid of those South Korean soldiers. Yes, your mind is strong. But you must tell me, I must know— why do you dress yourself like that?"

The young man offered a bemused smile.

"Look at your friend," Sun-ho said, pointing at another young man. "He's dressed like a pop singer. And the other one is wearing eyeliner. Do you know what makeup is for?

Makeup is for foreign girls who are kidnapped to Pyongyang to be whored out to Party officials."

The young man's smile went away.

"You are Korean," Sun-ho said with disdain. "Koreans defeated the Jurchens. Koreans fought off the Manchu. We repelled the Mongol invasions. Six times the Mongols tried to conquer us, and six times we prevailed."

"Enough," DJ said. "These are just kids."

For Sun-ho, it wasn't enough. "We beat the Japanese," he said. "We took them at the Siege of Jinju, at the Battle of Okpo, and we swept them from the forests of Taebaek in '45. We even whipped the Americans!"

"The Americans?" The young man laughed. "You crazy *ajeossi*. We never fought the Americans."

That was when Sun-ho took a swing upward, toward the young man's throat.

DJ jumped between them, but someone grabbed his back and rode him to the ground. He felt an elbow around his throat and smelled the junk-food breath of the boy who choked him out. When he came to, he was on his hands and knees, Sun-ho patting him on the back. The boys were nowhere to be seen.

"There you go, you're back," Sun-ho said. "You were only gone a few minutes."

Saliva ran from DJ's mouth. He could feel grit pressed into his cheeks, and both eyes were trying to stream clear.

Sun-ho said, "It feels good to fight, doesn't it?"

DJ tried to say no, but a kind of retching sound came instead. He blinked and looked down at the pavement, dark with spit.

"What happened to our country?" Sun-ho asked. His voice sounded philosophical and faraway. "How did this happen to us?"

"You don't belong here," DJ said. "I get that. But there's no way to take you back. You have to start adjusting, you have to accept that things are different here."

"I'll tell you where we belong, Dongjoo," Sun-ho said. "We were made for another time, one before all this, when a man had a wife, some kids, and lived out his days in the village of his birth. In the summers, a man's family would feast on what his war pony could carry home. In winter, they'd huddle to keep warm."

Sun-ho helped DJ to his feet, steadied him.

"You can't just attack people," DJ said. "Life is different here."

Sun-ho ignored this. "What does a man need?" he mused as he brushed the dirt from DJ's clothes. "Some heat under his floor, a woman he comes to love, the ram's-horn bow he inherits from his father? We should have been born before this mess, Dongjoo. What I wouldn't give to live a thousand years ago. I'd serve a Goryeo king. I'd live a life of honor. If your growth was stunted back then, it was due to crop failure, not a dictator who steals your food. If your hip got broken, it was the work of an ornery ox, not the fucking secret police."

DJ said, "I would take you back if I could."

Sun-ho took a last glance northward.

"Nonsense," he said, and clapped DJ once more on the back.

Mina let DJ hear her play. They worked their way along the Daehwa-bound Orange line, playing accordion in the Apgu-jeong, Oksu and Geumho stations. Mina tended to close her eyes when she played, allowing DJ to watch how she leaned back to fill the bellows, the way her right hand was light on the piano keys and her left punched through the registers. The tunes were less patriotic today. When she played "Hwi-param" in Yaksu Station, an unseen man whistled along from deep within the tunnel. "Rainbow Bridge" brought forth a woman who'd defected from Hamhung and now had a stall in the market selling Northern-style tofu. Following "Bangeap Sumnida," a fellow from Nampo approached. He sold icy bowls of *naengmyeon* from a little cart. "You two are new, I can tell," he said, and tossed some won in the accordion case. "Be patient. It takes a while, but Seoul will offer you her teat."

When he was gone, they had a laugh about that.

The Dongguk station, it turned out, was beneath a soaring church clad in blue glass. Here, Mina sang the words to "Waiting for Him" as after-sermon parishioners made their way down to the trains. They formed a large circle as she sang, unaware perhaps that the "Him" in question wasn't their beloved Yesu-Nim. When Mina thanked them and they heard her accent, money poured into her case.

When the crowd cleared, Mina took the instrument idly through its scales.

"The people at my meetings want me to give up the accordion," she said.

DJ sat on the cool marble floor. He was still in the thrall of the song.

"Are you serious?" he asked.

"They say I'll never accept the South while my music pays tribute to the North."

"But what about your husband?" he asked. "Aren't you on a mission?"

"They say if my husband were here, his name would have been recorded at Hanawon."

Mina stopped squeezing the bellows, so the notes she fingered became only the soft clacking of buttons.

DJ said, "Even if he's not to be found, it matters that you looked, right?"

Mina seemed uncertain. "I suppose."

"You can't stop playing your accordion," he said. "That's one thing I'm sure about. That's who you are. Why not just learn new songs? Or better yet, write your own."

Mina laughed at this. "And what do you think I should sing about?"

"How about a woman searching for her husband? She

never gives up. In fact, she plays her accordion at every sub-way stop in Seoul."

"You think that would make a good song?"

"Are you kidding?" DJ asked. "It would get you on one of those contest shows. A beautiful woman makes a daring es-cape and then scours a new country, playing North Korean tunes in search of the man she loves. There wouldn't be a dry eye in the house."

Mina started playing again. "I only said I had to find my husband," she said. "I never claimed to love him."

I never claimed to love him. DJ heard those words through an entire dishwashing shift. The water was scalding hot. It pen-etrated his hands, gave him focus. And the racks of dishes never ended. DJ didn't have to think about them—the dirty plates came, clouds of steam rose, and there were Mina's words. The other guys in the back of the restaurant swapped stories all night, tales about chasing virgins, Gangnam Dis-trict dancers and episodes of slapstick in the *jimjilbang*. DJ en-joyed the stories, though he never joined in. What would he have to contribute about nightclubs, steam rooms or even the topic of women? Plus, he'd never told a story in his life, at least not about himself.

In his bunk that night, DJ lay studying the South Korean lottery tickets Sun-ho had given them. Back when he and

Sun-ho counterfeited Chinese tickets, they'd run off thousands, then deal them to peddlers across the border. Their press wasn't very sophisticated, so on one print run, all the tickets would be winners. On the next, everyone was destined to lose.

DJ noticed the guy in the next bunk staring at him. He was one of the young veterans. "So, you're from the North?" the veteran asked.

"That's right," DJ said.

"That's fucked up," the veteran said. "I guess you've seen it all. The famine and the mind control and the Dear Leader—all that shit's for real, huh?"

"Yeah, I suppose it is," DJ said.

The veteran nodded. He was quiet a moment. "So you're into the lottery?"

"I take an interest," DJ said. He offered the veteran a ticket. "Try your hand?"

"No, thanks," the veteran told him. "You only get so much luck in life."

DJ nodded. It was getting late. Around them were the sounds of men clicking off lamps and closing metal lockers. When he reached to turn off his light, the veteran spoke.

"You know who's crazy for lottery tickets?" he asked. "Malaysians. All our contractors were Malay. Over in Iraq, I mean. They were Muslim, but friendly, I guess, so they outfit-ted our base. I was Zaytun Division. Anyway, they couldn't gamble, but the lottery was somehow okay. That's all they seemed to care about. Come Friday, there was a sandstorm of discarded tickets blowing around the base." The veteran tossed him a coin.

"What's this for?" DJ asked.

"That's a scratcher, right? You need something to scratch with."

DJ rolled to his side so the veteran could see. The ticket had three columns, and you got to scratch a jewel from each. DJ picked a diamond and then a sapphire and then another sapphire.

"What's the verdict?" the veteran asked.

"I lost."

"Believe me," the veteran said, "that's a good thing. Don't ever waste your luck. When I was over there, everything was booby-trapped. Man, all I wanted was to get out. We weren't in combat or anything. That was the Americans. But anything you came across might blow up—a car, a Dumpster, a pile of trash. And shit blew, trust me, I saw it. I had to take pills to sleep. The funny thing is, now I can't stop thinking about that place. When I close my eyes, Iraq is all I see."

DJ studied the losing ticket. He scratched away the remaining top coating and saw that South Korean tickets were different. If he had picked a diamond, a sapphire and an emerald, the card would have paid twenty thousand won. Every ticket was capable of winning if you played it right, which meant your fate was no one's but your own.

The next day DJ met Mina in front of his dormitory. They'd agreed to work the Black subway line, heading toward Onsu, but when she arrived, she seemed in no hurry. She sat on the smokers' bench, accordion case in her lap.

"What kind of men sleep here?" she asked. "Are they scoundrels? Are they hiding out?"

DJ hadn't seen the question coming. "I think they're just guys with problems," he said.

"Do you believe in second chances?" she asked. "Can people change their nature?"

DJ leaned against the bus shelter. "Those are two different questions," he said.

"This is the kind of place my husband would stay in," Mina said. She watched a couple of haggard-looking men emerge from the dorm and wince from the cold. "When I was a girl, I was known as someone who would push back. If you took my food, I would return the favor and then some. People knew not to cross me. That was my whole reputation. When my husband left, people shook their heads. When he disappeared with our savings, they clucked their tongues and said, 'That poor man. Mina will hunt him to the ends of the world.' That's who I was. And that's what I did."

"Yeah?"

"The funny thing is, no one here knows me. I don't have to be that person."

"Quit looking for him, then. Quit playing the subways."

"But then who would I be?" she asked.

DJ had no answer for that.

From down the street came honking and shouting. They turned to see a black BMW sedan slowly making its way toward them. It was headed the wrong way down a one-way street, its driver yelling at everyone in his path. When the car pulled up, they saw Sun-ho at the wheel.

A driver pulled up in front of the BMW and lifted his arms in confusion. Sun-ho leaned on the horn and left-handed a fistful of chicken bones onto the guy's hood.

DJ approached the sedan. "You trying to get yourself killed?"

"No," Sun-ho said. "It's lunchtime." He held up a bucket of Kentucky Fried Chicken.

"It's not Friday," DJ said.

"Tell that to the wind," Sun-ho said. "It's blowing north today. Get in before it changes its mind."

The backseat was packed with balloons, so Mina and DJ squeezed in front with the accordion. Sun-ho dropped the car in gear and raced into oncoming traffic. Pressed up against Sun-ho, DJ noticed the new down coat he was wearing.

"Looks like someone's been shopping," DJ said.

"One of those sexy Gangnam moms took me to the Shilla duty-free store. I still haven't recovered. Plus, those ladies keep giving me their old Samsungs," Sun-ho said, handing DJ and Mina each a phone.

"What do I do with this?" DJ asked.

"Do I need to explain everything?" Sun-ho asked. "When

you acquire a Samsung, you're deemed a good defector. You're granted immediate citizenship. Next the government gives you a Hyundai, a flag and a Bible."

DJ lifted his hands. "Who pissed in your porridge?" he asked.

"With a Samsung," Sun-ho said, "you can update your speed-dating profile and receive texts from Yesu-Nim Himself. With that blessing, you'll become an important South Korean businessman and start your own Internet. Finally, you'll achieve celebrity defector status. Yes, you'll start your own show, *The DJ Hour*. Here you'll have soulful interviews with beautiful defectors like Mina here."

Mina shook her head. "See why I thought he was your father?"

Sun-ho said, "Oh yes, it's easy to make fun of old Sun-ho—until the day you need him. Do you remember that day, DJ? The day you needed me?"

With a right turn, Sun-ho joined a proper traffic flow onto a northbound highway ramp.

"I don't forget," DJ said.

"What day is this?" Mina asked.

"Oh, this is a very entertaining story," Sun-ho said. "DJ tells it best, don't you, DJ?"

DJ threw Mina a look.

"Go on," she said.

"The story starts with a man named Jong-il," DJ said.

"I have never met this Jong-il, by the way," Sun-ho said. "If he exists."

"Jong-il and I went to engineering school together," DJ continued. "Jong-il's father was very cunning. He named his son after Kim Il-sung's son because no one could ever give offense to someone who shared the Dear Leader's name. Jong-il was smart, and the two of us were very competitive. One week I was the top student. The next it was Jong-il. We fought constantly for the top spot, always trying to outdo each other. But there was respect, too. If I discovered there would be a surprise exam, I would tell Jong-il, and he would do the same. In the end, I finished number one."

"Sounds like this story will have a happy ending," Sun-ho said. "I bet everything's going to work out just fine."

"So Jong-il ends up in Wonsan, making fake pharmaceuticals. The pill part is simple—they simply use laxative powders, which machines then shape and color. He shares his labs with Man-seok, also from our school, who makes real drugs, like ecstasy. The key to faking medicine is the packaging, so Jong-il uses my press to make four-color labels and blister foils."

"Your press?" Mina asked.

"Long story," DJ said. "One day Jong-il calls me. He says there's been a mistake. He says there was a mix-up, that some bad medicine went to Pyongyang rather than China, and people in the capital are sick. He says that heads are rolling and Man-seok's team is gone. He says trucks have come for him; they're pulling up out front. *'Run,'* Jong-il tells me. Then the call is over."

"Does Dongjoo inform me of this?" Sun-ho asks Mina. "Of course not. He comes to me and says to cut the power, send everyone home, grab all the lottery tickets and bring the car around. Dongjoo, he knows design and accounting and specs and all that. I know people. That's what I deal with. I know when someone's lying. I would have known right away this was a trick—first there is a mess-up in production and then also a mess-up in shipping? These are people who don't mess up. Who gets our operation when we suddenly defect? Jong-il does, that's who."

"Mess-ups happen," DJ said. "We made them. What about the Lexus train? What about Mahjong Madness? Did you forget burning those ten thousand tickets?"

Sun-ho says, "So we're driving north for the border, just like we are now. 'Faster' is all Dongjoo will say. He tells me nothing."

"So much was in my mind," DJ said. "My parents, the workers, their families. The idea of running was a strange dream—possible and impossible at the same time. It was only when we neared the border that it became real. It was only then that I thought about Sun-ho and how I couldn't leave him behind."

"Admit the truth," Sun-ho said. "You were thinking, *Sun-*

ho knows the border guards, he crosses all the time. While you yourself have never crossed."

"I was thinking how ugly it would be that after years of friendship, I would go free and you would not."

"You had never seen the outside world. You didn't know a single person in China. You didn't know the first thing about the real world. You were afraid."

"I was afraid they would kill you."

For a moment, Sun-ho simply drove. The only sounds were balloons mobbing one another in the windy backseat.

"So he doesn't inform me that we're defecting. Can you believe that? I had no idea I was leaving home forever. I don't get to say goodbye to anyone, I don't get to see Willow or even hear her voice one last time."

"Who's Willow?" Mina asked.

Sun-ho said, "Why don't you tell Mina what you told the border guard?"

"That was a mistake," DJ said. "I never denied that."

"We're at the bridge," Sun-ho told Mina. "On the other side is China. I cross once a month to deliver lottery tickets and to sign for car shipments. So I'm passing cigarettes all around, just like normal, when Dongjoo rolls down the back window and says, 'We'll never see you again.' To the border guard. The guard says, 'What?' Dongjoo says, 'And you're going to die here.' The guard gets this serious look on his face, and when he places a hand on that holster, I step on the gas.

That's why I couldn't just drop Dongjoo off in China and hand out some more cigarettes on my return."

"I said it in a sad way," DJ said. "I was thinking, *I'll never see these hills again, I'll never see Chongjin again, I'll never see my folks.* And that guard, he was just a boy, he couldn't have been nineteen. I said exactly what I was thinking, that we were leaving and that every one of them would die there."

"What happened?" Mina asked.

"What happened?" Sun-ho barked. "This happened. We're stuck in South Korea!"

Mina flinched at his anger. "I mean, was it a trick? What happened to your business? Is Jong-il in charge?"

DJ stared through the window at the grey, blue-roofed suburbs. "We don't know," he said.

"I know," Sun-ho said. Through his teeth, he said, "I *know.*"

Overcast skies hovered above the DMZ parking lot, with low grey clouds moving steadily north.

Sun-ho parked behind a row of tour buses. From the back-seat, he wrestled a large array of silver Mylar balloons printed with many variations of *Happy Birthday*. Despite the cold, Sun-ho removed his new jacket and tied it on. "My mistake last time," he said, "was launching from the border, where the guards patrol. This jacket has a long journey ahead, and an extra kilometer won't make a difference."

DJ watched the balloons twist in the wind, straining to

deliver their lightweight cargo. He'd imagined the burger and now the jacket floating off to a field worker, but the wind was due north, a flight path taking it over Panmunjeom and Gaesong City on a vector to Pyongyang. In his imagination, the balloons were headed directly for his parents in Potong-gang, and when the cargo got closer, when he imagined his folks on their balcony, arms open and facing south, when the bird's-eye view was close enough to see their faces, their expressions, how they'd aged—there was nothing; his imagination simply turned off.

Mina pointed across the parking lot. "What's going on over there?"

DJ turned to see. Past the buses was a group circled around several tall, clear balloons, each a couple stories high. Surrounding them were video cameras and a microphone on a pole.

"I bet it's one of those celebrity defectors," Sun-ho said. "With her big eyes and sad story, out to get famous by telling the world how victimized and pathetic we are."

When they neared, though, they saw that the defector was a man, about DJ's age and Sun-ho's size. He wore a suit and a smile and a name tag that read *Seo*. He was directing the filling of balloons from brown cylinders, and the loading of baskets with thousands of flyers.

Seo approached Sun-ho and handed him a flyer. It read *Kim Jong-un Is a War Criminal*, followed by quotes from a UN report.

"You're from the North, I can tell," Seo said. "Come, help us spread the word."

Sun-ho gave back the flyer. "What do you think people are going to do with these? It's cold in the North. Unless you're including matches, those leaflets will be worthless."

"You're wrong," Seo said. "We must get the word out."

"They know they're suffering, they don't need you to tell them the regime is bad."

"Do they know?" Seo asked. "In secret, I suspected. But I had no way of *knowing*. Perhaps if I had come across a flyer, sent from the South by people who cared—well, my suspicions would've been confirmed. Maybe I would've acted sooner."

"This is a jacket," Sun-ho said. "Jackets are good things to send in the winter. It's lightweight, down-filled. Look, it says North Face right here. North Face is the best. In this pocket are some energy bars." Sun-ho opened a pocket to display two Samsung phones inside. "There's also a map." Sun-ho reached into another pocket and removed some Fortune Smiles.

"Are those lottery tickets?" Seo asked.

Sun-ho looked down, frustrated. "The map's in the other pocket," he said.

Seo asked, "No offense, but your plan is to send oppressed people a designer jacket and a long shot at good fortune? What they need is the truth."

"I don't believe in fortune," Sun-ho said. "These tickets are all winners."

"How could you know that?"

Gritting his teeth, Sun-ho stood silent.

"Kim Jong-un is a human rights violator," Seo said. "The UN made it official. The most important thing we can send is news. First you free the mind. Then the body will follow."

"Thanks for the philosophy," Sun-ho said. "How about we do a thought experiment? Let's release our balloons at the same time and then imagine the people in the fields who see them floating in. One balloon carries pamphlets. The other delivers a warm down jacket stuffed with cell phones, food and winning lottery tickets. Let's imagine which one the citizens run toward."

"There's no way you're launching your balloons with mine."

"Why's that? Are you scared of the truth?"

"What is today's date?" Seo asked.

"February thirteenth," Sun-ho said.

"And you were born in North Korea?"

Sun-ho got a suspicious look on his face. "Yeah."

"And who was born on February sixteenth?"

Sun-ho grimaced. "Kim Jong-il," he said.

"And what is the message printed on your balloons?"

Sun-ho couldn't bring himself to say it.

"I'm trying to send dispatches of truth and solidarity," Seo said. "You'll appear to be sending gifts and well-wishes in honor of the Dear Leader."

"So it might seem to some," Sun-ho said, and released the jacket, which sailed quickly north. Then he neared Seo, so the two were in each other's breath. "There is a bit of truth and solidarity you can share with me," Sun-ho added. "Tell me where you get those big balloons."

Two nights later, the cell phone Sun-ho had given DJ rang. DJ sat up in his bunk. There was only the sound of men snoring and a faint city-glow through the security windows. He had the eerie feeling he'd awakened in the North. For a moment, he felt that beyond the metal bunks and concrete room stood the steel skeletons of abandoned factories, and past that the icy calm of the moonlit East Sea. On nights he'd wake like this in Chongjin, he'd drink scorched rice water and stare out the window at the fields of cars they had to work on, cars once owned by people whose lives he tried and tried to imagine.

The phone thrummed in his hand. DJ pulled the scratchy wool blanket around him. He touched the screen. "Yes," he whispered.

"This is Assistant Inspector Kang, at Samseong Station. We have a gentleman in custody who won't give his name. This number was the only contact in his phone."

"What did he do?"

"It says here he was picked up for entering traffic," Kang said. "Looks like he was yelling at drivers for obeying the stoplights. Probably alcohol-related."

"I know him," DJ said. "I'll be right there."

The station was on the Green line, so DJ arrived quickly. The officers were orderly and efficient. One took him past a large holding tank to a row of individual rooms. There he found Sun-ho lying alone on a metal bench. His eyes were open; DJ sat on the floor and looked into them. He saw a weary calm that suggested Sun-ho had been through a battle with the police, that the blank look had come after a long-avoided surrender.

"Is it true, my friend, have you been drinking?"

Sun-ho shook his head.

"Come, they'll let me take you home."

"I'm going to spend the night," Sun-ho said. "I don't mind it here. It's warm, and a man can stretch out."

"What, on this metal bench, locked in a holding room?"

"I need something from you," Sun-ho said. "Will you do me a favor?"

"What kind of favor?"

"Why would you ask that? Do you forget everything I've done for you? Don't you remember Najin? How about Comrade Seok? Have you forgotten the May Day shipment?"

"I saved your ass many times, too," DJ said. "Your temper got you into a lot of trouble."

"Just come to Gangnam tomorrow night, okay? If you

come to one of my meetings, you'll understand. This will all make sense. I'm in the tallest building on Dosan-daero, near Seolleung-ro. I'll meet you out on the street outside, just after sunset."

There was something wrong about it all, DJ thought, but he nodded. "You have to do something for me," he said. "Give this place a chance. It takes getting used to, I know. But today I saw a bus stop for an old woman. The bus had hydraulics or something—it knelt low so the woman could climb on. That would never happen at home. The North would never make a machine that bowed down to a person."

But Sun-ho didn't listen. "And bring your new girlfriend," he said. "A touch of the accordion never hurts—trust me, the Gangnam ladies will love that."

"She's not my girlfriend," DJ said. "She has a husband."

Sun-ho grunted. "She *had* a husband. Everything in the North is gone. That goes for us as well. Your parents, whom you can't bring yourself to talk about—they're gone. Everything I had, everything I was, none of it exists here." Sun-ho rolled so he faced the wall. "Now go," he said.

"I can't just leave you in jail."

"No? Why not?"

"It feels like I'm abandoning you."

Sun-ho glanced back, smiling for the first time. "You say that word like it's a bad thing."

———

The next night, DJ did as he'd agreed. When darkness fell, he and Mina made their way to Apgujeong in Gangnam. Here Shinsegae glowed in gold and purple light while Luxury Hall crawled with scrolling color. There were stores clad in metallic armor and stores whose colored tiles climbed down the walls and spilled into the street. In one shopwindow they saw a pink teddy bear with diamonds for eyes; in another, cupcakes coated with flakes of gold. You didn't have to be North Korean to know that entire families rose or fell for less than what some were willing to pay for a jewel-crusted hip-hop baseball cap.

Mina donned the accordion and, revealing a streak of dark irony, played "Following the Party to the End" as they strolled by the window displays.

On Dosan, near Seolleung-ro, Sun-ho called out to them.

"Come, my friends, come," he shouted.

When they approached, Mina played a riff from "Nowhere Without You."

"So, where's this good-time meeting?" she asked.

DJ stared at Sun-ho's North Face jacket. "Didn't you send that north?"

Sun-ho smiled. "That was a spare," he said.

DJ looked up at the glimmering tower. "You live here?"

Sun-ho joined him in admiring the building. "Nice, huh?"

He produced a key card and used it to unlock the building's mirrored front doors. Instead of heading for the elevators, Sun-ho took the fire stairs, swinging his bad leg down

each step before holding the rail with two hands and dropping the good. DJ and Mina trailed him for two flights until
they came to a concrete corridor for infrastructure access—
here were the distribution panels, the fire sprinkler valves, a
freight elevator. Sun-ho used his card to beep open a tiny
janitorial closet that smelled of fast-food wrappers and dirty
clothes. Taking most of the closet space was a molded plastic
chair on which rested a large black backpack. Plastic bags and
jugs of water hung from the ceiling, and there was room for a
single stack of cardboard boxes. From a box, Sun-ho grabbed
a couple of cell phones, which he pocketed.

DJ asked, "What is this, some kind of storage unit?"

Sun-ho displayed two dirty automotive fan belts.

"For the weight," he said, "there's nothing stronger than a
Toyota fan belt."

Mina took quiet stock of the closet. "Are you living out of
here?" she asked.

Sun-ho swung the pack onto his back. Then he turned to
DJ. "I'm sorry I only have one chair," Sun-ho said, staring
with a strange seriousness in his eyes. "I can get another if
you like. Do you want me to get another chair?"

DJ didn't know what to say. "Is there a lack of seating at
the meeting or something?"

Sun-ho didn't answer. He grabbed the chair and closed
the door, but before it swung shut, DJ got a glimpse of what
had been under the chair: a water jug, half filled with what
looked like urine. He wondered about Mina's question. Could

someone live in a closet? Could a person sleep sitting up? He and Mina exchanged a look.

Sun-ho was already headed down the hall with his chair, then pressing the call button of the service elevator.

"How long have you been in this building?" DJ asked.

"It's a very exclusive address," Sun-ho said.

When the elevator doors opened, the three of them stepped inside. Sun-ho swiped his card to press the roof button. Soft tones marked the floors as they flashed past.

"The meeting's on the roof?" DJ asked.

Sun-ho handed DJ the key card. "So you can get out of the building," he said. The card was marked with a name and an apartment number.

When they arrived, the roof was dark and windy.

"I don't understand," DJ said.

"There is no meeting," Mina said.

Sun-ho said, "You think I would go to one of those brain-washing sessions?"

"What about the Gangnam ladies?" DJ asked. "Do they exist?"

"I'd never betray Willow like that."

DJ stepped out onto the roof. The tar under his feet was soft. Fragments of cloud blew past, their bellies aglow with the light of traffic and commerce. Beyond the curtain wall was a skyline of twinkling amber. And then the dark rope of the Han River.

As his eyes adjusted, DJ noticed two brown cylinders: helium tanks.

Right away, Sun-ho started to strap the plastic chair to an outcrop of conduit with a rope tether. He cow-hitched the fan belts to each arm and began filling a towering clear balloon with helium from a tank.

In disbelief, Mina turned to DJ. "Are you going to stop him?"

That was a good question.

"Are you really doing this?" DJ asked. "Assuming you don't die from the cold or the lack of oxygen or the landing, don't you think they'll kill you?"

"Traitors," Sun-ho said. "That's who they kill. Not heroes."

"You can't really believe that. They kill anyone they like."

"Okay, I'll grant you that," Sun-ho said. "But you don't have to worry about me."

Sun-ho tied off the first balloon with a braided cord and attached it to a fan belt. The chair lifted, held only by the rope tether, where it danced on plastic toes. Sun-ho began filling another, the gas hissing, the balloon bent and whipping in the wind.

"Willow is much younger than you," DJ said.

Sun-ho didn't respond.

"You two have barely spoken."

Sun-ho called to Mina. "Do you know 'Arirang'? Would you play 'Arirang' for me?"

With a look of bemused wonder, Mina opened her accordion case and began to button the first slow chords, and then from the piano keys came the ancient melody.

"Yes, beautiful," Sun-ho said, attaching another balloon. "Dongjoo said you were talented. Did you know this song is from the Joseon Dynasty? Six hundred years, that's how long our people have been singing it. Do you know the words, will you sing it for me?"

" 'Arirang,' " Mina sang. " 'Arirang, Arariyo.' "

Sun-ho rolled the tank to the chair so he could anchor it with his weight. Backpack in his lap, he began to fill another balloon.

"Listen to reason," DJ told him. "Willow's father is in the Party. Anyone his daughter married would have to be a member. It would never work."

Sun-ho looked up from his plastic chair. "Don't you believe in new beginnings?" he asked. "Where's your sense of possibility?"

To signal an end to such talk, Sun-ho began singing along with Mina, a duet accompanied by the accordion and the hiss of helium. DJ looked up to the balloons as they filled—angry, they spun and tugged in the turbulent air.

When six balloons were filled, you could almost see the chair's weightlessness.

Sun-ho turned those wide, sad eyes upon DJ. " 'A thousand ri with every stride,' " he said. It was the start of a propaganda slogan they'd all been forced to say a thousand times.

DJ asked, "Why are you going in the dark?"

"Light, dark, it doesn't matter," Sun-ho said.

DJ felt his eyes getting hot. "It does matter," he said. "I don't want you to go. You're all I have."

Sun-ho nodded. "Think of it this way. I'm what you had of the North, and you're what I had of the South. We'll always fit together like that. We'll always be a team."

DJ shook his head. "I can't believe you're doing this."

"Come on," Sun-ho said. "'A thousand ri with every stride.'"

DJ was silent.

"'A thousand ri with every stride.'"

DJ finally finished the sentence: "'The winged horse Chollima flies.'"

Sun-ho smiled, warm and large. Then he loosened the knot that freed the tether. But he did not float into the sky. The chair's legs rattled. Then they started skittering across the roof, picking up speed until Sun-ho was slammed against the curtain wall, the balloons violently whipping.

DJ ran over and put his hands on the chair to weigh it down. "You're going to get yourself killed," he said. "You can't even get off the roof, let alone to North Korea."

Sun-ho smiled again. "A simple mistake," he said. "I forgot to give you this." He lifted the backpack and held it out to DJ. When DJ reached for it, Sun-ho paused. "Don't get on the ferry," he said, his eyes large and intense. "If you follow their rules, you'll become one of them."

DJ took the heavy pack, and when he did, Sun-ho was gone, snapped up into the sky, spinning wildly and swinging until he was no longer visible.

DJ felt the weight of the bag, recognized the metallic clatter of its contents. He didn't need to look inside to know it was filled with catalytic converters. He kept looking at the place in the sky where Sun-ho had been. There was no way Sun-ho could get what he really wanted; there was no way he could sail a thousand years back in time. Maybe the closest a person could come was North Korea.

Mina stopped playing. She locked her bellows and joined DJ at the wall.

Clouds came and went. Before long, the sky no longer resembled the sky Sun-ho had disappeared into.

"That would never happen in the North," Mina said. She shook her head, a look of wonder in her eyes. "Everything there is planned out. They've got it all rigged. This, though, this was . . . spontaneous and unexpected, this was *real.*"

DJ let his eyes drift across a horizon of buildings—thousands of lights, millions of them. The darkened apartments still made more sense than the lit ones. And there was no single light to guide you.

"You never think about going back?" DJ asked.

They were standing side by side, gazing north.

"Back?" She shook her head. "I feel like I just got here."

"Yeah," DJ said. "Me, too."

ACKNOWLEDGMENTS

I wish to thank the John Simon Guggenheim Memorial Foundation and Stanford University for their generous support. I'm also indebted to the Kalmanovitz Library at the University of California, San Francisco, where portions of this book were written.

I've been the beneficiary of many fine editors: Tyler Cabot and David Granger at *Esquire* for championing "Nirvana"; Christopher Cox at *Harper's Magazine* for his judicious edits of "Interesting Facts"; John Wood and Steven Albahari at 21st Editions for lovingly hand-printing "George Orwell Was a Friend of Mine"; and special thanks to Cheston Knapp and Michelle Wildgen at *Tin House,* where "Hurricanes Anonymous," "Dark Meadow," and "Fortune Smiles" first appeared. "Hurricanes Anonymous" was reprinted in *The Best American Short Stories.* "Nirvana" was reprinted in *The Best American Nonrequired Reading.*

This book could have no finer editor than David Ebershoff, and Warren Frazier is the prince of literary agents. The support of the Stanford writing faculty has been invaluable to me, particularly Eavan Boland, Elizabeth Tallent and Tobias Wolff. Thanks also to Gavin Jones. I'm grateful to Ed Schwarzschild, Todd Pierce, Neil Connelly, Scott Hutchins, Skip Horack and Russ Franklin, all of whom read versions of these stories and offered sage advice.

Special thanks also to Dr. Patricia Johnson, Dr. James Harrell and the Honorable Gayle Harrell. Phil Knight is my source for wisdom and inspiration. Stephanie is my Pleiades, my Polaris, my Hōkūleʻa and Southern Cross. Thanks especially and eternally to Jupiter, James Geronimo and Justice Everlasting.

About the Author

ADAM JOHNSON teaches creative writing at Stanford University. He is the author of *Fortune Smiles, Emporium, Parasites Like Us* and *The Orphan Master's Son,* which was awarded the Pulitzer Prize in fiction. He has received a Whiting Writers' Award and fellowships from the National Endowment for the Arts and the Guggenheim Foundation. His work has appeared in *Esquire, Harper's, Playboy, GQ, The Paris Review, Granta, Tin House, The New York Times* and *Best American Short Stories.* He lives in San Francisco.

Facebook.com/adamjohnsonbooks

About the Type

This book was set in Baskerville, a typeface designed by John Baskerville (1706–75), an amateur printer and typefounder, and cut for him by John Handy in 1750. The type became popular again when the Lanston Monotype Corporation of London revived the classic roman face in 1923. The Mergenthaler Linotype Company in England and the United States cut a version of Baskerville in 1931, making it one of the most widely used typefaces today.

R